© 2024 Aibo/Slipshot
On the web: https://slipshot.io
TikTok: @slip.shot
Instagram: slip.shot

SlipShot vol 2.0
Published in the United States by Mint Cookie Industries.
All rights reserved. No part of this publication may be reproduced, stored in a retrieval system or transmitted in any form or by any means, electronic, mechanical, photocopying, recording or otherwise without the prior permission of the publisher or in accordance with the provisions of the Copyright, Designs and Patents Act 1988 or under the terms of any license permitting limited copying issued by the Copyright Licensing Agency.

This is a work of fiction. Names, characters, business, events and incidents are the products of the author's imagination. Any resemblance to actual persons, living or dead, or actual events is purely coincidental.

Cover Design by: Gabriel Juarez, Ryan Sunada-Wong

Character Design: Ryan Sunada-Wong

Illustration, Theme Design: Ryan Sunada-Wong, Gabriel Juarez

Book Design: Changying Zheng

ISBN-13: 979-8-9870845-4-0

AIBO

Contents

CHAPTER 1 SCARS 11
CHAPTER 2 ARRIVAL OF AN OLD FRIEND 19
CHAPTER 3 FIRST BLUSH 27
CHAPTER 4 RECOLLECTIONS AND MEETINGS 34
CHAPTER 5 AN AWAKENING 49
CHAPTER 6 A DIRECT CHALLENGE 55
CHAPTER 7 PATHWAY TO GRIDDISH 67
CHAPTER 8 LESSONS 77
CHAPTER 9 PLOTS AND MACHINATIONS 80
CHAPTER 10 MEETINGS AND SERENDIPITY 87
CHAPTER 11 INFILTRATION 96
CHAPTER 12 AN ARGUMENT 106
CHAPTER 13 A FIGHT 112
CHAPTER 14 WE MEET AGAIN 121
CHAPTER 15 A TENUOUS FEELING OF HOME 124
CHAPTER 16 ONE 130
CHAPTER 17 A NEW PROJECT 134
CHAPTER 18 DESCENT 142
CHAPTER 19 RUSHING HOME 151
CHAPTER 20 A CHECKERED PAST 154
CHAPTER 21 A MOMENT OF LIGHT 158
CHAPTER 22 CONFRONTATION 167
CHAPTER 23 FALLING INTO FAMILIARITY 171
CHAPTER 24 SUDDEN LOSS 175
CHAPTER 25 HOME 179

CHAPTER 26 QUESTIONS	184
CHAPTER 27 CONVALESCENCE	190
CHAPTER 28 TO BEGIN THE QUEST	203
CHAPTER 29 A DISCOVERY	207
CHAPTER 30 A VISIT	213
CHAPTER 31 ADAPTING	218
CHAPTER 32 WAFTRING LIQUOR	228
CHAPTER 33 EXPLANATIONS	233
CHAPTER 34 FIRST MISSION	237
CHAPTER 35 MAKING PLANS	241
CHAPTER 36 BLOOD AND SEDUCTION	246
CHAPTER 37 A NEW ARRIVAL	261
CHAPTER 38 AN APPEAL	269
CHAPTER 39 AN INTRODUCTION, A BEGINNING	273
CHAPTER 40 A MEETING	289
CHAPTER 41 GROWING CLOSE	293
CHAPTER 42 RISING CONCERN	298
CHAPTER 43 REVEALING TRUTH	303
CHAPTER 44 MISSING	311
CHAPTER 45 ARRIVAL & DEPARTURE	318
CHAPTER 46 A FINAL MEETING	324
CHAPTER 47 THE GREAT RE-FRAG	332
CHAPTER 48 A NEW PLACE	335
GLOSSARY	342

CHAPTER 1

Scars

Var 7, Farth, Nissy

Cythiria Crenshaw tore the top from the paper box and pulled out a bright pink colored bandage. She peeled away the backing, twisting and pulling at the gauzy fabric, which crumpled up into a sticky ball.

"Shit," she hissed as she ripped the twisted and tangled bandage away and tossed it on the ground. She reached into the box for another, pulling more gently at the paper backing.

She gazed into the mirror. She frowned as her eyes flitted across the face that stared back at her. Her short black hair, her dark eyes, lips whose corners always seemed to be turned downwards. And those two scars. Those two round dots right in the center of her forehead that just never went away. She never remembered a time when she didn't have the scars on her forehead. Never remembered a time when they didn't just randomly ache, or when the burning pain was accompanied by deep grinding sounds somewhere inside her skull. Like someone had taken two heavy rocks and rubbed them together until they were worn down to crumbled debris.

She sighed and shook her head. She held each edge of the bandage between her thumb and forefinger and pressed it against her forehead. The ends of the bandage barely covered the two round scars.

Cythiria scoffed. "I look stupid," she said as she glared at the image in the mirror. "Like a real idiot." She paused. "And I really hate pink."

She stepped away from the mirror and threw herself onto the creaky bed of the small, messy room. In the corners, and upon chairs were strewn piles of dirty clothes, old t-shirts, cargo pants, an occasional waffled boot. She buried her head in her arms. The scars hadn't tingled for a while. Not too badly, at least. Not like they used to. The deep grinding sounds were less common now, more like a distant, lonely hum. Every so often, the grinding would come back. A good punch against the wall would help settle that. The pain of scraped and bloodied knuckles would be a good distraction. But it wasn't always like that. It took a while to get used to. If this is what you call getting used to.

The images of myself are broken, like looking into a shattered mirror, each shard a piece of a reflection. Which reflection is my own? Which one is true? Or are they all true?

And still, the day it all began, it seems so far away. The first day I can remember, it was…maybe a dream. But still so real….

~

The sky was dark. A cool, damp breeze whispered along the grassy meadow, carrying with it a lonely, distant hum. The air was fragrant, almost pungent, a florid scent that came and went with the breeze. The fall through the Slipshot was sickening, disorienting. It was the first time for the child Cythiria.

In the distance, there were tall buildings. Across the sky, a bright white streak, like a distant, milky river that cast its own gentle light upon the flickering towers. It crossed the horizon. It seemed unending, stretching for all eternity into the future.

There were two people. No, three. And then the burning started.

My body was small, my hands tiny, the hands of a child. Cythiria's head burned like she never felt before. Like fire shooting from those two scars on her forehead. She couldn't contain it. She couldn't escape from it.

That woman, the one with the fiery red hair, held Cythiria in her arms. Her eyes were frightened. Maybe more than Cythiria's own. She asked Cythiria a question. Cythiria couldn't hear her, not while her head felt as if it were being ground to dust. And there was a man. No, two men. One rushed towards Cythiria. He stood behind her, gazing into her face. He looked lost, afraid. And the other man? He's just a dark phantom in Cythiria's memory. A shadow. He said something to her. He said, "Slaves are strong. You are strong. You will survive."

Slaves? I didn't know what he meant by that. Is a Slave something special? Is it something that I should strive for?

On her hands and knees, she watched the blood drip from her forehead onto the ground. Why was she here? Where did she come from? Why do her memories only start from that moment? And when she tried to reach further back, to a time before she first came to this place, she could only feel her stomach twist and turn and grow queasy to the point where she would only want to heave and vomit.

He carried me back. The man who was afraid and tired. I could only hold on to him and wait and hope the pain would go away.

⚬

"Hope the pain would go away," mumbled Cythiria. "As if. Geeze, was I a stupid little kid or what!" She jumped up from her bed. It squealed and creaked under her sudden movement. She looked around and jumped towards an old chair that was shoved into the corner. She picked up a pair of cargo pants, sat on the edge of her bed, and pulled them on. She reached for a wad of socks which had been tossed into a corner and pulled them apart. She smelled them, grimaced, and pulled them on one at a time. She reached for a t-shirt, which was strewn on the chair back. Its sleeves and collar were messy and ragged. She jogged towards the door of her room and picked up a jacket that had been tossed onto the floor. She pulled it on. It was white with racing stripes down each sleeve and along the front, with a big, roomy hood attached to it. She picked up a backpack that was leaning against the wall. She pulled it onto her shoulders one loop at a time.

She took a deep breath.

She reached for the door handle and pulled it. It rattled open. Cythiria stomped down a narrow hallway, paused and glanced around the messy living room, which was strewn about with various objects: plastic and metal crates each about knee height and stacked against the cracking wall. Some miscellaneous aprons and rags and a collection of cans and bottles, a large picture window covered by heavy, dusty curtains.

"I'm going!" she shouted.

A cluster of crates, which has been pushed into the corner, rattled. A woman with red hair and wearing a brown cap with a long bill popped her head up between columns of stacked crates. She stepped out into the living room. Her cheek was smudged with grease and her hair was pulled to a high ponytail that seemed to flow out of the back of her cap. She looked Cythiria up and down.

"First day of high school, huh?"

"Yes, Jillian," pouted Cythiria.

"You can always call me mom."

"Sure." Cythiria rolled her eyes.

"What's with the bandages?" said Jillian, glancing at Cythiria's forehead. She reached her hand up and poked the bandage with her finger.

"Ow!"

"Does it hurt?"

"What do you think?"

"I should take you to the doctor."

Cythiria sighed quickly. "I don't want to see any more doctors. All my life, it was all about the doctors. But none of them did anything, they just poked and prodded at me all day."

"Cythiria, I…."

"Never mind." Cythiria paused. "I'm fine."

Jillian hesitated. "Cythiria, you should try to do better this time."

"Better?"

"Your grades."

"Whatever," she grumbled.

"I know you're not exactly the school type, Cythiria, but you need to try to get better grades. It's your last chance to get into a good college."

Cythiria sighed. "You know I have a hard time concentrating." She reached up and touched the bandages on her head.

"Well, you have to overcome it somehow. That's the only way that, well, you'll ever get out of this slum that we live in."

"It's not a slum," whined Cythiria. "I mean, I kinda like it."

She stepped forward and touched Cythiria on the cheek. "I just want you to have opportunities, you know."

"Whatever."

"Alright." Jillian patted Cythiria on the head. Cythiria rolled her eyes. "I'm off to deliver a shipment. Might not be back for a few days. Gotta warm up the rig, and then I'm hittin' the freeway!" A broad, toothy smile crossed her face and her eyes twinkled.

Cythiria let an ever so faint smile curl across her lips. "Be careful," she mumbled.

"Hah! Careful is my middle name," said Jillian.

"Sure." Cythiria turned and walked out of the living room down a narrow hallway. She paused at the door, sighed again, and pulled open the latch.

She stepped out onto a landing. She sniffed the air, which smelled of smoke mixed with an almost fragrant, humid sea air. Before her, a cracked and mottled street separated her from the blue grayness of the Nissy Bay, its agitated waves held back by a thick, steel dike. In the distance, rusting gantry cranes like giant metal horses filled the horizon. Above, a wide, milky streak stretched across the blue sky like a long, wispy cloud, the planetary ring of Farth.

She paused, turning towards a rustling sound to her side.

"Hey, Cyth," came a warm voice.

"Hey, dad." She glanced at Fredrick. He held an empty trash bag in his hand and wore a dirty, probably white apron. His dirty blond mane bounced on his shoulders with each step. He pushed a wayward lock of hair to the side and around his ear.

"Off to school?"

"Yep."

"Cool. Since you're in high school now, maybe they'll have sports programs."

Cythiria snorted. "Maybe."

"You should join one."

Cythiria moved her eyes up and to the right, just short of a full roll. "We'll see."

"It might be good for you."

"Sure it will. Like it'd do *me* any good."

Fredrick paused. "It might help you get your mind off things, you know."

"My *mind* probably needs to be on things."

Fredrick chuckled. Cythiria's face cracked a smile. "Well, I'll let you go," Fredrick said. He reached out and stroked Cythiria's arm. He held her gaze a moment, smiled, and then turned towards the front door. Her eyes followed him as he stumbled up a short flight of steps and then entered their house.

Cythiria sighed. She glanced at the pocked and mottled road before her, and the short, cracked wall that held Nissy's sea at bay. She pushed her thumbs into the shoulder straps of her backpack and walked, her heavy, waffled boots thumping with uncertainty upon the uneven sidewalk.

Squat, dilapidated bungalows gave way to graffitied garages and rusty-fenced lots, populated by dusty, corroded buses and cars permanently deposited therein. Cythiria sniffed the smoky, oily air and coughed, pulling her hood up over her head.

The two scars on her head tingled. She lifted her hand and brushed the bandage with her fingers. She gazed up at the sky, squinting through misty haze at the white-blue streak that stretched across the entire horizon, the ring of Farth.

"I feel different, all of a sudden," she mumbled. "Like, lighter." A smile curled up on the corner of her mouth. She breathed deeply. "I wonder what it could be. Like a change, somehow." She shrugged her shoulders and then pulled the hood back up onto her head, returning her gaze to the sidewalk.

Cythiria arrived at a dark stairwell which led into an underground cavern, the Nissy subway. She heard the whistle and clatter of cars as they raced through tunnels. A warm, dry breeze wafted up the stairs, knocking Cythiria's oversized hoodie off her head. She pulled it back on as she descended the stairs, avoiding glances with seated vagabonds and crooning buskers, their voices and twangy accompaniments cutting through the drone and murmur of the underground caves.

She stepped over yellowed and muddied puddles. She sniffed the stale, putrid air, glancing at upturned garbage cans and rotting trash strewn angrily across the platform. She glanced at graffitied walls, tagged and marked again and again, their original shape and color buried under arrays of reckless dark and inky hand strokes.

A warm blast of air blew through the platform, followed by the whistle and grind of an approaching train. Cythiria waited until it arrived and squealed to a stop. The slim, silvery doors spread apart with a quiet whoosh! Cythiria stepped in and wrapped her arm around a pole. She placed her hands in the pockets of her hoodie as she gazed out the window and the flashing lights that rushed by in a *chaotic blur*.

CHAPTER 2

Arrival of an Old Friend

Griddish, Ashen Fissure, the Slipshot to Var 7

Rive Amber gazed up at the Slipshot Silo to Var 7. A narrow smile crossed her face as she dismounted the Vérkatros, which had paused at the edge of the Silo's platform.

"Cythiria," Rive murmured. "It's time you returned home. I, as well as Griddish, have waited for you long enough."

She stepped onto the round, metal-tiled platform. Her confident, measured stride created a tinny echo along the platform's surface. She paused at the array of black Transposals, the posts that would absorb the plasmic arcs which would strike from the tip of the Slipshot Silo and then open a portal to Var 7.

"But first, the Slipshot must be initialized."

Rive walked towards the Silo until she reached its smooth, shimmering walls. She touched the surface with the palm of her hand, stroking it in circular fashion. She turned her hand, formed a fist, and knocked. From it replied a thin, rattling, metallic sound. She reached into her pocket and pulled out a device that was shaped like a cylinder. An Init Caster, or an IC, it fit inside the palm of her hand. She held it up and blinked her eyes momentarily, sending a command through the Tenddrome to initialize the device. She thrust it forward and it grew into a staff about half her own height. Aware of the presence of the initialized IC, the Silo popped open a hatch along its side. She touched the end of the IC to an awaiting socket and pushed. A

door, invisible to the eye before it was initialized by the connection of the IC, hissed open. Rive stepped inside.

The cool, stale air felt heavy and thick. Rive sniffed. She could smell the traces of burning metal which was typical to any Slipshot. Except these smells were stale and cold, as if they had been formed long ago and forgotten.

She squinted into the dark, wide chamber. The gentle Griddish light from outside the open doorway illuminated an oval shaped pod. She walked towards it. Its hatch was open. She looked inside, at a small seat. *The Slipshot and the Slave work as one. They, like us, are simply nodes within the Tenddrome. Yet, Slipshot and Slave speak different languages.* Rive remembered the lessons. She was herself a Mechanic Class Slave before the war. But now, she was a *Bestiar*, a warrior of her own making.

She scoffed.

She turned and saw a smooth panel, which appeared to hover in the dark, its black, gleaming surface reflecting the light that spilled in from the outside. She walked up to it and stroked its surface. She held up the Init Caster. A hatch opened on the surface of the panel, and She touched the awaiting socket with the tip of the IC.

The Silo groaned and rumbled, and the ground rattled beneath Rive's feet. She looked up. Tendrils of energy licked the sides of the Silo, trilling an electric tune, twisting and winding until they formed a sphere of azure energy within its center. She felt a pull, as if tiny fingers were reaching down and plucking at her hair and skin and clothes.

She returned her attention to the pod and walked towards it. She stepped in, turned, and sat. She glanced around. *The Slipshot begins where the Slave ends. The Slave ends where the Slipshot begins. The two shall act as one, since both are Nodes within the Tenddrome.*

Rive breathed deeply. She closed her eyes, her breath lowering to a slow and steady pace. Her muscles relaxed, their tenuous fibers feeling as if they were unwinding, turning, and stretching, as if she herself were morphing into a knotted, twisting mass of fleshy tendrils.

She could hear the hatch hiss to a close. The air grew still, the silence deep. The darkness seemed to expand to an almost inky, liquid state. In the distance, small dabs of light bounced and streaked a chaotic rhythm. They grew closer, encompassing her, wrapping their cold, blue light around her like vines. And then they scattered.

She could see the dome of Griddish from above and the blackness of space beyond. She saw twisting funnels of light stretch in all directions, from Griddish to their associated Vars, forming umbilical connections from parent to children, connections she would not otherwise see, were she not so deep within the Tenddrome and connected to the Node which is the Slipshot to Var 7.

With her eyes, she followed one thin tendril of light to a distant Var. She could see the blue skies, the oceans, and the bright planetary ring of Var 7. She could feel the cold breeze of its atmosphere, the warmth of its beaches, the heat of its desert sands.

And then, her vision faded to black. She opened her eyes. She could feel her heavy pulse pound in her ears. The Slipshot was now connected to Var 7. She pulled the door of the hatch open and stepped out, her eyes blinded by the sharp, blue light of the Silo's energy mass, the sphere that twisted and turned inside its walls. She walked towards the door of the Silo and stumbled out onto the platform. She walked towards the point of convergence of the Transposals, glancing down at the black stain where Slipshot portals have opened and closed since the beginning of the Var's time.

"Well, here we go," she mumbled. She reached into her pocket and pulled out a small, oval shaped capsule, the Capsa. She turned it in her hand and pressed it between her fingers. She squeezed it and tossed it onto the platform. It bounced, a hollow, tapping sound, and then stopped. It popped and from its thin shell burst a plasmic arc, igniting the posts and joining the Silo's topmost portal in a shower of light. At the point of convergence, above the blackened ground, a thin, dark sliver formed and then spread apart, growing into a portal many times Rive's width and height. She gazed into the portal, which was so black that it tricked her groping eyes, always evasive, always defying. She could feel it pull at her hair and skin and clothes. She could hear the sounds of Griddish as they warped and folded into indecipherable knots.

The Slipshot to Var 7 is finally open again.

She stepped and then fell forward into darkness. She gasped and choked, her breath sucked out of her lungs as if she were squeezed inside a vacuum. And then, the bright blue sphere known as Var 7, Farth, appeared, encircled by a glossy, glimmering white ring. She felt a chill and then a blast of wind. Her lungs heaved greedily for oxygen as she plunged through wispy, white clouds. She braced herself, and then, a moment later, her booted feet landed squarely on brown soil.

She stood tall and gazed along the horizon, at the choppy, blue waters of the city's bay, the clusters of tall, lean towers that blinked a constant pink and blue glow, at the streaky, white planetary ring that stretched from one horizon to the other.

She smelled deeply of the air, which carried a scent of decaying sea. "Nissy," she mumbled, as a scowl curled on her upper lip. *So, this is the city where Cythiria resides. I suppose I should get used to this place. I have a lot of work ahead of me.*

ARRIVAL OF AN OLD FRIEND

CHAPTER 3

First Blush

Var 7, Farth, Nissy

Cythiria glanced along two dark, windowed monoliths which rose from the well-paved street. In a shrubby courtyard, clusters of students stood and chattered a steady hum, backpacks hanging from their shoulders. Cythiria paused and shuddered, and then stepped forward.

"Hey, hey," she heard, as she brushed up against one of those backpacks. "Check out the little hottie," said its owner, smirking as he turned and nodded his head. His eyes moved up and down her body.

Cythiria felt her neck and cheeks grow warm. She lowered her head, hoping she could sink deeper into her hoodie and disappear.

"Fucking moron," she grumbled.

She stepped forward and walked into the blocky building. In the dank halls, which echoed with the din of busy, excited voices, large digital projections scrolled the names of students along with their assigned classrooms. She waited for hers to appear, found it and gestured with her hand. She glanced at the floor, which flashed a sharp, LED yellow line and an animated arrow under her feet. She pushed her hands into her jacket pockets and stepped forward.

"Hey," she heard next to her. Her body jumped from the suddenness of the greeting.

"Hey," she mumbled.

"I feel like we got off on the wrong foot," came the voice of the backpack owner from a moment ago.

"You think?"

"I wanna make it up to you, you know?"

"I don't know."

"How about we meet up at lunch."

Cythiria rolled her eyes. "I don't do lunch."

"For real?"

"Yup."

"Ha! Me neither." He laughed nervously. "Lunch is lame."

Cythiria grit her teeth. She pulled one hand out of her pocket and held it towards him, palm forward. "Gotta go." She followed the flashing yellow line and the arrow to a glass door, which opened automatically with a whisper before her.

"Will I see you again?" came the voice, a higher pitch now.

"Doubt it," she said. The door closed behind her.

She sighed. She glanced around the room. Clusters of students stood and waited, chatting nervously among themselves. A few had settled into the sleek, plastic-looking workstations, which were equipped with arrays of holographic emitters, headphones, and headsets that covered the eyes like some die-cast blindfold. Some of the workstations had scribbles scratched into their sides. Others had marks drawn into arcane shapes and patterns. Beyond, a wide picture window looked out onto a cityscape. Tall, sleek buildings stretched towards the sky as busy streets snaked among them, filled with vehicles that moved at a steady, almost mechanical pace through intersections and around clusters of distracted pedestrians.

The fluorescent yellow arrow under Cythiria's feet flashed and animated in the direction of one of the workstations. Cythiria stepped towards it. She pulled her backpack off her shoulders and dropped it on the floor. She glanced across the aisle at another workstation, and astride it, a student. Her long, brown hair was pulled to a pair of side ponytails. Wavy tufts flowed down her cheeks from each side of her forehead. She wore bright red lip gloss, and her hazel-colored eyes contrasted with dark, wispy eyelashes. She turned her head towards Cythiria and looked her up and down. The corners of her lips turned to a discriminating frown.

"Hey," said Cythiria, nodding towards her.

She nodded back.

"I'm Cyth. Crenshaw."

She turned her eyes and frowned. "Cyth." She glanced across Cythiria's forehead. "So, what's with the bandage?" she said curtly.

Cythiria raised her hand to her head. "Um, I had an accident."

"Accident?"

"Long time ago." Cythiria paused. "You got a name?"

"Chelsea. Brimwater."

"Chelsea. Nice. I'll call you Chelss."

Chelss snorted and rolled her eyes. "I wish you wouldn't." She gazed out the window.

"You a first year?" said Cythiria.

Chelss scoffed. "Well, obviously."

Cythiria felt her neck and face grow warm. *Why wouldn't she be a first year? She's in the same classroom as me. Keep it cool, Cyth.* "Yeah, me too."

Chelss snorted again.

A gentle, ringing chime filled the classroom. The light in the room faded. The generic din of chatting voices settled to silence as the students made their way to their workstations. A projected image, cast upon an otherwise empty slate on the wall, materialized.

"Welcome to class 4a, year 1," came the gentle, calming voice. "You have been assigned a workstation. If you have not seated yourself yet, please do so now." The voice paused. The room grew quiet.

Cythiria stepped into the workstation. The seat was covered with a thin, soft, rubbery material. The workstation seemed to wrap itself around her, as if she were seated inside the cockpit of a racecar or an airplane. The walls cast a gentle, calming light, and a cool, airy breeze swirled around her. She shivered, and the breeze warmed, as if the workstation itself read her bodily response to it. She sighed, and her eyes started to droop. On each side was a small window. She looked out either side. On one, some student she hadn't met. On the other, Chelss. She felt her heart thump! inside her chest.

"In front of you," continued the voice, "Is an array of three screens. You will use these regularly during lessons. In addition, you have been assigned a headset and a pair of earphones. We will begin role, so please apply the headsets now."

Cythiria glanced through the widow at Chelss. She watched her as she gently pulled on the headset, making sure that the long tufts of hair streamed over its bands and not under them. Cythiria followed, pulling it on carelessly until it settled upon her head.

A warm glow of red light was followed by a series of quick, blue flashes.

Cythiria felt a deep, rumbling grind in the back of her head. She grimaced. Her forehead tingled and burned and then she heard a *pop!* followed by a deep sting, as if she had been cut with a jagged knife.

She jumped up and ripped the headset off. She tossed it across the room and tumbled out of the workstation. A gentle, chiming, rhythmic *burrrrr* sounded through the room, followed by the sound of the voice. "Please return to your workstation. Number 15987, Cythiria Crenshaw, please return to your workstation."

She fell on the cold, concrete floor and pushed her back up against the wall. She could feel a tickle on her forehead and then her cheek and lip. She lifted her hand and wiped her cheek and then glanced at her crimson covered fingers. She started to tremble, pulling her legs up against her chest and wrapping her arms around her knees. Her ears and head pulsed and throbbed, and the deep grinding sound in her head rose to a more feverish pitch. She heard a voice, close by, urgent, a thin, wispy sound that cut through the chaotic, noisy din of her own mind.

"Hey, Cyth, are you ok? Cyth!" She could feel a body press close to hers, an arm wrap around her shoulder, a hand grasp her arm. She could smell a gentle, florid scent, a comforting perfume. She turned her head and looked up towards the sound of the voice. She looked into those hazel eyes. They were wide, urgent, yet soft, nurturing.

"Cyth! Are you ok? Talk to me!"

And then, darkness.

CHAPTER 4

Recollections and Meetings

Var 7, Farth, Nissy

Cythiria sat on the hard pallet. The white room was unnaturally silent, except for the occasional *blip* and *tweet* of electronic monitoring equipment, or the *huzzz* and *fizzle* of digital projections onto blank, white slates. It was as if the room existed in a vacuum, or somewhere out in space, or maybe in Cythiria's head. Especially when her head felt like it was being stuffed with cotton just before the grinding noises would begin.

She pulled her legs close to her chest and wrapped her arms around her knees. She gazed over her socked feet towards the floor, her dark eyes distant, distracted. A crimson-stained, gauzy bandage was wrapped around her head, her hair matted against her cheeks and neck. She sighed.

"Thanks for helping me," she said, glancing momentarily at Chelss, who sat next to her. "You didn't have to come here with me, you know."

Chelss shrugged. "It's ok." She paused. "Besides, the computer wanted to know what happened to you, so it hoped I could be of help, I guess. I suppose it assumed we were friends or something."

Cythiria felt her heart *thump!* again. "I'm sorry you had to see me like that." She felt her stomach turn as she gazed into those hazel eyes, gentle, yet urgent. She felt a tender hand stroke her shoulder and then her back.

"It's ok."

"That was pretty bad."

"I've seen worse," said Chelss.

Cythiria turned her head towards Chelss. "You have?"

Chelss paused. "Well, no."

Cythiria's face cracked a smile, which was followed by a chuckle, and then a laugh. Chelss's frown, which seemed a permanent fixture, turned reluctantly to a wide smile, awakening round, dimpled cheeks.

"Um, you said your injury…," Chelss started, hesitating. She glanced at the bandage wrapped around Cythiria's forehead. "You said that you got it a long time ago."

Cythiria sighed, lifting her hand to her forehead. She stroked the bandage as it rustled under her touch. "Yeah." Cythiria paused.

"Look," said Chelss, as she started to stand up. "I don't want you to tell me anything you don't want to. I mean, maybe I should go."

"No!" said Cythiria, looking up at Chelss, her eyes pleading. "Sit down. Please." She took a deep breath. "I don't really know myself. I mean, I have these memories, from when I was a little kid, but they only go so far. I remember…" Her voice cracked, as tears welled up in her eyes. "…I remember my head was hurting really, really bad. And I couldn't make it go away. Someone was there with me. Maybe my parents. But they couldn't do anything.

"Since then, it's been off and on."

"What's been off and on?" said Chelss, her hazel-colored eyes wide, filled with concern.

"Those feelings. Kinda like what happened today." Cythiria sighed deeply. "It's hard to explain. Like, this grinding sound in my head. Some days it's constant, like it won't go away. And then, I just lay there all day. I don't want to get up and go out or do anything. Or maybe I just can't. Like there's this weight on me that I can't get off." Cythiria gazed at the floor.

Cythiria felt Chelss's soft hand on her arm. "Have you seen anyone about it?"

Cythiria scoffed. "Plenty. Jillian was always bringing me to see some doctor about it. All they'd do is poke and prod at me all day when I was a little kid. 'We can always do plastic surgery to remove the scars,' they'd say. But even then, I knew that wasn't the problem. Jillian knew too."

"Jillian?"

"My…er…mom."

"I'm so sorry." Chelss's hazel-colored eyes teared up a bit. "I didn't know."

Cythiria uncurled her body and sat up straight. "No worries. It's not your fault. Besides, you probably saved me."

"No, I…."

"Not that you'd want to. I mean, look at me."

Chelss's lip quivered. "It's not that. I just…."

Cythiria and Chelss turned towards a fizzling sound. A projected image of an almost-robotic human head was cast upon the blank, white slate. "Number 15987, Cythiria Crenshaw. Upon further examination, it is recommended that you take leave for the remainder of the day. Information about your incident has been forwarded to your legal guardians. A pod will be provided and return you to your place of residence. Number 15988, Chelsea Brimwater, please return to the classroom."

"How nice," mumbled Cythiria. "Nothing like having a personal touch." She pulled her boots on one at a time and stood up from the pallet.

"Look," said Chelss, "I don't have to go back to class. Let me take you back to your house."

Cythiria smirked and raised her hand. "Nah. I can handle myself. Besides, you'd get in trouble, number 15988. Might even get yourself suspended. Or worse, expelled."

Chelss hesitated. She glanced at the bandage on Cythiria's forehead and then glanced away. "Your injury."

"Psssshhhh," snorted Cythiria. "I've had that for at least eight years now. No one was able to fix me then, and I'm pretty sure some school computer AI or whatever isn't about to do it now." Cythiria paused, gazing into Chelss's hazel eyes. "I'll be fine. I promise."

Chelss nodded. "So, I'll see you tomorrow?"

Cythiria forced a smile. "You bet!" Cythiria stepped forward, and Chelss followed close behind. Cythiria stopped and turned to face Chelss. "How about we exchange contact info?"

Chelss hesitated. "Um…sure." She took out a device from her pocket and held it up. Cythiria reached into her pack and produced a similar device. She touched its surface to Chelss's. "Awesome. If I ever need help again, I'll call you first."

"Sure," said Chelss, smiling mysteriously.

"See ya!" Cythiria lifted a hand and waved as they passed their classroom. She walked through the dim corridor to the courtyard. Outside, the air was humid and smelled of smoke and rotting garbage and urine. The hum of cars and pedestrians echoed along the urban canyon that was Nissy.

Cythiria paused as she watched a dark, glassy vehicle pull up to the curb. The door slid open. She glanced inside the driverless cockpit, pulled her oversized hoodie over her head, and turned sharply down a side alleyway, her heavy, waffled boots tripping over unevenly placed cobbles and clusters of rubble and detritus.

"I ain't gettin' in that thing," she mumbled. "I'd rather walk. At least I can be anonymous out here."

She turned at a graffitied street corner and walked towards the cavernous entrance to the subway station, a broad smile crossing her face. *Bet I look pretty bad ass with this bandage on my head. No one's about to fuck with me now. Probably think I just escaped from the psycho ward, hee hee.*

Cool, white lights flashed hypnotically through dirt-smudged and graffitied windows. The whoosh and sway of the subway car, along with her warm, oversized hood, brought Cythiria's eyes and head to a steady, rhythmic droop. She nodded and drooled until the flashing lights were replaced by the warmth of Nissy's sunny, mid-day light.

Tall, slim, and sparkling needles seemed to stretch past a milky white slash, Farth's ring that cast its own light even in this bright day. Shimmering office buildings gave way to squat, single storied warehouses and shops as the train car emerged from its underground cavern and skirted along elevated tracks. The train paused at a station, its hovering mechanism squealing to a stop. The doors slid open, as passengers crowded out, some pushing and shoving, others shouting at unseen enemies, perhaps only visible to their purported victim's eyes. Others stepped in and darted and dashed to open seats, or grabbed hold of handlebars, their hands buried deep in their pockets or holding devices to which they paid their undivided attention.

Cythiria opened the top flap of her pack and reached in, grabbing hold of a handheld device. She stroked its surface, and the screen lit up. "Sweet," she mumbled, tapping "C-h-e-l-s-s" and a heart emoji under the newly entered line item. "My only contact except for dad and Jillian."

A woman paused in front of Cythiria. Cythiria stuffed the device back into her backpack and glanced up at this newly arrived person. Her eyes were dark and brooding. Cythiria scoffed, tilting her chin downward so that the hood would enrobe her head even more completely than it already had.

"You got some nice arms," Cythiria heard. She glanced up, towards the direction of the voice, catching the dark gaze of the woman who stood above her, and casting her own derisive glance.

"Whatever," she snorted. "Like you can even see them."

"Nice body, too."

"Hey, lay off, what are you, some kinda freak?" Cythiria shouted, the hood of her hoodie falling from her head.

The woman sneered. "You should use that to your advantage."

"Fuck off, ok. Just mind your own business," said Cythiria, turning in her seat.

The woman paused. "What's with the bandage?" she said, raising her forefinger and poking it.

"Ouch! That hurt! What the fuck's your problem?" said Cythiria, as she started to stand up. The woman placed a firm hand on Cythiria's shoulder.

"You ever think about fighting?"

"What?" scoffed Cythiria.

The woman looked Cythiria up and down. "I figure with your arm reach you'd have quite the advantage in the ring."

"Look, I don't know…."

"Lots of girls like to fight. For some, it's soothing."

Cythiria paused. "I…."

"Their minds are often agitated, restless. Like, they're looking for something. Something they've lost, something they wish to regain."

"Regain?" Cythiria's shoulders slumped. Her face relaxed as she gazed up at the woman who sneered down upon her.

The subway hovered to a squealing stop. "See that over there?" said the woman, nodding over her own shoulder towards the window behind her. Cythiria looked. On the street below, a squat, dirty brick building stood. On its roof, a plastic-looking, sun-bleached prop in the shape of a trophy. "That's my gym. Why don't you stop by sometime?"

Cythiria returned her gaze to the woman's, upon whose face cracked a derisive grin. "My name's Rive. Ask for me when you arrive."

Cythiria scoffed, half-heartedly. "As if…."

The woman turned and stepped out of the train car. Cythiria followed her with her eyes, watching her lithe gait, her disdainfully tilted chin, her confident, intentional step. The door whooshed! to a close and the train lurched forward. Cythiria continued to watch the woman named Rive.

As if I'm gonna go to some trashy gym because some freak on the subway told me to. Like that's ever gonna happen!

…*Something they wish to regain.*

Cythiria kicked her feet in the air, jumping over the subway turnstiles. She pulled her hood close over her head as she landed on the other side, her waffled boots echoing a solid thunk! on hard, metal tiles.

She stepped onto the street. Bright blue LED lights, emanating from humming cars, flooded the roadways with an almost piercing glow. Above, neon flashing lights cast warm blues and yellows on the smudgy, broken sidewalk. Beyond, the milky white slash of the planetary ring cast an almost ghostly glow on distant towers that stretched towards the sky like ambitious spikes.

Cythiria glanced around, jaywalking between speeding cars until she reached a dented and rusty steel door. It was tagged with graffiti, its original design buried under newer markings, signatures of new owners wanting to claim the barren brick walls that constructed this dingy alley.

The ground under her feet felt slick. Cythiria held her breath as a warm, humid breeze pushed the smell of garbage from nearby dumpsters in her direction. She took a more gingerly step forward and then kicked the door open, diving into a dark corridor which was lined with waxy boxes and rusty metal shelves piled up with various cans and instruments.

She sniffed. The smell of spices filled her nose and she smiled. As she walked down the corridor, the dark shadows were cast aside by a warm glow, and the echo of her *clunking!* boots was replaced by the shouts of voices, the hiss of frying oil, and the clang of utensils striking copper pans. The smell of spices gave way to deeper aromas, like saucy tomatoes, baking breads, melting cheeses. She smiled as she nearly tripped over a waxy box of vegetables and a wrapped-up slab of some kind of meat.

"Hey, if it isn't our little Cyth!" came a deep, rumbling voice. Its owner, a man with a barrel chest and arms like tree trunks, wore a dirty apron that was probably pristine white at some point in its life, as well as a worn and ragged t-shirt. Sweat poured down his forehead and dripped along his cheek and neck. He carried a cauldron of opaque, steaming yellow liquid. He set it down on the ground before her. Cythiria felt hot droplets splash against her face. She smiled as she wiped them away. He reached his hand to his forehead and wiped, then flicked his wrist so that the sweat splattered on the floor of the kitchen.

"Disgusting, you fucking animal!" came a shout from a man who turned away from a fiery stove. "Can't you see we got a lady here now, ya pig!"

"Fuck off!" the man shouted, as he turned towards Cythiria. He leaned forward and raised a thick, hairy eyebrow, his slightly crossed eyes focusing on the bandage on Cythiria's forehead. "What the hell happened to you?" he grumbled. "You get in a fight? Knocked 'em on their ass?" He raised his hands and balled them to a pair of Cythiria-head-sized fists.

Cythiria reached towards the bandage on her forehead. "Nah, just a little accident."

The man stood straight and put his forefinger to his chin. "An accident, or on purpose!"

"Um, definitely an accident."

The man snorted. "Well, if you say so. You eat yet?"

"Nope."

"Fredrick!" yelled the man. "Bring your princess something to eat. Jesus fuck, what an asshole." He turned towards Cythiria. "Am I right?" He crouched down and picked up the cauldron and made his way to a wide pit near the dining room entrance of the kitchen, placing it down roughly, its contents splashing and hissing and steaming as they struck the fiery surface below.

Cythiria turned and walked towards a corner of the kitchen and sat herself down on a crate, filled most likely with cans or some other shipment that regularly arrived at the kitchen. She took off her jacket and sat back. The steam and fire of the kitchen made her flush, and her neck and back started to prickle from forming droplets of sweat. She started to nod, her eyes drooping at the loud and steady din of the kitchen, the clanging pots and pans, the hiss and roar of fire, the grumbling shouts and groans, the *thump! thump!* of the dining room door as it was cast opened, and then flip-flopped to a close.

"Hey," came a voice that startled her awake.

Her eyes snapped open. "Oh, dad." He was wearing a long apron. It was still kind of white, although it too was quickly losing its pristineness. His dirty blonde hair was tied up to a tight ponytail and he wore a peaked, puffy hat upon his head. Strands of hair managed to sneak out from the inner band of the tightly arranged cap, clinging to his sweaty nose and cheek, which was scruffy and unshaven. His eyes were droopy, tired looking. He held a plate in his hand.

"You could have gone home if you wanted to."

"I know."

"They told me about your…accident," he said, nodding towards the bandage on her head.

"Yeah, well, that's the way it goes when you're all messed up like me."

Fredrick smiled gently. "You're not messed up, Cyth."

Cythiria scoffed. "I'm sure Jillian had a meltdown when she heard about it."

"I…." Fredrick paused. "I didn't tell her yet. She being on the road and all, I didn't want to worry her."

"As if she'd worry about me."

"Your mother loves you very much."

"She loves her *rig* very much," she said, derisively.

Fredrick smiled as he glanced down at his hands. "Here, I made this for you." He handed the plate to Cythiria. She smiled and took it, picking the contents up in her hand. It was a thick, crusty sandwich, warm with melty cheese and a spicy, tomatoey aroma. She bit into the crunchy crust, munching loudly and voraciously. She felt warm and she smiled as the food settled her grumbling stomach. When she was finished, she set the plate aside and stretched her body out on a stack of crates, putting her hands behind her head. She sighed deeply. Her forehead started to tingle, just a little bit, and her eyes started to droop. A moment later, her little corner was filled with the sound of a droning snore.

The subway whooshed and rattled as it hovered along its superterranean tracks. Fredrick pulled his jacket close to his body as the chill of the night settled into the otherwise empty car.

He felt a bump against his shoulder. He glanced down at Cythiria, her head resting on his shoulder, slightly turned up so he could see her face. Her eyes were closed and bordered by thick, dark eyelashes. Her mouth was slightly open, emitting a gentle snore, as rivulets of drool dripped down her chin and onto his jacket. He smiled as he reached over and pulled her hood over her head, pausing as he glanced over the gauzy bandage that started to show two crimson dots in the center.

He sighed deeply. *Those scars. If only I could have done something. If only....*

It's true, I would have sacrificed her. If for no other reason than to save my own world. But even then, there was nothing I could have done. Nothing to stop the Vérkatrae from coming down and tearing my whole reality apart.

"Why are you doing this?" Fredrick looked pleadingly towards the woman. Rive Amber, she was called. Her eyes were tired and worn. The corners of her lips were turned to a deep frown.

"Why? It is the way of Griddish," she said, her gaze distant, distracted. Fredrick glanced around the wide, metal-tiled platform, the tall, thin spire that was known as the Slipshot Silo. It seemed to reach forever skyward, endless in its ambition as it endeavored to touch the very apex of the dome that encased all of Griddish. The other Mechanic Class Slaves looked only at their handiwork, at the tools and parts that they carried around, wiping their hands on smudgy aprons, rubbing scruffy chins, nodding and scowling towards those two Varlings who had just arrived from Var 8, Earth. Among them stood countless Vérkatrae, some tall and bulky with heavy, rounded shoulders and red, glowing and shifting eyes running along their chassis. The Sleepers. Others stood closer to the ground, their bodies and limbs coiled to a tight spring, ready to trounce and consume and tear their target world apart. They were known as Constructors. They were waiting until summoned.

And summon them, *she* did.

"But circumstances change. *I* am giving you a chance. A new beginning."

"But all I want is to return to my own world," said Fredrick. He looked at Jillian, as she stood by his side, her eyes distant, wandering, her face without expression.

"That, I am afraid, is not possible. Your world is not as it once was." Rive paused. Her voice cracked. "War is coming to Griddish. You can either choose to be a refugee and die here, or you can have another chance."

Another chance?

Fredrick held the child Cythiria in his arms. She gazed at him with those dark, mysterious eyes. She would blink, enter the Tenddrome and return without effort. At least, that is how Fredrick understood it.

The Tenddrome. The manner in which all Slaves connect to one another. Without the Tenddrome, Slaves have no identity, and their memories, shared among all the Nodes that make up the Tenddrome, are not their own. The Tenddrome is like a cocoon that provides safety and comfort. But it is also binding.

That is how Rive Amber described it. *When we came here, as we fell through the Slipshot, to Farth, to Var 7, as they, the Slaves and Engineers of Griddish called it, Cythiria screamed.* In a single moment, her connection to the Tenddrome was broken. Was that the reason for the scars on her forehead? If only I could have done something. *If only I could have stopped the pain.*

If only….

Fredrick reached over and stroked Cythiria's thick, black hair. Her head wobbled with the pulse and rhythm of the subway car. *She's so big now. She's almost a woman. Almost. But still….*

The subway car rattled to a stop. The sliding door whooshed open. Fredrick jumped up and shook Cythiria's shoulder. She moaned. "Come on," he said, turning his back to her and crouching down. "Get on. I'll carry you."

Cythiria sluggishly reached forward and wrapped her arms around Fredrick's neck. Fredrick lowered his arms, hooking each around one of Cythiria's legs, and pulled her up into a piggyback. He stood and jogged out the door just as it was sliding to a hissing *slam!* He stood on the platform.

The weak, buzzing light cast a blue, reflective tinge on the damp surface. He looked up at the milky white slash, the ring, blinking his eyes at its cool brightness, and glancing at the dark, pulsing lights of ambitious skyscrapers. Cythiria clung to his back.

"Am I too heavy," she mumbled with a slur.

"Nah."

He stepped forward, down a broken escalator, across a cracked, cobbled street, and through an intersection that was choked with humming cars and clusters of pedestrians, milling around among blinking yellow and blue neon. He turned down a corridor cluttered with dumpsters and bags of detritus. It led to a dark, quiet street. Fredrick sniffed the air. It was fragrant, almost florid, and rancid with decaying sea life. He could hear the *thump!* of the sea against the steel dike. Above, the milky white slash that illuminated the night sky. In the distance, those blinking towers that made up the cityscape of Nissy.

Fredrick stumbled up the stairs of the single-story bungalow and kicked the door open. He walked to Cythiria's room, turned, and dropped her on the creaking bed. He bent over her, pulled her up by her shoulders, and stripped her of her hoodie.

"Dad," she mumbled, as she opened her eyes sleepily. "What's wrong with me?"

Fredrick snorted gently. "Nothing, Cyth."

"Why does my head hurt so much?"

Fredrick sighed.

"And why can't I remember anything from when I was a kid?"

Fredrick stroked Cythiria's head with his rough and calloused kitchen hand. "Someday you will, Cyth."

Cythiria's eyes closed as she sunk into slumber.

CHAPTER 5

An Awakening

Var 8, Earth, San Francisco

A dry, hot breeze whisked up a cloud of dust, filling the air with fine, choking particles. In the sky, rocky shards floated in close proximity to the surface, often crashing to Earth in a bright, cacophonous boom and crackle.

The Golden Gate Bridge was a mass of twisted, rusting metal, clinging to a waterless ground in a web of frayed and split cables. The city itself, its once grand buildings, were simply piles of rubble, worn away by a biting, relentless wind that stroked away the details of its surface to sandy mounds.

Matere Songgaard, former Engineer Class Citizen of Griddish, sighed as he recalled the days before the Vérkatrae arrived. The chilly evening fog, the bay filled with blue water and small, white boats, was a memory long passed.

He squatted over a dented and rusty metal basin, turning it slowly on the dusty, gravelly floor of the makeshift shelter. He groaned as he felt a contraction in his arm. Pain like an electric shock shot from his wrist to his shoulder. He fell back, kicking the basin over as its viscous, amber contents spilled onto the ground, filling the shelter with a pungent, oily smell. Matere coughed as he pushed himself up onto his buttocks and feet with his good arm.

He stumbled through a narrow doorway to the outside. The bright sun hurt his eyes as he squinted at his arm, his body bent over as he grasped at his forearm with his other hand. He tugged and pulled at the sleeve, the feeling of electric shocks coursing through every fiber of his limb.

He tore away the ragged, dirty sleeve. His eyes widened as he gazed at his arm. It pulsed and throbbed in front of him, while fibrous tendrils twisting and turning like trapped snakes, forming themselves into new, amorphous shapes.

Matere grit his teeth and then bellowed, falling to his knees in a cloud of dust. A moment later, his arm stopped pulsing, and the twisting and turning fibers settled to a state of quiet, the shape of his limb returning to that of a normal arm and a hand.

Almost normal, except that the fibers behaved more like Vérkatrae. They were warm and soft and hard at the same time. And although they held the shape of a human arm and hand, their color and texture were more alien than human.

Matere sighed. He could feel the tickle and prick of sweat dripping down his forehead. He reached his hand up to wipe it away. He glanced up at the deep, blue sky, at the clouds of asteroids that would quietly glide by. They were close, and they were often torn from their orbit and cast to Earth's surface in a show of streaking lights and hammering booms! He gazed across the dusty, yellow hills, the stony mountains and gorges that were once covered with seawater, at the distant artifacts of human civilization, broken and crumbled skyscrapers, rusting hulks of battered bridges. All remnants of a world that existed before they arrived.

᙭

It seemed so long ago that the Constructor Class Vérkatrae arrived. Their destination was Earth.

The ground seemed to rattle and quake under their feet. Matere took Betel's hand and pulled her up the side of the scrubby hill, his ankles turning as he stepped on pocks and stones. His breath was short, raspy, droplets of sweat dripping down his forehead and neck.

He climbed to the top of the hill. Betel followed. He gazed across the cityscape, the skyscrapers, clusters of small white houses, and beyond, the Golden Gate Bridge.

Cars stood still on the roads and freeways, while large, bulky machines walked among them, emitting deep groans that vibrated the ground beneath their feet.

"Sleepers," mumbled Matere, as he glanced sidelong towards Betel. "They've awakened."

Beyond them, a wide, dark hole split open across the sky. A moment later, hordes of nimble, fast, four-legged machines, their noses close to the ground's surface, flashed plasmic arcs before them as they emerged from the dark gash. Matere sniffed. The wind smelled of burning metal. In the distance, the ground shattered and split and boulders the size of towns were thrust towards the sky. The bay turned to cloud and steam, and it was boiled away under the invasion of the Vérkatrae.

"Constructors," said Matere. "Once they've arrived, there's no turning back."

Lines of constructors moved across the landscape, razing the city as they advanced up the hill towards them. Matere glanced at Betel. He reached into his pocket and pulled out his Plaxis Strand, flicking his wrist and igniting it with a plasmic hiss and whistle as it cut through the air.

"At least we can bring them one last fight."

Betel nodded and reached for her own Plaxi and ignited it.

The *screech!* of the Vérkatrae as they tore apart matter echoed along the remaining hills and valleys. Matere poised his body for the attack, slicing at the machines as they reached the top of his and Betel's hill.

The machines split into pieces, their severed arms, legs, heads falling to the ground under Matere's slicing Plaxi. And then, their shapes morphed. Pieces once separated from each other grew together to form new parts, joining other Vérkatrae, or combining with each other.

Matere, his breath short, his arms aching from the onslaught, stood back-to-back with Betel. He could hear her raspy breath. He could feel her body shudder. He watched as the ground seemed to fade beneath the advance of the Vérkatrae.

And then, from some unseen angle, one lurched forward, crashing into them. Matere tumbled and then lay on the ground, gasping for breath. He looked up. He saw an amorphous countenance and cold, glowing eyes, a gaping mouth as plasmic arcs licked its own head and neck. Matere pushed at its face with his hand, and with his Plaxis Strand, struck the neck, severing the head from its shoulders.

The head melted away like liquid, bubbling and flowing onto Matere's arm, twisting and twirling like some enraged cyclone. Matere screamed. Betel fell to her knees next to him. She dropped her Plaxi.

"Matere," she said hoarsely, as she watched his face twist and contort. "Matere!" she shouted, turning her gaze to his arm, and the Vérkatros that attached itself to him, her eyes wide with terror.

And then they just stopped. They just returned to the Slipshot and were gone. They didn't finish their task. They didn't deconstruct this place like they normally would. That was their job, their purpose. So, why?

Matere heard the scrape of shoes through loose gravel behind him. He turned to face the sound.

"You ok?" came the warm, reassuring voice of Betel.

Matere snorted. "Hardly." He held his arm up, clenching his fist. He gazed over its almost mechanical texture, the skin of a Vérkatros that ran from his shoulder to the tips of his fingers. "It's never done that before," he mumbled.

"Done what before?"

Matere sighed. "Like it had a life of its own. Like it had awakened."

Betel paused. "Perhaps your arm has gained its own agency. Which would make sense in light of the original Vérkatros attack."

Matere shook his head. "Then that would make my arm itself a Vérkatros? And if that's true, what does that mean for me?"

In the small shack, Betel and Matere sat at a squat, hand-hewn table. Matere stretched his arm across its top. Betel, who sat opposite Matere, took hold of it by the wrist and glanced closely over its texture. Its sinews twisted and turned upon themselves like viny tendrils, its weirdly mechanical parts embedded within and obfuscated, defiant of any form of observation and categorization. The color was a type of gentle, calming azure.

"If it is a Vérk, then it'll likely act on its own will," she mumbled as she continued to examine Matere's arm. "But like everything from Griddish except us, this Vérkatros is also a Node within the Tenddrome." Betel paused. "But, as far as we know, without the Slipshot, there is no way for any Node to establish a connection back to any other Node in Griddish." Betel sat up and sighed deeply. "So why awaken now?"

"Why indeed?" said Matere, glancing cautiously towards his own arm. "I've lived with this thing since the day it took over, like it was some kind of a parasite that I couldn't get rid of. Still, it never moved like this before."

Betel sat up. She rubbed her chin with her finger as she glared intensely at Matere's arm. She sighed quickly. "Could it be that the Slipshot is open again?"

Matere paused. "Open? But why? Haven't the Vérks done enough damage?"

"They never finished the job," said Betel. "They were supposed to turn this world back into primordial gas. Yet here we stand on solid ground." Betel glanced up at the sky and the cloud of asteroids that passed within her view. "For the most part."

Matere lifted his arm off the table and held it up, glancing over it, his gaze sharp, critical. He curled his fingers into a fist. "I suppose we should find out."

"Find out?" said Betel, tilting her head to one side, her cool, gray eyes sharp and penetrating.

"If the Slipshot really is open or not."

Betel's eyes lit up. "You mean?"

Matere stood up, letting his arm fall to his side. "Indeed. Let's go get the Perispikes."

CHAPTER 6

A Direct Challenge

Var 7, Farth, Nissy

Cythiria walked through the narrow, stuffy hallway. She turned and stumbled up a flight of stairs. She bowed her head and sank deeper into her hoody. She lifted her hand and brushed her fingers against her forehead. The large gauze wrapping was gone now, replaced by a pair of small bandages that she had arranged in criss cross fashion.

She pushed her hands into her jacket pockets. She could hear the voices of students, grumbling, laughing, chatting, their nervous, busy feet shuffling and milling around. She sniffed. The air was warm, humid, smelling of sweat mixed with pungent cologne. Cythiria lifted her hand to her mouth and coughed.

Cythiria felt her heart beat quickly in her chest as she gazed down the hall. It was Chelss, leaning against the wall, her long, brown hair pulled to a pair of wavy ponytails. She was staring at a device that she held in her hand. Cythiria paused, wanting to turn around, go in another way, or run home. She took a slow, deep breath and stepped forward.

"Hey," she said, pausing in front of Chelss, whose hazel-colored eyes glanced up distractedly from the device and caught her gaze. Her long, brown hair tumbled down upon her shoulders. Her red lips curved to a pout. Her dark, wispy lashes accentuated her eyes with an almost burning mystery. Cythiria felt her stomach flutter.

Chelss nodded and then returned her attention to the device in her hand. "Glad to see you're ok," she muttered.

"Yeah, well, eventually I'd get over it, you know."

"Um hm," she said flatly as she tapped and stroked the screen of her device.

"If it was up to me, I'd ditch this school and just get a job somewhere. I've only been here a day and I already hate it."

Chelss glanced at Cythiria, her eyes flitting up and down her face, a subtle scowl growing across her face. She returned her attention to the device in her hand.

"Oookaay," mumbled Cythiria. She started to step away and then paused. "Hey look, if you don't wanna talk to me, all you have to do is say so…."

Chelss paused. "Just forget it."

Cythiria turned and stomped along the hall, her heavy, waffled boots echoing a thick, hollow *thud!* She pushed through a cluster of students and stumbled into the classroom. She tore her backpack off her shoulders and threw it at her workstation. The backpack crashed and tumbled onto the floor. Cythiria sat on it and leaned against the workstation. She crossed her arms and pouted.

"What's her problem?" she grumbled. *Just a few days ago she was super nice to me and now…. Did I do something to piss her off?* Cythiria gazed out the window of the classroom, her eyes flitting along the towers that reached towards the milky white band in the sky. She sighed.

"Fuck this, I'm outta here," she muttered, as she scooped up her backpack and slung it onto one shoulder. She stomped out the door of the classroom and turned down the corridor, crashing against oncoming students. Pushing forward, she passed Chelss, who was leaning her back against the wall. She felt her heart thump and her throat tighten. She looked down as she buried

A DIRECT CHALLENGE

her hands in the pockets of her hoodie, trying not to turn her head towards her fellow student, the object of her overwrought passion.

She stumbled into the courtyard. The hum and whisper of moving cars and the patter and babble of human voices echoed through the urban canyons. High pitched tweets and sirens cut through the generic din, punctuating the steady rhythm of Nissian life with flashes of disruption. Cythiria stepped forward, turning down a narrow street corridor, its cobbles damp. She sniffed. The putrid smell of rotting garbage attacked her senses. She coughed and sank deeply into her hoodie.

She dived down a flight of slippery stairs into the subway's neon lit cavern. The chaotic sounds of buskers, of poorly tuned, twangy stringed instruments, or the heavy, steady *thump! thump!* of drumsticks striking upturned buckets tittered along the hard, tiled floors and walls.

She stepped towards the turnstiles, placing one hand on each and swinging her legs over the gate, her head buried deeply in her hoodie. She paused at the railway track of the subway. She could hear the *whoosh!* and squeal of the train as it approached her platform. She could feel the warm, dry air brush across her face and catch her hoodie. It slowed and paused and the doors slid open. Cythiria walked in and plunked herself down on a seat.

The train lurched forward and dove into the darkness of the tunnel. The hiss and squeal of the hovering mechanism echoed along the walls. The sharp, LED lights flashed hypnotically, and multi-colored animations played advertisements through the car's windows.

Cythiria sighed as the train rocked side to side. *Why does Chelss hate me all of a sudden? The way she looked at me, as if I was some kinda freak. I mean, I guess I am some kinda freak.* She reached up and stroked the crisscrossed bandages on her forehead with her finger. *I don't think I'll ever be normal. Probably everyone at that fucking school hates me now. Geeze, I'm gonna get it once they find out I cut class. Jillian is gonna freak out. Dad might get upset too.* Cythiria grimaced as she felt a sharp jolt of pain shoot through her head. She could hear a low, grinding hum somewhere between her ears, somewhere in the soft flesh that made up the inside of her skull. Sometimes, her head felt like it was stuffed with cotton, like all the sounds in the world, all her thoughts, her inner voice, were being muffled by some gauzy fabric. She pulled at her ear lobe and shook her head. She felt her stomach turn. *I don't blame Chelss. She'd have ME to deal with, and that's no fun for anyone.*

The train shot out of the tunnel onto an above ground track. The echoing hiss and whistle were replaced by a vibrating hum from deep within the chassis of the subway car. Towers and skyscrapers gave way to warehouses and fenced lots, sleek passenger cars to large trucks and rigs. The streets below were cracked and looked slickened and oily.

The train squealed to a stop. Cythiria pursed her brow as she glanced out the window at the squat building with the plastic-looking trophy mounted to its roof. She jumped up as the doors hissed to a close, kicking a booted foot between them, and squeezing out onto the platform. The train lurched forward as she watched it fade and disappear down the track.

She turned and dashed down the stairs, through a dingy, gray corridor. She jumped the turnstile and emerged onto a street corner. The hum and rattle of large trucks echoed along the streets and among the squat buildings. She crossed the intersection, nearly tripping over oily, cracked bitumen until she arrived at a glass door whose pane was cracked from the bottom to the top.

She took a deep breath. *Something they've lost. Something they wish to regain.* Those words, from that woman, echoed through her head. *Is this really what I want?* She scoffed. "I mean, I'm just gonna check it out. I don't have to commit to anything, right?" she mumbled. "Maybe this isn't even the place." She glanced up at the sky, at the milky white streak, the planetary ring that crossed it. "Still early. I'm sure the school is calling dad right now. He's gonna talk to Jillian, and that's when I'm gonna get it." She took another deep breath, steeled herself, and pulled open the door, which clattered with a hollow clang from a brass bell clapping against its pane.

Cythiria stepped in. She glanced around the wide chamber. Long punching bags hung from the ceiling, attached with thin cables to creaky, wooden rafters. Lifting weights were stacked in the corners and placed upon racks. In the center stood a round-shaped ring. To its posts were joined sheets of intertwined wire that looked sharp to the touch. The sound of whipping jump cables, the slap of gloves against pads, the grunt of strained voices echoed through the room. Cythiria sniffed the air. It was stale and smelled of mildew. She crinkled her nose and did a quick pirouette towards the front door when....

"I see you made it."

Cythiria paused. She turned towards the voice. "Um...."

"And so soon." The voice's owner strolled forward with a quiet yet determined stride, her hands clasped behind her back. She stopped.

Cythiria looked at the face of the woman who stood in front of her. *Rive* she remembered from that day on the subway. Rive held her chin high and her nose in the air as she glared down at Cythiria with sharp, critical eyes. A scowl spread across her face and her lip curled to a frown. Her jaw clenched, and her upper lip quivered as if she were about to spit. Her black hair was tied to a tight ponytail. Her stance was certain, confident, her body taut, as if it were about to spring into combat at any moment.

Her eyes. Those dark, glaring eyes softened for a moment, as if recalling a distant, regrettable memory, or a loss of something precious. Her brow pursed to a melancholic curve, releasing their otherwise stoic tension for a single, passing moment.

"Yeah, well, I was just leaving," said Cythiria, poking her thumb over her shoulder towards the door.

Rive stepped towards Cythiria. A wry smile crossed her face. "At least grant me an opportunity to change your mind."

"An opportunity?"

"A wager."

"Well, I, um...."

Rive stretched her arm towards the ring, as if she were about to present a grand spectacle. "If you can strike me once in there, then you'll be free to go as you please."

"*Strike* you?"

"Indeed."

"As in, hit?"

"What else?"

"With my fist?"

"You may choose your own weapon."

"And if I do hit you, you'll let me go?"

"If not, then you will become my newest student."

"It kinda sounds like you're taking me prisoner."

"Prison, as you put it, is a state of mind."

Cythiria raised her brow. "Um, look, I don't have a lot of money, so…."

"Who said anything about money?"

"You know, I don't know about this. I mean, it seems kinda unfair, like, I wouldn't want to mess up that pretty face of yours or anything." Cythiria grimaced.

Rive's eyes sparkled for a moment and then returned to their stoic glare. "It doesn't hurt to try. What could you lose? Seems to me, you only have something to gain. Isn't that why you came here in the first place? To gain something you lost? To be strong again?"

Cythiria paused. *To gain something I lost. To be strong again.* What did Cythiria lose? Herself? Who was she? She didn't know. She didn't know why she had those scars on her forehead. She didn't know why her head hurt so bad that sometimes she just wanted to blow it off her own shoulders and get it all over with. She looked at Rive, gazed into those dark, unfailing eyes, that confident glare. *If only I could be strong. If only….*

"Fine," she said. She pulled the straps of her backpack off her shoulders and let it drop onto the concrete floor. She pulled off the hoody, once sleeve at a time. She sat on the floor and pulled off her heavy, waffled boots. She stood up.

A cocky smile crossed Rive's face. She turned and bowed, stretching her arm invitingly towards the ring. She held Cythiria's gaze with her own sneering glare. Cythiria stepped forward. She walked up to the wire fence and paused. She took a deep breath and stepped in through an open door.

She felt the smooth canvas under her bare feet. She heard the door of the ring slam shut as Rive stepped in. Her legs and feet started to tremble. Rive stepped towards her and stood close. A tiny smile seemed to crack her otherwise stoic frown. "Just be yourself," said Rive.

"Then I'll certainly die here."

Rive lifted her hands towards Cythiria's forehead. "But first…." She pinched the crisscrossed bandages on Cythiria's head and ripped them off.

"Ouch!" shouted Cythiria, stepping back.

"Now, let's go."

Rive crouched, her legs spread to a combat stance. She lifted her fists and held them close to her chin. She glared at Cythiria as she circled.

Cythiria also crouched and lifted her fists. She felt her heart pound heavily in her chest, the warmth of adrenaline course through her body. The cotton stuffiness that seemed to always fill her head cleared, and the deep grinding sound that echoed between her ears faded. She felt light, as if a heavy burden had been lifted from her shoulders and her chest.

She clenched her teeth and grinned as she circled. She locked eyes with Rive. She lurched forward, leading with a right jab. Rive ducked and stepped under, turning and then facing Cythiria from her side.

"You have to do better than that," said Rive, her voice taunting. "One strike, and you're all mine."

Cythiria pirouetted and stepped back. Her breath was short, raspy. She crouched, raising her fists to her face in a defensive stance. She felt the prickle of breaking sweat on her neck and back. The scars on her forehead stung from its salty dampness.

She lurched forward again, her left fist low as she aimed with an uppercut. Rive stepped lithely to the side. She could feel Rive slip closely by. She could feel her breath stroke her cheek, the breeze from her body brush against her own.

"Stop toying with me," Cythiria growled.

"Toying? All you need to do is strike me once. Is that so hard?" Rive smirked as she stepped back, lowering her fists tauntingly to her side and nodding provocatively towards Cythiria. A cocky sneer spread across her face, baring sharp, white teeth.

Cythiria clenched her teeth. She jumped towards Rive and reached for her waist. Rive stepped aside and raised her foot, tripping Cythiria so that she tumbled to the floor.

"Fuck!" Cythiria slammed her fist on the mat. She stood up, lowered he head, and lifted her fists up. And then, like a blur, Rive lurched forward. Cythiria felt a crack against her jaw. She tumbled backwards and feel on the mat. The world around her turned to white sparkles, her eyes rolled up in their sockets, her limbs stiffened. A moment later, maybe longer, Rive stood above her, holding out an open hand. Cythiria sighed and took it. Rive's arm was strong, unmoving. She pulled Cythiria up as if she were nothing but a slender twig.

Rive looked into Cythiria's eyes with her own dark, critical gaze. Her stoic expression softened, a thin smile curved up along the corners of her mouth. "Be here before dawn tomorrow," she said.

"What?" protested Cythiria.

"It's part of the deal," said Rive. She lifted her hand and placed it on Cythiria's shoulder. Her grasp was strong. "I won. You lost. So, now you belong to me."

"You know that wasn't fair," said Cythiria.

"Life is not fair. We are not always born with the tools we need to survive. We need to forge them, and then hone them." Rive Amber turned and walked out of the ring, disappearing down a dank, gray corridor at the back of the wide chamber. Cythiria stepped gingerly towards her pile of things. She sat down and pulled on her boots and her jacket. She sat and sulked and then stood up. She pulled the backpack onto her shoulder and walked towards the front door, kicking it open with her foot. The brass bell clattered against the windowpane. She glanced up at the sky, at the ring that was now a shade of golden yellow as the sun set on Nissy and evening settled in. She raised her hand to her jaw, touched it hesitatingly, and grimaced.

※

A gentle breeze whispered along a dark, cobbled corridor. A man leaned against the wall of a dilapidated brick building. The wall was covered with layers of graffiti and tags perhaps decades old. A neon light buzzed and hummed to life, casting pink and green light on the hard, glistening surfaces.

His head was like smudgy, oily smoke, its shape always morphing and incomprehensible. He pulled his hood over his head. "It's been a long time, my dear Mechanic Class Slave," he mumbled as he watched Cythiria walk across the street and enter the dark gateway of the train station, hopping over the turnstile and disappearing into its shadows. *You've grown much since that day when you first arrived here, crying because of the fire that burned those holes into your head.*

I see you've placed your trust in an old acquaintance. Do you recall her? I doubt you can, not after you lost your connection and your identity to the Slipshot. Everything that Griddish touches is corrupt, including its own children. This universe will only be saved once we've seen the end of Griddish and all its creations.

The man let the hood fall to his shoulders. His head morphed as dark tendrils twisted and turned to form a human shape. Eyes, a nose, a mouth materialized from dark nothingness. His face was stoic, framed by a silver beard. His hairless head glistened in the ring's milky white light.

I'm afraid I can't let you continue this little relationship with your newly discovered old friend, Cythiria. Friends? Can Slaves really be friends with each other? The man paused. *So today, I am Jeremiah Onu again. I suppose I should seek out my old confidants Fredrick and Jillian. I believe we will have much to discuss.*

CHAPTER 7

Pathway to Griddish

Var 8, Earth, San Francisco

Matere glanced along the horizon, at the dusty ravines that littered the landscape where the city once stood, its remains long ago obliterated by the Vérkatrae advance.

How long ago was it? A lifetime, maybe?

Shards of rock floated in the sky, casting weak shadows on the ground below. One, dislodged from its orbit, whistled and popped as it entered the atmosphere in a show of bright, white light. A rusty, corroded car limped and puttered by, its engine stuttering and groaning as oily smelling smoke spewed out of its tailpipe.

Matere waved at the driver and waited for the car to pass. He turned towards Betel. "I think this is the place."

"Are you sure?"

Matere sighed, his eyes grew distant, as if recalling a memory. "It's been a long time since the Slipshot last anchored itself to Var 8. It was near Opal's apartment…."

"…Chinatown."

"Or what was once Chinatown." Matere glanced along the horizon. "This hill we're on, it feels familiar. Imagine back then if the water from the bay was gone. It might look something like this," he said, a tone of reminiscence in his voice.

"It's worth a try," said Betel. "Even if we're off, and if the Slipshot actually is open, then it should find us when we light up the Perispikes."

"Let's hope."

Betel pulled the strap of the backpack off her shoulders and let it fall onto the gravelly ground. It clanged heavily. She opened it up and pulled out a device about as long as her forearm. It was shaped like a spike. She pointed the tip at the surface of the ground and pressed a switch that was hacked onto the cylinder. A sharp *clang!* and the Perispike burrowed almost instantly into the ground. Betel reached into the pack and pulled out another Perispike. She tossed it to Matere. He stepped about ten feet away, held its tip above the ground, and depressed the switch. Betel placed two more, tossing another to Matere until they had five Perispikes placed in a pentagonal arrangement.

Betel wiped her forehead with her hand as she gazed up towards the bright sun. She sighed. "You ready for this?"

Matere nodded. "Let's do it."

She bent down and pressed another switch which was also hacked into the shaft of the Perispike. An arc of light emitted from the Perispike and connected with each spike in the array. A blue tinge reached towards the sky from the Perispikes and converged at the top, forming an azure dome. A deep quiet filled the space around them. Outside, flocks of birds seemed to be frozen in place as they flew through the sky, and a certain stillness seemed to settle on the world outside.

"That should align Var 8 to Griddish," said Matere. "Now, all that's left is to hope the Slipshot is actually open."

Betel reached into her backpack and pulled out an oval-shaped capsule, the Capsa. She lifted it up, holding and turning it between her thumb and forefinger. She squeezed it and then tossed it towards the center of the dome. A moment later, it popped, and from it emerged a plasmic arc, which reached towards the top of the dome. A thin, dark line formed in the center and then split and crackled apart, opening a dark hole. Matere gazed into it and then pulled his eyes away. He glanced at Betel.

"So, the Slipshot *is* open after all," she said, her gray eyes shifting as she considered. She glanced at Matere's arm, which appeared to fade and then twist and split. "I guess that Vérkatros on your arm knows."

Matere held his hand up in the air, and his eyes followed his arm. "I guess it does."

Matere turned towards the open Slipshot portal. He felt it pull on his hair and clothes and skin. He heard the sound of Betel's voice, which twisted and morphed into indecipherable knots. He reached out his hand, taking Betel's into his own.

"Well, this is it," he mumbled. He glanced at Betel and smiled. And then, they fell into the Slipshot.

Matere held onto Betel's hand. He felt squeezed and compressed, as if he were being pushed through a long, narrow tube. Below him, the blue sky of Var 8, its yellow and gray surface, its clouds of orbiting meteors, its cracked, planetary sphere that looked like some broken wheel, pulled away. Above was darkness, but then, a gentle light poured out from a small portal, which widened as he approached. He reached for it, kicking his arms and legs as if swimming through thick, viscous fluid. He tumbled onto a hard surface, scraping his arms and face. He looked up. He heard Betel *plunk!* behind him.

He stood up and looked around. The Slipshot, the dark portal that deposited them here, faded away. The black Transposal posts that circled the platform under his feet were now quiet. He glanced at the Silo, the tall thin tower that stretched towards the underside of the dome, its apex rising to a sharp point. Just below that, a round portal that looked like some all-seeing eye. The round, tiled platform, upon which sat the Silo, was quiet. He tapped a booted toe against its metallic surface. It returned a hollow, tinny echo. Square, blocky buildings that were built along the perimeter of the platform stood empty, quiet, devoid of Mechanics who normally peopled them as they sought out parts to undertake repairs on the Vérkatrae, the Slipshot, or any number of machines that ran Griddish.

In the distance, along the horizon, he glanced at the cityscape that was Ashen Fissure, its once white buildings now a tangled heap. He glanced at Betel. She shook her head.

"A lot has changed, Matere," she said as her eyes followed the horizon. "Griddish, it seems, is no longer what it once was."

Matere sniffed the air. The smell of burnt metal faded as a gentle breeze *whooshed!* through the grass and along the surrounding hills.

His ears pricked at the sound of footsteps. He glanced quickly at Betel and turned towards the sound.

A man stepped towards him, his heels clicking on the metal-tiled surface of the platform. A smirk spread across his face. He stopped in front of the two, scoffed, and pushed his hand through his thick, black hair.

"Well, well, well, if it isn't our little Engineer Class Citizens Matere Songgaard and Betel Longshrew Piper come back from the dead. How was the afterlife?"

Matere scoffed. "And you are?"

Natty snorted. "I'm sorry. I didn't introduce myself. Name is Natty Mick, former Mechanic Class Slave," he said, smirking. He pushed his hand through his thick, black hair again.

"Mechanic Class Slave," mumbled Matere disapprovingly.

"Oh, but I've been upgraded. I'm now a Bestiar, thanks to one Rive Amber."

Matere and Betel exchanged glances.

"Are you the one who opened the Slipshot?" said Betel, her voice tense, her gray eyes sharp.

Natty snorted. "Surely you didn't think it would just open itself. I mean, how silly would that be?" He stretched his arms and yawned. "To be honest, I'm surprised you showed up so soon. I guess it didn't take you long to figure it out."

"So, then, since you've been expecting us," said Matere, "Can I ask you a question?"

"You can ask as many questions as you like," scoffed Natty. "As Var 8 Varlings say, 'knock yourself out.'"

"What is your purpose? Why set up this little charade of yours?"

"Why, indeed?" Natty stepped close to Matere and glared at him with dark eyes. His top lip trembled as if he were about to spit. "I suppose it was time for you to come home."

"Come home?" said Matere, raising his brows. "Come home to this?" He nodded towards the ruins where once Ashen Fissure stood.

Natty scoffed. "I suppose I could've let you rot on Var 8." He smirked, pushing his hand through his hair yet again. "I guess you could've just died on that half planet."

Betel grit her teeth. She stepped forward and glared at Natty with her cool, gray eyes. "Why didn't you finish the job? Do you realize how much suffering you caused?"

"Suffering! I would think allowing so many people to survive would fit right into your grand world view." Natty lifted his hand and touched it to his chest, mockingly. "You Engineer Class Citizens never change. You walk a fine line between total chaos and strict protocol. You're completely oblivious to how the world really works," he said, his lip curving to a snarl.

"It wasn't us," said Matere. "Sending the Vérkatrae to Var 8 was not our plan."

Natty shook his head. "As if you could so easily wash your hands of what happened. Being the inventor of the Beauty Worlds, of Var 7, Var 8, and who knows how many others, that does not let you off the hook one bit." Natty paused. "Nonetheless, it really wasn't our idea. It's just that, well, war started. And the Vérkatrae were no longer concerned with their duty to dismantle Var 8. Simply put, they gave up and left."

Matere and Betel exchanged glances. "Gave up?"

"The Vérks are not as simple as you would think," Natty sighed ostentatiously. "Who knows what goes through their little brains?" Natty stretched once more and placed his hands on his hips. "So, I guess I should welcome you back home." Natty reached his hand towards Betel, who slapped it away, scowling. "Such venom," he smirked. "Not becoming a woman of your stature, Betel Longshrew Piper. Or should I say, *Councilwoman* Longshrew Piper." He scowled, glancing along her body from shoulder to toe. "I see you look like one of *them* now, like some impoverished Varling. Whatever happened to the sparkling regalia that you once so proudly donned?"

The sound of grinding dentine issued from Betel's clenched teeth. Natty saluted and then turned. His sharp heels echoed a clicking rattle on the metal-tiled surface of the Slipshot Silo's platform. He waved as he mounted upon the back of a Vérkatros about twice his own height. It turned on six legs and paused. It rose from the ground and retracted its legs into its chassis, hovering silently away.

Matere sighed. "What do you suppose that was all about?"

Betel shook her head. "I don't know, but he's suspicious as hell."

Matere turned towards Betel. "Well, I aim to find out."

"It could be a trap."

Matere sighed. "Perhaps. But if these Mechanics are out to get us for some reason, then it won't take much to get caught."

"Bestiars," corrected Betel.

Matere tilted his head. "Huh?"

"They call themselves Bestiars now."

"Indeed. Which makes this whole situation all the more interesting. There hasn't been a new class of Slaves for eons."

"Be careful, Matere," cautioned Betel.

Matere faced Betel and smiled widely, baring white teeth. "As if I could be anything other than careful."

Betel sighed and rolled her eyes. "That's what I'm afraid of."

Natty Mick sat on the Vérkatros, its body vibrating gently as it hovered along the grassy Ashen plains. The body dipped and rolled as the dark walls of Sanguine Heap came into view. To Natty's left, the broken cityscape of Ashen Fissure burst up from the ground like shattered teeth, the once glistening white towers now burnt and corroded. Even further beyond the walls of Sanguine Heap, echoing pops, flashes, and vibrating rumbles carried on in rhythmic fashion, and then settled to an eerie quiet.

Natty sped towards the walls of the fortification, whooshing silently through steel arches into its main courtyard. Bestiars stood in militaristic order, Plaxis Strands ignited, their bodies glistening with sweat.

Natty paused the Vérkatros, blinking his eyes for a moment as he issued the halting order through the Tenddrome. He swung his leg jauntily over the back of the Vérkatros and jumped onto the cobbled surface of the courtyard. He walked towards the inner gateway, through dank corridors that smelled of musk and sounds of chanting, clashing voices.

He stepped through a hall, his heels tapping with certainty on the hard, stone floor. He glanced out of narrow windows that overlooked the plains of Ashen Fissure. The horizon was littered with dormant Slipshot Silos, their numbers choking the otherwise verdant hills of Griddish. He scoffed.

He entered a dark chamber. Inside, a gentle, green glow flickered along the floor and walls. He approached, stopping at a panel from whose surface was projected a holographic screen. Within it, characters flitted up and down like nervous insects.

Upon the panel were arrogantly tossed crossed and booted feet, their owner, a taut body and a scowling face.

Natty paused. "So, you're back."

"Only temporarily. The Vars are like poison to us Slaves, especially when the Slipshot is closed."

"And what about your little project?"

"Cythiria? I'd say I'm making progress."

"So, she's still alive?"

Rive paused. "Damaged, but alive."

Natty scoffed. "So, how is she useful to us?"

"She is critical to our success."

"Even as damaged goods?"

Rive sighed. "She survived this long on Var 7 with a closed Slipshot. That's not an easy task." Rive paused.

"And?"

"A hunch."

"About?"

"The Vérkatrae."

"What about them?"

"Cythiria is neither a Slave nor a Varling. Or, maybe she is both. Griddish is old, Natty. We need change."

Natty scoffed. "And you think some brat from Var 7 can change Griddish? Are you insane, Rive?"

"Maybe."

Natty snorted and shook his head. "Whatever. Honestly, I'm only here to inform you that Matere and Betel have arrived."

"Indeed. I sensed a change in the Slipshot's status."

"Well, he's pretty pissed. And so is Betel. Frankly, you should have just left them to rot on Var 8. There's no way they would have been a threat from that worthless shit hole of a half planet. But now, they're running around free in Griddish and likely to raise some real havoc."

"I'm counting on it," said Rive. Natty rolled his eyes. "In fact, Matere is the key to our success. Both he *and* Cythiria."

CHAPTER 8

Lessons

Var 7, Farth, Nissy

Cythiria glanced up at the dark blue sky. The brightness of the milky white ring started to fade as Farth's warming star rose on the horizon. Shallow, white lights gleamed intermittently from windows on tall towers, and red and yellow lights mounted on their apexes blinked slowly and hypnotically. Whispers of cars and distant rumbles of trucks echoed along the deep, urban corridors. A fresh, dewy smell was quickly dismissed by the rise of dust and smoke from the spinning mechanisms of cars and the churn of machinery inside nearby warehouses.

Cythiria took a deep breath as she gazed at the door of the building upon whose roof was mounted the large, plastic trophy, faded and yellowed in areas awash with regular sunlight. "Welp, here we go," she mumbled as she pulled back her shoulders and jutted out her chin and chest. "Again."

She pulled at the glass door, and the hollow metal clapper rang against its pane. She stepped in and glanced around the dim chamber, squinting towards some lights that emanated from the back. She could hear the *flip! flap!* of fast punches on bags and the rapid *whip!* of jump cords through air. She sniffed the mildewy, musky air and coughed quietly as she held her hand to her nose.

She dropped her backpack on the floor. It echoed a heavy *thump!* She stepped towards the ring that stood at the center of the chamber. She reached out and touched its wire fence and then rubbed her chin, recalling that day.

She gasped.

Something wrapped itself around her neck and pressed against her throat. She felt the air grow thin in her lungs. She reached her hands towards it, grasped it, and pulled. It was strong, sinewy, throbbing.

"I'm so glad you showed up," came the slithering whisper from beside her head, tickling and taunting her ear. She tried to face it, but she could not turn her head while she was clenched within this iron-like stranglehold. She could feel a body pressing against her from behind. It was hard, solid, unmoving. She relaxed, her breath shallow, her quick pulse pounding in her ears.

"I…."

She felt the once unbreakable grip relax. She fell onto her knees and placed her hands on the floor in front of her, forcing deep breaths as she coughed and choked. She glanced up.

"I've been waiting for you," came the voice of Rive Amber. Her otherwise dark, glaring eyes looked soft, almost warm for a moment, a gentle smile curling up on one corner of her mouth.

Cythiria turned and sat on her haunches. "Yeah, well, I've been busy."

"Too busy for yourself?" Rive reached an open hand towards Cythiria, who took it, and was hoisted onto her feet as if she were nothing but a weed.

"Too busy for everything, except keeping my head straight."

"I see."

Cythiria scoffed. "Not your problem."

Rive raised her hand and placed it on Cythiria's shoulder. "Now that you belong to me, your problems are my problems."

Cythiria shuddered. "Creepy," she muttered. She looked into Rive's cool, dark eyes. "Fine, well, I don't know. It's just that my head has always been a problem for me. When I was little, my parents brought me to see doctors, but they couldn't ever do anything about it."

Rive frowned. "Your parents?"

"Yeah," said Cythiria, smiling distantly, "Fredrick and Jillian. I know they tried their best, but…." She paused and rubbed her nose, which grew a distinct shade of pink.

"There are a few people you can rely on," said Rive. "First and foremost among these is yourself."

Cythiria shook her head. "I'd be dead by now if that's the case," she mumbled.

Rive smiled gently. "And now you have me." And then, in a blur, she cuffed Cythiria on the cheek. Cythiria tumbled back, falling onto the mat.

"The fuck was that for?" Cythiria grumbled, holding her hand to her face.

Rive stepped forward and stood over Cythiria. She glared down at her with dark, burning eyes, her nose and chin high, a scowl growing on her lip. "Just a reminder that even friends can turn against you." She paused. "Come on. We've got a lot of work to do."

Cythiria sighed. "Great," she grunted as she pushed herself up on her feet and stood. *Fucking psycho.* The room spun and the space around her seemed to sparkle. "What the hell did I get myself into?"

CHAPTER 9

Plots and Machinations

Griddish, Ashen Fissure, the Ruined Council of Engineer Class Citizens

The once verdant hills were scorched dark brown. The stale smell of burnt grass wafted along the cool breeze, brushing gently against Matere's matted, white locks and his sandpapery cheek. His eyes followed the shattered edges of the once crystalline dome and the sparkling debris that littered the ground around it. He glanced at Betel who looked upon the ruin with wide, unbelieving eyes, her jaw slack.

"It's hard to believe when it happens to your own home," she said.

The two stepped forward, their booted feet falling upon the broken, steel-cobbled surface of the main avenue of the Council known as Midriff Stump, echoing a hollow, rhythmic clink! Along the road, burnt corpses of once oval-shaped vehicles lay in nests of debris and puddles of rotting fluid. Bodies, now decayed, lay strewn upon the road, their white regalia stained rusty crimson and black. Ruins, which were once gleaming, white buildings that housed the daily accouterments of Engineer Class Citizens of Griddish, littered the sides of the broken boulevard, their innards tossed about like so much detritus.

Their eyes followed the length of the avenue, where it terminated. On one side of the road, to the right, the crumbled council chambers of Governance lay in ruin. On the other, the once black, cube-shaped buildings known as Development stood broken and shattered, reaching towards the sky like decaying teeth.

A distant, echoing pop cracked through the air. Matere and Betel jumped and turned towards it.

"They must have moved," said Matere. "That man, Natty Mick, said that war had started." Matere sighed. "We were never prepared for war. How would we be able to fight against any threat?" He glanced along the ruins. "This is quite obvious now. The others must be in hiding."

"What do you suppose started it?" said Betel.

Matere scratched his rough, sandpapery chin. "He also said that the Vérkatrae gave up on dismantling Var 8 completely because they were no longer concerned about it. Could it be that the Vérkatrae have risen up against us? Or maybe their aim is to destroy all of Griddish."

Betel sighed. "That would be unlikely. By destroying Griddish, they would be destroying their own existence. And as far as we know, they could never make that kind of a decision anyway." Betel's eyes shifted sharply. "At least, as far as I can remember from the original spec."

"Then how?"

Betel shook her head.

Matere glanced towards the shattered ruins of Development. "Maybe we can find out."

"Over there?" said Betel.

"What other choice do we have? At least I can see if my old laboratory is still around."

Matere glanced along dark walls of the chamber. He sniffed the damp, musty air. He walked to the window, which was now shattered, its shards

scattered across the floor, cracking and grinding under his booted step. He gazed along the once grassy hills that were now scorched brown. A cool, smoky breeze brushed against his face and hair. He coughed as he gazed into the distance, at the rows of Slipshot Silos that stretched towards the upper dome, their tips thin and needly.

He turned. Betel stood crouched over a panel in the center of the chamber, her gray eyes shifting over some arrays of exposed circuits, their silvery, slithering tendrils twisting and winding among each other. She sighed and pulled at a hatch. From inside, a nest of wound, viny coils popped out. She stepped back, took hold of the entanglement, and yanked. A holographic sphere fizzled and sparkled into view, casting a cool, electric blue light on the dank walls of the chamber.

"Impressive," said Matere. "And how does one of your stature know how to do that?"

Betel stood up and gazed coolly at Matere. "Oh, come now, my dear scientist." A mocking smirk crossed her face. "Before I was ever a technocrat, I was an engineer, learning all those tiresome things that the rest of you learned in school. I, on the other hand, decided to become useful and get out while I still could."

Matere snorted. "Useful, huh?"

"Indeed." She turned toward the holographic sphere and gestured. "So, we want to find out about the Vérkatrae." She gestured. Lines of characters filled the screen vertically. "The early spec of the Vérkatrae, when they first came into existence at the time that Griddish was constructed, says that they were simply helper machines designed to provide logistical support to the various classes of Slaves. The bulk of Vérkatrae were placed under the command of the Mechanics."

Matere shuddered. "Like Opal Fremmitty."

"Indeed."

"And we all know about the trouble she caused when she was on Var 8, as well as her ensuing tragedy."

"Yes, we do."

Matere rubbed his sandpapery chin and frowned. "Still, that man Natty said that the Vérkatrae were no longer concerned about their duties. That would mean they *decided* to abort their Var 8 dismantlement project."

Betel shook her head. "Vérkatrae have never been able to make their own independent decisions. Not, at least, according to the original spec, since that would go against their main purpose, the reason for their existence." She paused. "It's as if they had a collective moment when they decided to abandon the Var 8 dismantlement project. That in itself is quite the contradiction."

Matere sighed. "And even more puzzling is this war. We can see its damage all around us. We can smell it. We can even hear the rumblings in the distance. How is it that they became involved? There was always tension between Slaves and Engineers. But how do the Vérkatrae fit into the equation?"

Betel pursed her brow. "Indeed, how? And with their power, what's to prevent them from wiping Griddish from existence entirely?"

"Or even the universe as we know it." A wry smile crossed Matere's face as he gazed with raised brow towards Betel. "There's only one way to find out."

"And that is?"

"Infiltrate the Slaves. Spread some chaos and see what comes out of it."

Betel sighed and shook her head, an ironic smile spreading across her face. "So, the standard approach?"

"There is no standard approach, my dear."

Betel paused. "So, what's your plan?"

Matere sighed. He scratched his stubbly chin with his fingers. "What is the Slave's biggest weakness?"

"The Tenddrome?"

"Perhaps. But why?"

"Because of the Tenddrome, Slaves cannot act in secrecy, at least while in Griddish. Unless they've somehow mastered it to the point where they can slip in and out unnoticed. By its very nature, it undermines their personal identity."

"Which means that they are harder to isolate."

"Or manipulate."

"And that makes infiltration impossible."

"Indeed," said Betel.

Matere turned towards the holographic sphere and gestured. It flickered. "Unless…."

"Unless what?"

"Ever heard of a place called the Dusk Quadrant?"

Betel sighed deeply. "The Dusk Quadrant is ancient, Matere. And it belongs to the Slaves, even *if* it still exists. It could have been destroyed in this war, or simply abandoned. And besides, it's their turf, so to speak. Do you really think you can get inside?"

Matere paused. "The Dusk Quadrant is the only place where Slaves can maintain their own secrets, where they can disconnect from the Tenddrome and do whatever they like. Without the Tenddrome, they are at their most vulnerable." He looked at Betel. "I see this as an opportunity."

Betel locked onto Matere's gaze for a moment. "If the Tenddrome hasn't evolved since we were last here, that is. The passage of time is different in Griddish than it is on the Vars, Matere. Events happen at the same speed, but they are perceived differently."

A wry smile crossed Matere's face. "It couldn't hurt to take a look."

Betel paused. "Ok, Matere. I suppose we have no other choice."

CHAPTER 10

Meetings and Serendipity

Var 7, Farth, Nissy

The scent of dirty frying oil wafted along the bright alleyway. Clusters of people stood over steaming stalls, pointing at items hanging from inside display cases. Shouts and whistles and the generic din of people chatting and laughing echoed through the urban canyons.

Cythiria sniffed the air. Her mouth watered as she looked over the rows of carts, at faces buried in steaming bowls, mouths wrapped around papered packets.

"Grrrrrrrghhhh," she felt from her stomach. She placed her hands in her pockets and walked through the alley, her booted foot slipping on the oily surface. She paused as she glanced at a bench pushed up against a graffitied wall. She gasped lightly and held her breath. Her stomach turned and she felt her heart beat heavily inside her chest. *She* was sitting on the bench. Her long, brown hair was pulled into ponytails that flowed playfully from either side of her head. Her hazel eyes, peering through thick, curly eyelashes, distractedly scanned the throngs of people as they flowed through the alley. In her hand she held a clear cup, her crimson-painted lips wrapped around a thin straw as she slurped up a toxic green colored liquid.

Cythiria took a deep breath and stepped towards her.

"Hey, Chelss," she said, raising her hand in an awkward wave. Her voice was a pitch higher than usual, and it cracked. *Geeze, what an idiot. I sound like a prepubescent boy!*

Chelss glanced towards the voice. She pulled the straw away from her lips. A subtle smile crossed her face and her eyes lit up. A moment later her face returned to its resting position as she glanced unimpressed towards the crowds.

"Hey," said Chelss coolly, returning her gaze to Cythiria. "Haven't seen you at school for a while."

Cythiria felt her neck and cheeks flush as she locked onto Chelss's hazel-colored eyes. She forced her hands into the pockets of her hoody, fighting the urge to use them to cover her face. "Yeah, well, you know, I can't really do that whole plug-and-play thing."

"I see. Your parents are ok with that, I mean, you not being at school?"

"Well, um…." Cythiria glanced down at her shoes. "They don't really know."

"Really?"

"Well, they haven't said anything. They work a lot. Jillian's never really home. Dad is always at the restaurant, like, cooking and stuff."

Chelss nodded knowingly. "I'm jealous."

"You are?"

"Well, it looks like you slipped through the system. Seems kinda hard, with all the tracking they do." Chelss smiled wryly. "I'm sure they'll catch up with you sooner or later."

"You think?"

"I do." She paused. Her eyes flitted up and down Cythiria's body. "You look kinda different."

"Oh, yeah, well, I've been training," said Cythiria, a proud tilt to her chin, an arrogant smirk on her lips. Her body seemed to inflate, her balled fists resting squarely on her own hips.

Chelss raised her right eyebrow. "Training?"

"Yeah, there's this gym I've been going to."

"Gym?" said Chelss, turning her body towards Cythiria while she remained seated on the bench, her eyes lighting up.

"Yeah. I'm learning boxing, kickboxing, combat sports, that sorta thing."

A smile curled up on the corners of Chelss's crimson-colored lips.

Cythiria pulled off one sleeve of her jacket. Her heart raced and she spoke quickly, as if she were trying to get as much information out while she still held Chelss's attention. Her own body felt warm and pleasant. "See?" she said, her voice cracking nervously. She pulled the sleeve of her shirt up to her shoulder, revealing a bear arm. She flexed.

"Nice," said Chelss. She moved to sit on the edge of the bench.

"And take a look at this." Cythiria lifted her shirt, revealing chiseled abdominal muscles.

"Wow."

"You can touch it if you want," said Cythiria.

"Erm…."

Cythiria flushed. She pulled her shirt down and slipped her arm back into the jacket sleeve. "Yeah, well, so that's what I've been up to. You should come by the gym sometime. It's this little place out on the south subway line. You can't miss it. Old looking building with a giant trophy-looking thing on the roof."

Chelss smiled widely and laughed a song-like chuckle. "A trophy?"

Cythiria swallowed hard. The warmth of her face and neck spread to her armpits, where she started to break a sweat. She wanted to cover her face with her hands but fought the urge to do so. "Yeah, don't ask me why. Don't really know what that's all about."

"Cool." Chelss and Cythiria locked eyes for a moment.

"Hey, hey!" came a voice from behind them. "Cee, I got your doughnuts." A man pushed between Cythiria and Chelss and sat on the bench next to her.

"Cee?" muttered Cythiria.

Chelss shrugged her shoulders.

The man handed Chelss a paper tray of three fried, sugared balls of dough. She glanced nervously at Cythiria and took the tray, gazing into it distractedly. The man lifted his arm and put it around Chelss's shoulder and pulled her close to him. He took one of the sugared balls and shoved it into his mouth, his lips smacking loudly. He smiled arrogantly as he glanced up at Cythiria, his gaze running up and down her body.

"Who's this?" he said, smirking. His eyes moved up to the two scars on Cythiria's forehead.

Chelss frowned. "A friend."

"Yeah?" said the man. He lifted his arm off Chelss's shoulder and moved his hand to her thigh, stroking inside slowly and firmly. His smirk grew wider.

"I...," stammered Cythiria, "...I've got to go." She turned, locking her eyes onto the sidewalk in front of her. She walked quickly though the crowds of people, her head down, bumping carelessly among them. *Idiot! Idiot! Idiot! I'm so stupid! Why did I think…?* She felt her face flush hotly. She felt her heart pound loudly in her chest and blood pump through her ears. She felt her stomach turn and her mouth water salty. She felt a deep, grinding vibration rumble through her head. She turned into a dark alley, stopped, and pressed her back against the cold, brick wall. She balled her hands into fists and struck them against her own temples. *Stupid, stupid, stupid!* She slid down the side of the wall and sat on her haunches, pulling her knees close to her chest, wrapping her arms around them, black locks of hair flowing carelessly down her cheeks. She sighed deeply as the grinding sound in her head settled to a distant, lonely whistle. The two scars on her forehead burned and stung for a moment. Cythiria reached her hand towards a tickling sensation on her nose. She touched it. It felt damp. She looked at the crimson-colored fluid on her fingers. "Such an idiot," she mumbled, as she listened to the sound of vehicles whoosh by, the generic din and mumble of people. She felt the sun as it poked through the cloud-like ring of Farth and cast a warm light on the Nissian streets below.

"*Left hook!*" shouted Rive. The slapping of leather on leather echoed along the gray, stone walls of the gym. "Use your hip. Pivot!"

Cythiria gasped for breath as sweat poured down her forehead, neck, and back. She curved her right arm and struck the pads that Rive held in her hands. Her arm ached, her fist, wrapped in thinly padded gloves, were red and sore and cracked and bleeding in places. She charged forward.

"High kick!" shouted Rive, as she held the pads high. "Use your shin, don't strike with your toes. Center your hips. Strike with the power of your core."

The skin on her shins burned and cracked, opening old and new welts as she struck the pads, hissing and gasping with each stroke.

Rive paused at the hollow clap of the old bell against the windowpane of the front door, lowering her padded hands to her side. She turned towards the sound and scoffed. "Looks like you have a visitor," she grumbled.

Cythiria turned her head towards the door. Her eyes opened wide, and her heart seemed to stop.

"Chelss?" she whispered.

Chelss's long, brown hair, pulled to a tightly braided ponytail, flowed easily down one side of her head and onto her shoulder. She wore loosely fitting workout pants and a jacket that hung off one shoulder, revealing a fitted tank top. Her hazel-colored eyes gazed towards her apprehensively as a gentle smile spread across her crimson lips.

Cythiria turned towards Chelss, who walked towards her, pausing at the edge of the padded floor mat. Cythiria could feel her neck and cheeks grow warm and a hollow ache fill her chest and stomach. She lifted her gloved hand to her head and pushed her hair back awkwardly, wiping away the sweat on her forehead in the same stroke. She took a quiet breath and stepped to the edge of the mat.

"Hey," she said.

"Hey," replied Chelss.

Cythiria swallowed hard. "About the other day, I…."

"Don't worry about it."

"I didn't mean to interrupt your date or anything."

Chelss snorted. "The guy was an asshole. Took too many liberties, you know?"

Cythiria nodded, unknowingly. She paused. "So, what brings you here?"

Chelss smiled, her eyes locking momentarily with Cythiria's. "Well, you said you work out here. I mean, how could I miss the place? That trophy thing, right?"

Cythiria chuckled. "Yeah. How'd you know I'd be here now?"

Chelss paused, tilting her head to one side. Her long, braided ponytail fell off her shoulder and flowed down her back. "A gut feeling?" She smiled.

"Really?"

"Well, you haven't been in school for a long time, so I figured where else would you be?" Her eyes moved up and down Cythiria's body. "I mean, the facts speak for themselves, and you don't seem all that social anyway."

"You could have texted."

"After the last time I saw you, I thought it might be better if I just showed up. You seemed pretty embarrassed."

Cythiria snorted awkwardly. "Yeah, I guess." She gazed into Chelss's hazel-colored eyes. The sound of steady, quiet footfalls broke her from her reverie.

"Well, since you have an audience, *Cythiria*, why not show off your skills?" came the voice of Rive, with particular venom on Cythiria's name.

Cythiria turned to face Rive. She looked at her, glancing up and down her body. Her hands were gloved, her feet bare. She glared at Cythiria, her chin high, a quivering scowl growing on her lip. She lifted her hands towards her face, her dark eyes sharp yet calm as she glowered.

Cythiria swallowed hard. She felt her legs tremble and her stomach turn. Her heart beat heavily in her chest. She glanced once at Chelss, who looked at Rive with a raised, critical brow. She sighed quickly. "My coach." She took a deep, calming breath, turned her hip, and planted her feet. She lifted her hands towards her chin and crouched.

A thin smile curled up on one corner of Rive's mouth. She stepped sideways, her gaze cool yet burning. She threw a jab. Cythiria slipped to one side and stepped back.

"Come on, Cythiria, don't you want to impress your new *friend*?" she said, her words infused with spite. "You can't win by moving backwards."

Cythiria pushed forward with a front kick. Rive ducked and struck Cythiria in the leg with a foot. A whipping *smack!* echoed through the gym. Cythiria stumbled and fell on one knee, then jumped onto her own two feet. She crouched and reset her stance.

"Do you think *she's* impressed by you, Cythiria?" said Rive. "I don't think so. You have to do better than that."

Cythiria clenched her teeth. Her body started to tingle. Her core felt hot, and adrenaline rushed through her body. She surged forward. Rive stepped aside, tripping Cythiria with a low kick to her ankle. Cythiria tumbled forward, turned, and then surged towards Rive. She threw a high kick to Rive's head, which she blocked with her glove. Rive's eyes twinkled with admiration for a moment, a slight smile crossed her face. Rive struck back with a right undercut to Cythiria's midsection. Cythiria fell back onto the mat. She gasped for breath, and then pushed herself onto her knees. She stood, her breath short, her eyes brooding. She ground her teeth.

"Scowling at me won't change anything, Cythiria," said Rive. Her lip curled and quivered as if she were about to spit.

Cythiria lurched forward with a right jab. And then, she felt a crushing blow to her midsection. She fell to the ground, gasping and choking, tears streaming from her eyes. She curled up, hugging her own torso with crossed arms, coughing and sputtering. Just above her, glaring eyes, a cocky smile, a face so close she could feel a cool, steady breath on her cheek. And then, a whisper that tickled her ear, words that twisted and turned like hissing snakes. "Don't ever forget, Cythiria. You belong to me." The face faded. Cythiria blinked hard. Rive stood above her, glaring, her chin held high. She scoffed. She turned, pausing for a moment. "Get yourself ready. I've scheduled you for your first fight." With a light, confident stride, she walked away.

"Wow, that was intense," she heard. She looked towards the sound of the voice. Next to her, a pair of hazel-colored eyes looked admiringly into hers. She could feel the tickle of long hair as it brushed against her face, a cool, calming breath that gently stroked her cheek. "You were pretty good."

Cythiria gazed a moment more into Chelss's eyes and then forced herself to look away. She pushed herself up onto her side and then sat on her haunches, her arms resting on her knees. She took a deep breath. "You think?"

"Yeah."

"I didn't stand a chance against Rive." Cythiria paused. "Well, apparently, she's got me schedule to a real fight." Cythiria turned her head and looked at Chelss, whose face was infused with the brightness of a broad smile, showing small, white teeth. Cythiria didn't remember ever seeing those teeth, not like this, not while framed inside a smile. She felt a growing warmth in her chest. "Will you watch me fight?" she said.

"Of course," said Chelss. "Count me in."

Chelss stood up and held out a hand to Cythiria. She took it and was pulled up onto her feet.

"Cool," said Cythiria, placing a gloved hand on Chelss's shoulder. "I…I'm glad you're here."

"Me too."

CHAPTER 11

Infiltration

Griddish, Ashen Fissure, the Dusk Quadrant

"So, this is the place they all come to forget," mumbled Matere, standing atop a hill as he glanced across a wide depression. "The famous Dusk Quadrant."

Wide, grassy plains sunk to a deep valley. In the center stood an arching gateway. Above the valley, in stair-step fashion, wide panels hovered, casting progressively darker shadows the closer they came to the gateway. In the distance, countless Slipshot Silos littered the horizon.

From the portal, small dots of people that looked like insects emerged and entered, a regular, spare flow. A distant pop was followed by a deep rumble.

Matere turned towards Betel, who gazed upon the portal with cool, gray eyes.

"Shall we go check it out?"

Betel shook her head. "What if the Slaves notice us? These are dangerous times for us, you know."

"They won't because they can't," said Matere. "Once they're inside, they're shut off from the Tenddrome. That's the reason they go there in the first place. So, they won't know that we aren't Nodes within their system. We'll just be just two bodies among many."

Betel scoffed. "You hope. They still have their eyes. They can see that we're different, Matere. It doesn't matter if they're shut off from the Tenddrome or not."

"It matters a great deal. Most of them will be, how shall I say it, under the influence. Once they step inside that door, they won't have a care in the world. That's the whole point of the Dusk Quadrant, according to the original spec. It was designed so that they could let loose, so to speak."

"It's hard to imagine that designed creatures need to let loose," grumbled Betel.

Matere paused. "The original Engineers designed them in their likeness. So, it shouldn't be a mystery. One need only look in the mirror, Betel."

"And suddenly the great Matere Songgaard has grown so high and mighty," said Betel, a mocking tone in her voice.

Mater sighed. "We'll just wait until there's a clearing so we can sneak in while no one on the outside can see us."

"Specs change, Matere. You should know this by now. The Slaves and the Tenddrome are not the same as they were when the original Engineers implemented them. Systems have evolved. They're bigger and more intelligent now. If we go in there, we'll be getting into something that we know very little about."

Matere paused. "Well, what else then? We have to try to understand what's going on here. And the way things are headed, it could be the end of Griddish if we don't do anything. This could be the Slaves' one weak point."

Betel sighed deeply. "And once we're inside?" she said.

Matere sighed. "We'll see."

Betel shook her head. "That's what I was afraid of."

Matere and Betel paused at the tall archway, which opened up a glowing portal that led into the Dusk Quadrant. Matere whistled as he gazed up at the archway's ambitious height, seeming as if its sole purpose was to reach the very top of the Griddish dome.

A pair of Slaves stumbled out, glancing suspiciously towards the pair as they tumbled down the levels of the portal's landings, and onto the grassy depression below. Matere and Betel exchanged glances. Matere took a deep breath. "Well, here we go," he said as he stepped in, Betel just behind him.

Matere glanced along the cool dark corridor, which descended in a steady slope. Along the wall, electric torches were mounted, buzzing and flickering a weak, sickly light along the floors and ceilings. Another pair of Slaves stumbled by, glancing towards Matere and Betel with bleary, unfocused eyes.

"So far so good," Matere mumbled. "As long as no one saw us coming in, I think we're ok."

"Well, someone did see you come in, if you didn't forget. Those two Slaves, maybe?"

"I mean *see* see. Honestly, I don't think either of them really saw anything."

"You hope," said Betel.

The two continued to descend until the gentle slope flattened out. They paused as they came upon a glimmering, watery surface, like that of a dark lake. They could hear a steady, rhythmic hiss, the gentle slap of water against a shore. Above the lake, the ends of which they could not discern in the dimness, bright spheres like planets spun and twirled in darkness, punctuated by points of light splattered about like stars. Small, shadowy figures sat along the edge, Slaves tangled in coupled embraces, or single, distracted, and staring into space, their eyes distant and wandering. Matere turned to Betel.

"See, I told you," He whispered. "They're all out of their minds."

Betel frowned. "Don't get too comfortable yet. You don't know how this environment is affecting them, or how long it lasts. For all we know, there could be a switch that brings them back instantly. Then what will you do?"

Matere snorted and shook his head. "If such a switch existed, I'd like to get my hands on it. Then we wouldn't have to go through this charade."

"A charade you love far too much, my dear Engineer Class Citizen. Let's not forget about Var 8. Your patterns are too predictable, Matere."

They turned and continued down the corridor, which grew warmer the deeper they progressed. Matere sniffed the air and crinkled his nose. A spicy smell like that of cinnamon invaded his senses. His legs started to feel weak, as if they were about to collapse under his weight, and he felt as if he were spinning. He shook his head and bit his lip.

"That smell," he mumbled. "It's powerful. Its effect is…undeniable. It must be Waftring." He turned and reached his hand towards Betel, who took it into her own. Her cool, gray eyes looked glassy, unfocused. The light of the corridor changed from shallow, flickering blue to warm, red hues. Matere felt his own heartbeat and a pounding sound in his ears. He felt his eyes droop, and the world around him started to flicker and sparkle. The walls seemed to move, as if they were made of water. His arm twitched and throbbed. He glanced at it. It seemed to split apart in a mass of uncoiling, slithering tendrils. Matere felt his stomach turn. His throat tightened. His skin itched from breaking sweat. His breath was short, raspy. He wanted to run.

And then he stood in a wide chamber. A cool breeze brushed against his face and through his damp, sweaty hair. A line of gates, many times his width and height, lined the edge of the chamber, the entirety of their fronts filled from top to bottom and side to side with a single character, perhaps a number.

He sighed. "We made it through, somehow. I don't really recall how exactly we got here."

Betel nodded. "Hard to believe Waftring could be so powerful."

"You noticed that too."

"Indeed, I did."

"And yet, we're not Slaves. So how could it affect us so much?"

"There's a whole lot we don't know about the Dusk Quadrant, Matere. We've been over this. Are you sure you want to keep going?"

He smiled gently and then squeezed the hand he still held in his own. He stepped forward. He could hear Betel's stumbling steps behind him. He walked towards the first gate and paused. He looked it over and then pushed it. It was heavy, but silent as it opened. Inside was a narrow corridor that seemed to stretch forward into darkness.

He paused and looked towards his right. A door was cast open and beyond, a chamber. He stepped inside. The air was cool and stale. His vision grew clear, and his legs felt strong again as his body recovered. He took a deep breath. He turned to face Betel, who glanced around the room, her gray eyes sharp.

Matere smiled widely. "See, I told you you've nothing to worry about. Do you think any Slave would ever care about anything after a mind-bending experience like the one we just had?"

"I suppose not."

"And for all we know, they may have an experience a hundred times more intense than that."

"Perhaps. But we can't be sure, Matere. The Slaves have evolved and changed. They may have started out like us, designed in our own likeness. But they might also have evolved into something entirely different."

"Not according to those we passed in the corridors. It wouldn't fit their behavior."

Betel shook her head. "So now what?"

Matere glanced along the walls of the chamber. The ceilings were high and near them hovered dark spheres. Smaller spheres orbited their cores and silvery tendrils streamed from their outer shells. In the center stood a long table, and around it, chairs were scattered carelessly, some tipped over onto their sides. Divans lined the walls along with tables and clear, smudgy drinking glasses.

"Seems like the Dusk Quadrant was a lot busier at one point," said Matere as he gazed at the table. "A real party place, it looks like."

"Indeed," said Betel. "But how does that help us?"

"Well," said Matere, scratching his sandpapery chin with his now calmed arm, which had returned to its human shape, "Remember a little joint by the name of Temple Pizza on Var 8?"

"How could I forget?" said Betel, her voice saturated with irony.

"I think it's time we open up a new shop. We'll call it Temple Tavern."

"Selling?"

"Pleasures of the body."

"And to what end?"

"Information."

"What kind of information?"

"Anything that will help us to bring an end to this war."

Betel snorted. "And you're gonna do that all by yourself."

"Of course not," said Matere, smiling wryly. "I have you."

"And?" said Betel, crossing her arms across her chest, her posture infused with skepticism.

"And a bunch of Slaves who are looking to have a good time. It's perfect, Betel. Like igniting a Plaxis Strand in a Griddish gas station."

Betel snorted and shook her head. "There's no such thing as a Griddish gas station, Matere. Your metaphor is flawed."

"But there *could* be, if we built one."

Betel walked to the table and picked up a chair, setting it on its legs. She looked at the table and stroked the top with her finger. She rubbed her thumb and forefinger together. "It's gonna be a lot of work."

"Something we're not afraid of."

Betel shook her head. She walked through the main chamber to an arched doorway at the back. She stepped in. The ground was covered in debris and broken glass. On the wall opposite the doorway was stacked square, copper-colored casks, upon whose sides were drawn a pair of characters. Betel heard Matere step up behind her. He paused and then whistled.

"And with all that fermented Waftring, I'd say we have a pretty good chance," he said.

"The liquor of the Slaves."

"Hot, spicy, and gets you wasted real fast."

Betel turned towards Matere. "And here it sits. Why is that Matere? In a ruined area of the Dusk Quadrant. You'd think someone would've shown up to claim it."

"That would be us, my dear," said Matere, slapping his chest with his open hand.

Betel sighed. "It's too easy, Matere," Betel mumbled.

"I'd prefer to look at it as an opportunity. Good fortune comes to the bold!" said Matere, chin high, arm gesticulating as if to present a grand spectacle.

CHAPTER 12

An Argument

Var 7, Farth, Nissy

Cythiria lay on her bed, her eyes wide open as she stared at the ceiling. She kicked off the cover with her leg and turned, slapping the pillow to a fluffier state with her hand. The dim blue of morning light seeped through the curtains on her window. The two tiny scars on her forehead tingled. She lifted her fingers and stroked them. She sighed and sat up, groaning, her back damp and sticky with sweat.

"Great," she mumbled. "Just great. Not a second of sleep and this is my big day. My first fight. Rive's gonna have a fit when she sees me."

She stood up from the side of the bed and walked towards the mirror that hung from a rusty wire which was nailed into the wall. She gazed into it, at her dark, bloodshot eyes, and the two tiny scars on her forehead. "Geeze, I look like shit," she muttered. She slapped her cheek with her hand and reached for her box of bandages. She opened it, took one out, and peeled off its backing. She moved closer to the mirror and applied it to one of the scars. She took out another and crossed it with the one that had already been placed, and then repeated the process with the other scar. She stepped back and looked into the mirror.

What's happening to me? Some days, I just don't want to be here anymore. I just wish I could end it. Be done with it. What right do I have to be here anyway?

She frowned, crinkled her nose, and turned.

She looked around the cluttered, jumbled room. She crouched and rummaged through piles of clothes until she found a red and white, horizontally striped t-shirt. She lifted it to her nose and sniffed, grimaced, shrugged, and then pulled it on. She rummaged again, and picked up a pair of jeans, which had been wound up into a messy roll. She unfurled them and pulled them on. She walked towards the door of her room, picking up the hoodie that she always wore, pausing to pull it on and then crouching in front of a pair of whiteish sneakers, which she tied onto her feet.

She slammed the door open and walked out into the living room of the small bungalow.

"Where are you going?" she heard. The voice seemed tense yet forced to unnatural calmness. She turned.

"Dad," she said. "I, um, thought you were at work."

"I would be normally, but it seems like we have a little issue."

"Oh?" she said, smiling nervously and rubbing the back of her neck. "What ever could it be?"

Fredrick stood up and locked his gaze with Cythiria's, his blue eyes chilly, his mouth turned to a scowl. "I think you know."

"I…really don't."

"Come on, Cyth. I know you've been missing school."

"Oh, yeah, well…how'd you know that?"

Fredrick held up a tablet computer. "Seems that *someone* set up my account to block emails from the school. Who do you think did that?" He shook his head.

Cythiria felt her neck and face grow warm. "Well, I don't really know…."

"Cythiria, why would you skip school like that? What could be the reason that you would do that and not tell me?"

Cythiria sighed deeply, her shoulders and chest deflating. "I can't, dad. I can't deal with it."

"Why not?"

"I just…." She paused. "I can't plug into the network, like they want me to. It's painful."

Fredrick's face, tight with sternness, softened. "What do you mean painful?"

Cythiria raised her hand and touched her forehead with her fingers. She could hear the crinkle of the newly applied bandages. "I don't know how to explain it."

Fredrick sighed deeply. "The scars," he mumbled. "So, if you haven't been going to school, what exactly have you been doing?"

"Well, I'm going to this gym."

"A gym?"

"Yeah."

"What kind of a gym?"

"A fighting gym."

"A fighting gym?" Fredrick raised his brow and grimaced.

"Yeah, there's this chick named Rive who coaches, she's kinda weird, but she taught me all kinds of things…."

"Rive?" said Fredrick, his eyes growing wide, his face drawn and taught, his jaw clenched. "Rive who?"

"Um, Amber...."

Fredrick turned towards Cythiria and sighed deeply. "Cyth, I don't want you going to that gym anymore."

"What? Why?"

"I just...think it's not safe for you."

"Are you kidding?" said Cythiria, her voice growing in pitch, a scowl spreading across her face. "Now you're sounding like *Jillian*!"

"Cyth, I...."

"I thought you understood me!" Cythiria shouted. "I thought you were on my side!"

"I am on your side, Cyth." Fredrick stood up from his chair. "I'm always on your side."

"Not when you talk like her. You act like you don't even care." Cythiria's scars on her forehead started to tingle and burn. A distant, lone whistle echoed through her head. Tears formed along the corners of her eyes and streamed down her cheeks.

"Does Rive care about you, Cythiria?"

"Yes, she does. When I'm around her, my fucking head is normal again!" She raised her hands to her head and punched her temples with her fists. "When I'm around her, all this bullshit goes away. I feel like...."

"Like...?"

"Like I can live again. Like, maybe I can be normal again."

Fredrick sighed deeply. He shook his head. "Please Cythiria. At least wait until Jillian gets home and we can talk this over...."

"Fuck you!" shouted Cythiria. "Fuck all of you!"

"Cyth…." Fredrick reached towards Cythiria.

Cythiria slapped Fredrick's hand away. "No, I can't. I have to go. I have a fight tonight."

"A fight?"

"I knew you wouldn't approve."

"Cyth…."

She kicked a nearby chair and stomped towards the front door. She kicked it open and stumbled onto the sidewalk of the small bungalow. She glanced up at the white ring, her eyes following its ridged pattern until they settled on the long, slender towers of the city. She sniffed the sea air. It smelled of decay.

"Fuck all of them," she mumbled, as she turned and walked towards the subway station. *Fuck all of them. I'm not backing down from this. I don't care. Rive brought me here. I have to keep going.*

∞

Fredrick sat on the soft, lumpy couch of the living room. He placed his head in his hands and gazed at the floor. His stomach turned and his chest tightened. He sighed deeply.

A gentle chime broke him from his reverie. He turned towards it and gestured. A holographic image fizzled into view.

"I'm on my way," came the cracking, fizzling voice.

AN ARGUMENT

"Jillian," said Fredrick. He gazed at the staticky, projected image of her face, the shock of red hair that flowed from under her peaked cap, the gentle scowl that always seemed to cross her face these days.

Jillian paused. "Are you ok?"

"It's Cyth."

Jillian's voice tensed. "What about her?"

"Rive Amber is here, and she found her."

"Found her?"

Fredrick sighed. "Cyth got angry and went to see her."

Jillian paused. "You've got to stop her, Fredrick. You can't let her go."

Fredrick shook his head. "I can't stop her, Jillian. She's already starting to rebel against us. If I get in her way, she's just going to leave, and then who knows what'll happen? It's already hard enough as it is for her. She has so many questions, I can tell. But she doesn't ask. She just sits there, all gloomy, angry, in pain." Fredrick let out a deep, shuddering sigh. "Honestly, I don't know what to do with her."

Jillian paused. "I'm on my way home. When I get there, I'll talk to her." She lifted her arm and the projected, holographic image of herself fizzled away.

"That's what I'm afraid of," he mumbled.

CHAPTER 13

A Fight

Var 7, Farth, Nissy

The rickety chair creaked under Cythiria's weight. She sat, holding her hand out while Rive Amber wrapped it in long strips of fabric. She reached towards her head with her free hand. She pulled at the tightly wound braids of her short hair. The cornrows pulled at her scalp and itched.

She gazed distractedly forward. Her stomach turned and she could hear her own heavy pulse pounding in her ears. She sniffed. The air smelled dank and musty.

Buzzing fluorescent lamps cast a weak blue-white light on the walls and along the floor. The muffled sounds of impatient crowds, the jeers and stomps, echoed through the corridor, which ran adjacent to the small, spartan chamber.

Cythiria lifted her other arm towards Rive.

"Remember, keep your chin down and your guard up. Just like we practiced. Don't ever let that down."

She heard footsteps in the corridor and glanced nervously towards them. A young woman, about her age and size, glared at her through a large, shimmering, silky hoody and then walked on.

She sighed. The turning sensation in her stomach grew with each passing moment. Tiny, sharp prickles rolled along her neck and back as her skin grew damp with sweat. The two scars on her forehead tingled, and a deep humming sound echoed through her head. *Where is she? Chelss said she would come, but….*

Cythiria held up her hands while Rive pulled a padded glove onto each one. They felt tight, restrictive.

"It's time," Rive said, standing up.

Cythiria took a deep breath, letting it out slowly through pursed lips. She stood and turned. She could feel Rive stand close behind her, strong hands as they grasped her shoulders, a whispering voice slithering inside her ear like hissing snakes. "Now is *your* time, Cythiria." She felt a push from behind. She stepped forward and turned down a long, dark corridor.

The hum inside her head subsided. She felt light, her mind clear. The two scars on her forehead no longer tingled. Her stomach no longer turned. Her body grew warm, trembling with excitement. Her taut muscles felt strong, her step light.

The dark corridor exited into an arena. Dim lights cast a sickly yellow luminescence on the ground and the walls while holographic scoreboards flickered blues and pinks and numeric characters scrolled by like busy, nervous insects. Jeers and whistles echoed along the concrete bleachers.

She walked forward, her stride steady. She paused, gazing up at the ring. She glanced around at the spectators, her eyes following the rows of people as they looked towards the ring, drinking, eating, swearing, arguing, tossing debris into the aisles. *Where is she? She said she would be here. She promised me….*

She felt herself pulled towards a man. He gazed down at her, scowling. She felt fingers press against her cheeks, the slippery ointment that was rubbed onto them. She felt fingers in her mouth, a smooth, rubbery object forced between her chops. She bit down. She felt herself turned. She faced

Rive and gazed into her dark eyes. They were cold yet burning, her lips scowling. "Just do what we did in training. Hands up, chin down. Use your hooks. Pivot on your hips."

Cythiria nodded. In front of her, a short flight of stairs led to the ring. She stepped up, onto the apron. She paused and glanced around. *She said she would be here. Chelss promised she would come.* She bit down on her mouth guard. *Was it that guy? Is that why she's not here? Was it that guy who kept… touching her? Is that what she liked? I could do that, if that's what she wants.* Her chest tightened. *Fuck her! I don't need her here. I'll do this on my own!*

Cythiria ducked between taut ropes and stepped into the ring. She could hear the distracted, drunken jeers of the crowd. She saw a man dressed in black step forward. She heard echoing, staticky words, her name stated, more jeers and taunts. She looked at her opponent, about the same size and age as her, her eyes wide, focused, as she punched her gloves together and hopped on the balls of her bare feet. She felt herself pulled face-to-face with her opponent. She gazed into light blue eyes and at platinum blonde hair wound into tight braids like her own. She felt herself pushed back into her own corner. She heard broken, scattered words from Rive. Words like "relentless" and "pursuit." She glanced around the arena. *She promised she would be here. Where is Chelss? Why didn't she come like she said she would?*

She heard a bell ring.

She lifted her hands up, holding them close to her chin as she crouched and circled. She watched her opponent circle and duck. She released a quick jab. She could hear the muffled cheers of the crowd, the distant sound of Rive Amber's voice as it barked some inaudible commands. She circled, releasing a hook.

She felt a heavy strike to her torso. Her breath felt as if it were being sucked out of her body. She stumbled back. The cheers of the crowd rose to a fevered, drunken pitch. And then, she felt a crushing strike against her temples. She fell backwards. The world around her sparkled and faded. The muffled sound of the screaming crowd gurgled and bubbled. She felt as if she were being submerged in a pool of water. Her opponent moved towards her, screaming. The man in black stepped forward, blocking her with his arm. They moved slowly, as if they were running through thick syrup.

She saw the man wave his arm. The crowd released a muffled scream. She saw Rive's face hover above her own. "Cythiria! Cythiria!"

Cythiria slumped over in the rickety chair as she held a dirty towel against the side of her head. Rive Amber knelt in front of her, cutting a piece of white tape. Cythiria removed the towel and gazed down at it. A small, crimson stain appeared in its center.

"Are you disappointed in me?" she said, looking into Rive's dark eyes.

Rive paused. She placed her hand on Cythiria's neck. "I could never be disappointed in you. Remember what I said?"

"Lead with your jab?"

"I said, 'You belong to me.' That will always be true, no matter what." Rive stood up. "Let's go. I'll take you back to the gym where I can look at your ear more closely."

"I…I really just want to go home."

"Then I'll take you."

"I want to stop somewhere first." Cythiria hesitated. "I want to go by myself."

Rive scowled, a critical, burning gaze crossing her face. "Where?"

"I want to see dad. We sorta had a big argument."

Rive scoffed. She knelt and placed her hand on Cythiria's cheek. "There's only one person you can rely on in this world, Cythiria. That's yourself."

Cythiria sighed. "But…."

"I just want to make sure that you don't expect too much of people, or else you'll always be disappointed. And when you realize that you really need them, they might not be there for you." Rive tilted her head, her eyes widened with significance.

"I know, I just…."

"Wherever you go, take care of yourself first." Rive paused. She stood up. "I'll expect you at the gym tomorrow morning. I'll look at your ear then." She turned and then stepped out of the small, dimly lit chamber, her heels clicking confidently down the dark corridor.

Cythiria sighed. *Why didn't Chelss show up? She promised me she would.* The scars on her forehead started to tingle and burn. A deep, grinding sound like stone scraping against stone echoed through her head. She pressed her finger to her temples. "Not this again," she mumbled. *It's the same as it was when I was a little kid. That feeling.*

Not this again.

The dank halls smelled of must and urine. Briny, yellow dampness collected in puddles along the dented and cracked tiles. People in wheelchairs rolled along the floor, bumped into walls, or parked at desks where they slapped their hands or fists against smudgy window panes, screaming for help from disheveled nurses in frayed uniforms. Guards, their electric shock devices hanging from their waists, leaned their backs against soiled walls as they gazed on the crowds dispassionately.

"Jillian Crenshaw!" echoed the scratchy, tinny words from the loudspeaker. Jillian jumped up and stepped forward, pulling a reluctant child behind her.

"Come on Cythiria, hurry up."

Cythiria frowned, her short, black bowl cut bouncing up and down with each pattering stride. Her dark eyes scanned the corridor, and the two scars on her forehead shone a distinct shade of pink. She grimaced as she felt her head grow heavy, as if it were slowly being stuffed with cotton. The gentle, rhythmic grinding that echoed through her skull had an almost soporific beat to it.

Jillian paused at the front desk. Cythiria sidled up to her and wrapped her short arm around Jillian's leg. She gazed up at the person who sat behind the desk, barking instructions over a holographic screen. Jillian gestured. The screen flickered and then fizzled away.

Cythiria felt her arm yanked as she stumbled forward, nearly tripping over Jillian's fast-moving heels. The yellowed walls of the corridor seemed to rush by, as Cythiria gazed into open doors, at people sitting on undersized beds, and gazed around distractedly.

Jillian turned into one of the small rooms and paused. Cythiria felt strong, bony hands grasp her under her arms and hoist her up onto the examination table. She gazed into Jillian's blue eyes, casting glances along her flowing, red hair.

"Ok, now be good while we wait for the doctor," came the firm, yet quiet, words of Jillian as she stroked away dark locks of hair from Cythiria's forehead and around her ear. Cythiria giggled at her tickling fingers.

Cythiria placed her hands in her lap and gazed around the room, at the yellowed ceiling panels, the smudgy windows, and the cracked tiles on the floor. She sniffed. Her nose wrinkled at the omnipresent sour smell that seemed to penetrate every corner of the building's interior.

"So, you are…," came the voice of a man as he crashed through the closed door of the small room.

"Jillian Crenshaw."

"And this?" he said, nodding towards the child.

"Cythiria."

He wore a blue jacket and matching baggy blue pants. He reached into his pocket and pulled out a thin, stem-like device. He flicked it, and the tip grew to a blue luminescence. Cythiria gazed at the light and smiled. His bright blue eyes shifted over the forehead of Cythiria.

"And the symptoms are?"

"Well, she seems to have trouble hearing me sometimes."

"Seems?"

"Sometimes," Jillian paused. "I call her, when I'm in the other room, and I'll go find her, and she just sits and stares at the corner. I'll touch her shoulder and she'll jump up as if she didn't know I was standing right next to her."

The man gazed at Cythiria's forehead and pressed his finger against one of the scars. Cythiria jumped, and the grinding sound echoed deeply in her head. She choked back tears as she looked apprehensively at Jillian. He roughly turned her head with his hands. She felt a cold, sharp object poke at the inside of her ear. She jumped.

He stepped back, stood up straight, and gazed down at Cythiria. "Nothing unusual. As for the scars, you can always try plastic surgery."

"Are you sure?" pressed Jillian. "I mean, it's obvious there's something wrong with her...."

"Ma'am," said the man impatiently. "Unless there are more specific symptoms, there's nothing I can do. Maybe get a psychiatric evaluation if you have concerns over her behavior. As for her physical concerns, except for those scars on her head, there's nothing wrong with her."

Jillian sighed deeply and glanced at Cythiria, her blue eyes growing damp as they swept over the child's face. "Come on, Cythiria," she whispered, picking her up and setting her down on the floor.

*

Something is wrong with…me. Something is always wrong with me. Cythiria felt her throat tighten. She sniffled, wiping her nose with her finger as it turned a distinct shade of pink. *Even then, something was wrong with me. Stupid little Cythiria that everyone hates. Especially HER. I should have known Chelss wouldn't show up to my fight. Why would she? I know I probably wouldn't.*

Cythiria wiped her face with her hand and stood up. She walked over to a corner of the dimly lit room and picked up her jacket. She slipped it on, pulling the large, loose hood over her head. She turned into the long, narrow corridor. The acid yellow lights flickered and buzzed and the dampening, slippery ground sloshed lightly under the heels of her boots.

CHAPTER 14

We Meet Again

Var 7, Farth, Nissy

Fredrick sucked on the end of the lit cigarette. Its yellow-orange embers crackled and glowed under the weak, lavender lights of the alleyway. He glanced up at the milky white light of the planetary ring, as it cast an almost icy glow on the edges of the squat, dirty buildings around him.

He waited outside the tumbledown arena. He could hear the roar of the crowds inside, the stomp and rumble of feet on the hollow, metal floors. He paced the streets, back and forth, sucking down cigarettes till they scorched his fingers. He knew she was here. Rive Amber. And with her, Cyth. The fight had been advertised. Cyth was to be the easy loss to an up-and-comer.

Fredrick clenched his jaw. He felt a welling up inside of him. *How could she do this to Cyth? How could she sacrifice her this way?* Still, it was Rive Amber.

He took one last drag and flicked the cigarette butt towards a gutter. It sparkled as it bounced along the curb of the alley and then disappeared down a drain. His ears pricked up at the sound of steady, clicking heels. His eyes grew wide and his heart beat heavily in his chest as he watched the lithe movements of a shadowy, hooded figure.

He took a deep breath and stepped forward.

"What do you want with her, Rive?" he said, his voice tense, almost trembling.

The figure paused, the head rising to reveal dark eyes and a growing scowl. "I could ask you the same question, Varling."

"Why did you come back?"

Rive turned to face Fredrick, her body centered, confident. She reached her hands towards her head and pulled the hood down. "Surely you didn't think I would leave Cythiria in your incapable hands."

"She's adapting to her new world."

Rive scoffed. "You call *this* adapting? She barely understands her own thoughts. So much potential is wasted while she's here."

"It's not for you to decide, Rive. If you bring Cyth back to Griddish, you'll only make things worse for her."

"*Cyth?*" A mocking smiled curled up on the corner of her mouth. "Am I to assume that you two have grown close?"

"We…are growing closer."

Rive snorted. "How nice. I suppose I've arrived just in time, then." She paused. "Cythiria is a big girl. She can make her own decisions. Far be it from me to break up any parental bonds, no matter how weak they may actually be." Rive turned and pulled the hood on her head.

"Rive, please," said Fredrick. He reached his hand and grasped Rive's arm. "Please don't do this to her."

Rive glared at Fredrick's hand and then at him, locking his gaze with her own dark, burning pools. She tore her arm away from his grip and scoffed. "What must be, must be. There is no way around it, Varling." She stepped forward, her gait slow, steady, her heels clicking confidently.

"She was gonna lose that fight," Fredrick shouted after her, nodding towards the arena. "You know that. Why did you sacrifice her?"

Rive paused and turned her head partially towards Fredrick. She scowled. "This is nothing compared to what she will soon face. I've simply broken her in." She resumed her steady, confident gait and faded away into the night.

Fredrick sighed deeply and reached into his pocket, taking hold of a pack of cigarettes. He turned and crumpled the pack in his hand, pulling out one last, wrinkled cigarette, and lit it with a stainless-steel lighter that smelled of fresh kerosene. *I'm sorry, Cyth. If only you knew what was coming for you.*

CHAPTER 15

A Tenuous Feeling of Home

Var 7, Farth, Nissy

Cythiria paused as a chilly breeze whipped along the fluorescent-flooded streets. She dashed into a yellow-green lit cavern. She hopped over the turnstiles of the subway station and jogged up a broken escalator. A warm, dry wind blew through her hair and inflated her hood momentarily. The train *whooshed!* into the station and then made a squealing pause. The doors rattled open and Cythiria stepped inside. She leaned against the handrail, pulled her hoody over her head, and pushed her hands into her pockets.

She sighed deeply. *Did I do something wrong? Is that why Chelss didn't show up tonight?* Her ear throbbed under the bandage and the deep, grinding sound echoed through her head. The scars on her forehead tingled and burned. She felt an aching sensation in her chest, her throat tightening as she sniffed back forming tears.

The train rattled to a stop. The doors slid open and Cythiria stepped out of the train. She jogged down a dark stairwell, jumping over the turnstiles and onto the street. The neighborhood settled to a dark, purple hue. She looked up at the sky, squinting from the brightness of the milky white planetary ring. She glanced at the dark alleyway before her and ran towards it, her heavy boots slipping on the damp street. She paused and glanced around. She stepped forward, her heavy heels *clunking!* rapidly along the cobbled surface. She paused at the old, corroded steel door and kicked it open. She sniffed at the spicy warmth that emanated from the small portal and then dove into the dark, narrow corridor.

The kitchen was hot, as usual. The hollow clang of metal utensils on metal pans echoed through the dim and fragrant chamber, punctuated by shouts and cursing. The man with the barrel chest and tree-trunk arms stumbled towards Cythiria and paused. "Well, look who's here." He glanced at the large, white bandage that hung from her ear. "So, what do we have here?" He moved close and he looked over the bandage, raising his hand to his scraggly chin and scratching a sandpapery *ruzzzz!* "A fight, perchance?"

"Um…."

The man winked. "Freddy told me. He was a bit flustered. Like he was in a rush to get back here. He seems disturbed by something." He laughed. "Not that we need that lazy son of a bitch anyway."

"He knows about it? About the fight?"

"Of course. Why wouldn't he?" The man moved closer to Cythiria. "Don't tell him I said so," he whispered conspiratorially, "But he's a good kid. Really proud of his little girl."

Cythiria flushed. *His little girl.* Cythiria sighed quickly. "Well, I guess you nailed it, then," she said, forcing a smile.

"Who won?"

"The other girl," said Cythiria.

The man stood straight. "Well, look at it as a learning opportunity." He glanced up at the yellowed, smudgy, oily ceiling. "Like when I burn a perfectly good roux b'cause I got distracted. Teach me to keep my eye on my target." He glanced down from the ceiling at Cythiria's face, smiling warmly. He reached his giant paw towards Cythiria's head and mussed her short, black hair. "Hang in there, kid. You should trust Freddy. He's a good man," he said, winking. He turned. "Yo! Freddy! Your kid is here."

Fredrick stumbled out of a closet, which was adjacent to the kitchen, holding a ragged, water-stained, cardboard box in his arms. He set it on a worktable, sighed, and wiped his sweat-drenched forehead with his hand.

"Freddy?" snickered Cythiria.

"The man is insane," replied Fredrick. He reached towards the ties on his apron and untangled them. He glanced quickly at the bandage on Cythiria's ear, and then looked away. "I'm on break. Should we go outside?"

Cythiria nodded. Fredrick took off his apron and tossed it on top of the box. He walked through the dark corridor, pulling open the rusty steel door. He stumbled into the damp alleyway, paused, and then leaned against the wall, gazing up at the milky-white ring that washed the night city with a glimmering sheen.

"Beautiful, isn't it?" he said, distractedly.

Cythiria looked up. "Yeah."

He turned towards Cythiria. "Look, I'm sorry about what I said earlier." He reached his hand up and stroked Cythiria's dark hair. "You're so grown up now. You have to make your own decisions about life." He sniffled and his eyes seemed to dampen in the cool, white ring-light. "I wish I could've been there to watch you fight."

Cythiria shrugged her shoulders. "No worries. I know you gotta work."

"Your mom was worried. When I told her."

Cythiria scoffed. "I doubt Jillian would ever worry about me."

Fredrick's voice was soft. "She only wants the best for you. She'd much rather you be in school."

"I hate that place."

"Well, you have to go back eventually."

"I'll never go back there," she snapped. The grinding inside her skull grew to a more fervent pitch. Her head felt like it was being stuffed with cotton.

Fredrick sighed and then smiled gently. "So how did it go?" he said, looking at the bandage. "Not well, I take it?"

"I lost. First round. Pretty pathetic."

"Well, it's your first time, isn't it?"

"Yeah."

"I had to ask. Just think of it as a learning experience."

"That's what tree trunks said," quipped Cythiria.

Fredrick snorted. "But it seems like there's more to it than that. You seem a little distracted."

Cythiria paused. She sighed. "I met a friend."

"A friend?"

"Well, I thought so. She said she was gonna come and watch me fight, but she never showed. I'm kinda scared to text her."

Fredrick pursed his brow, jutted his lips, and rubbed his chin with his hand. "Maybe she just forgot."

"Somehow I doubt that."

"I'm sure you'll work things out." Fredrick reached up and touched Cythiria on the shoulder. "These things always seem to work out."

"Yeah, right," said Cythiria, a tone of sarcasm in her voice.

"Come on," said Fredrick. "It's getting cold out here. Let's go in. I'll get you something to eat." Fredrick turned, kicked the dilapidated steel door open and entered the dark corridor. Cythiria followed close behind. The warmth of the kitchen felt reassuring, and the general din of people working settled the grinding sound inside her head. She glanced around the corners of the kitchen and found a cluster of stacked boxes. She walked towards it and sat, leaning back, gazing up at the yellow, stained ceiling. Her eyes grew heavy as she dozed off and fell into a restless slumber.

"You go first. I'll lock up behind you," said Fredrick. Cythiria stumbled out of the dark corridor into the restaurant's rear door alleyway. She wrapped her arms around her waist, sniffing cold air that stung her throat as she inhaled. She exhaled a cloud of steam, which poured from her mouth and rose towards the purple, flickering lights. Above, the milky-white ring washed the city in an icy glow.

She heard a thump and a clang behind her, the rattle of keys on the old, steel door. She glanced left and right down the alley and paused. She held her breath. Her chest thumped heavily, and she heard her own pulse pounding in her ears.

A figure stood at the end of the alley. It was dark, almost wispy. Where its head should have been, black, smoky tendrils twisted and morphed into each other. A moment later, they merged into a solid mass. A shiny bald head that seemed to glisten in the ring-light, a white beard, glasses that flashed, and behind them, sharp, glimmering eyes.

She blinked hard. And then, it was gone. "What the…?" *Now I'm seeing things.* She shook her head and lifted her hand to the bandage on her ear.

"Ready?" she heard from behind her. She jumped, turning towards the voice, her hand over her chest. Fredrick looked at her face, which had been nearly buried into her hood. "You ok?"

"I…."

Fredrick turned towards the street and started to walk. "Come on, or we'll miss the last train home."

CHAPTER 16

One

Var 7, Farth, Nissy

One. I know you're here. Somewhere on this pathetic Var. And somehow, you are the center of Cythiria's plight. A catalyst, shall we say?

The door shut behind Rive Amber as she stepped onto the wet, bitumen street that was the driveway to her gym. The hollow clang of the bell echoed through the empty urban corridors as it slapped against the windowpane. Rive glanced up at the sky. The milky white ring cast a ghostly glow on the distant towers that clung together in chaotic clusters. Blinking pink and blue fluorescence shimmered, reflecting in scattered puddles along the street.

Rive sniffed the air. It smelled humid, smoky.

She turned down a narrow alley, her shoes slipping on the cobbled stone surface, walking until she emerged onto a small courtyard nestled among the graffitied walls of dark, empty warehouses and rusty, tumbledown chain-link fences.

She walked to the center and paused, glancing along the corners of the courtyard, at the places where the Perispikes had been placed and hidden prior. She closed her eyes momentarily as she sent the initialization command. A plasmic arc burst from the first Perispike and connected to each one in the array, washing the courtyard in an electric-blue light. A shimmering, azure wall rose from the Perispike array and formed a dome.

She reached into her pocket and pulled out a Capsa. She held it between her thumb and forefinger, squeezed it, and cast it onto the cobbled surface of the courtyard. It bounced once, twice and then stopped. It jumped. A stream

ONE

of plasmic arcs burst upwards towards the apex of the dome. A thin, vertical line formed, then spread apart, expanding to a dark void. Rive stepped toward it, gazing into its sheer blackness. She could feel it pull on her hair and skin and clothes. She took a deep breath and fell forward.

She felt squeezed as the world faded away and the air she once breathed was sucked out of her lungs. A moment later, she gazed up at a growing light, a shimmering gateway towards which she was drawn. A flash, and she stepped onto the metal-tiled platform. She gasped and coughed, falling onto her knees and then her hands, taking deep breaths and then heaving. She rolled onto her back and gazed up at the portal as it closed. Beyond the black Transposal posts from which the Slipshot was initialized, stood the Silo. It stretched upwards, eternally, its tip seeming to touch the apex of the Griddish dome.

She pushed herself up onto her knees and then stood. She breathed deeply of the calm, fragrant air. She gazed around the verdant hills, at the distant Slipshot Silos that littered the horizon. She heard a distant *pop!* and glanced towards the shattered cityscape of Ashen Fissure. She sighed deeply. *This war. We can only free ourselves from the Slipshot once we end this war. This is why I need you, Cythiria. I need you by my side. I need you to be there for me.*

She closed her eyes and entered the Tenddrome, issuing a request. A moment later, a Vérkatros emerged from the hills and hovered across the metal-tiled platform. It paused as legs emerged from its chassis and stood. She glanced over the Vérkatros, a scowl crossing her lips. *And someday, Griddish will be free from you.*

Buzzing torches were mounted along the dark walls of Sanguine Heap, illuminating Rive's chamber with an electric blue light. She sat on a squat

131

pallet, her legs crossed in front of her. She closed her eyes and took a deep breath.

The room faded to a thick, inky blackness. She opened her eyes and glanced around as she floated in what felt like a heavy liquid. In the distance, points of light appeared, a few at a time, popping into clusters and multitudes, turning, and disappearing and reappearing.

Rive turned to face the lights as they collected into a massive sphere. Plasmic arcs coursed through the sphere as the lights morphed into each other, then split apart again, forming new points of light.

The Tenddrome takes our lives and renews our lives. Can we ever be free from this relentless cycle?

And then, from the sphere emerged dark tendrils that groped and entangled the points of light, splitting and crushing them.

Rive opened her eyes. Her breath was short and raspy. "One," she mumbled. "Is that you? 1^1. Is that what you're called? That meaningless abhorrence that will be the end of us all? And yet, to some, you'll be welcomed with open arms."

Rive turned towards the sound of echoing footsteps as they grew close to her.

"You look like shit," came the voice. Natty Mick emerged from the darkness, smirking.

"The Vars will be the end of us," replied Rive. "They sap us Slaves of our life. Especially when the Slipshot is closed. The fact that Cythiria has survived this long is astounding."

ONE

Natty pushed his hand through his thick, black hair. "So why are you back in Griddish? Having trouble with your little *project*?" he said, a tone of sarcasm in his voice.

"It's only temporary. Soon, I'll be returning to Var 7." She took a deep breath and stood up. She stepped towards Natty, her otherwise confident stride faltering on the cold, stone floors. "I also need you to go to Var 7."

"What?" Natty scoffed. "I already went to Var 8 for you, and that place is pretty much a wasteland. Why do I have to go to that shithole Var 7 now?"

Rive paused. "One."

"One?"

"He is on the move. I've seen his effect on the Tenddrome. I suspect he's on Var 7."

"Suspect?"

"He was close to those two Varlings that took Cythiria."

"You mean, that you *gave* Cythiria."

"I want to know why he is involved with them."

"And then?"

Rive paused. "Perhaps the end of everything."

Natty snorted. "Isn't that what you want, Rive? The end of everything? The Tenddrome? The Slipshot?"

Rive glared at Natty, a snarl growing on her lip. "Please, Natty."

Natty bowed. "As you wish." He turned and walked out of the chamber.

CHAPTER 17

A New Project

Var 7, Farth, Nissy

"The fuck she think she's gonna gain from this?" Natty grumbled as he dismounted the hovering Vérkatros at the edge of the Slipshot to Var 7, Farth. His booted feet *clanged!* on the metal-tiled surface of the platform. From the distance, he heard an echoing *pop!* He felt the rumble of firefall in the ground, squinting at the bright flash of light that followed as he glanced towards it. "Shit's getting close," he mumbled.

He reached into his pocket and pulled out a Capsa. He squeezed it and tossed it towards the array of black Transposal posts, at whose convergence point would form the Slipshot portal. The Capsa clattered to a stop, jumped, and split open. From it burst a plasmic arc, which connected to the first post, following the array until it reached the Silo. From atop the Silo, an arc struck the convergence point, and in its center, a thin, vertical line formed and then split open. Natty gazed into the sheer blackness of the hole and stepped forward until he stood at its very edge. He could feel the pull of the Slipshot on his clothes and skin and hair. He took a deep breath, closed his eyes, and fell forward.

A moment later, he was gazing up at a night sky. The milky white ring cast a frosty glow on his supine body. Upon the sides of dark buildings flickered pink and blue, fluorescent lights, and above, a deep, purple LED glow.

Beneath him, he felt a soft, almost cushiony surface. He sniffed. The sour smell of rotting garbage pierced his nose. He jumped up, entangling his feet in loose bags, tripping forward to the edge of what came to be a metal container. He tossed his arm over the edge and gagged and heaved, pulling himself over until he fell on the cold, damp, cobbled street. He stood up, leaned against the garbage receptacle, and sighed.

"Fucking Vars," he mumbled. "Disgusting places. Why we haven't rid ourselves of them once and for all, I'll never know."

He stood up and stretched, gazing towards the milky white ring in the sky. *Now, all I need to do is find out where that asshole One is, and then I can get the hell out of here. And the ones who lead me to One could be the very same Varlings who lost their precious Var 8 to a dismantlement project. Or, nearly so.*

Natty paused at the entry to a dark alley.

"Finding the Varling shouldn't be too hard," he mumbled. He had, after all, confronted Rive. At least, that is what Rive said. Even in a large city like Nissy, people follow their routines, their regular paths. "We are all creatures of habit, aren't we," said Natty, out loud. He yawned and then stretched. "It's too bad we're all just so boring and predictable in the end."

The buzz of fluorescent light echoed weakly along the abandoned streets. Natty felt a chill as the night settled in and the cool, planetary ring cast a white light on the buildings and the damp streets around him. An aboveground subway train whooshed and rattled by.

The deep clang of an opening metal door broke the chilly silence. A few mumbling voices bubbled along the edges of the alley and dissipated. The clack of heels on bitumen *clicked!* and *clunked!* until they faded away. An orange ember seemed to float in the air. Natty sniffed. The smell of cigarette smoke scratched at his nose and throat as he stifled a cough.

"Bingo!" he whispered. *Don't we just love Varling colloquialisms! As if our own vocabulary isn't colorful enough....*

Into the deep, purple LED light, a figure emerged. Natty stepped forward.

"Well, if it isn't our little Varling so far away from home," he said.

The man paused and glanced towards the direction of the voice. "You," he said.

Natty smirked and pushed his hand through his thick, black hair. "That's right. Me. It's been a while, hasn't it…um…." He touched the tip of his left forefinger to his temple and then clicked his right fingers.

"Fredrick."

Natty snorted. "Right, *Fredrick*."

Fredrick paused. "Look," he started, "I don't want any trouble. I've got a job and I've settled in…."

"Trouble?" said Natty. A crooked smile spread across his face. "Now why would I, of all people, want to bring any trouble to *you*?"

"I know Rive is here…."

"Ah, Rive. Yes. Good old Rive Amber. I heard you two had a bit of a confrontation recently." He paused, turning his eyes towards the sky as if recalling a memory. "How is Cythiria, by the way? I hear she's a big girl now. Quite the grown up compared to that little shit you left Griddish with ages ago."

Fredrick clenched his teeth. His legs trembled. He lurched forward, raising his fist to strike Natty, who stepped to the side and delivered a heavy knee to Fredrick's torso.

Fredrick fell to the ground and wrapped his arms around his waist. He turned over and pulled himself up on his hands and knees, coughed and dry heaved, and then stood. "I'm not letting you take Cythiria," he growled.

Natty scoffed and rolled his eyes. "As if. Just so you know, I'm not here to break up any budding familial relationships or anything. Just keep in mind where Cythiria came from. It's unlikely she'll survive here much longer. When the Slaves are without their Tenddrome, they're as good as dead."

Fredrick scowled.

"Look, I'm also not going to waste my time on this place, so don't go thinking I've come with any of those awful Vérkatrae at my service. Besides, all that dismantlement stuff, well, that was from a different era of Griddish. We've moved on. We're no longer interested in managing the Vars and what not."

"Then why are you here? Why not just stay away if you hate this place so much?"

Natty stepped closer to Fredrick. "To be honest, it's not me so much. There are other elements out there, very dangerous elements, that are not satisfied with the way things are."

Fredrick paused. He reached into his pocket and pulled out a crumpled pack of cigarettes. He tapped one out and placed it between his lips. He reached into his pocket and flicked open a steel lighter that smelled of fresh kerosene and lit, casting an orange yellow luminescence on his face. He dragged deeply from the cigarette as it crackled and glowed under the dim light. He blew a puff of smoke toward Natty, who grimaced and waved it away. "So, what has that to do with me? I'm powerless against you and your Slipshot and the Vérkatrae."

Natty smirked. He pushed his hand through his thick, black hair. "Have you ever heard of someone by the name of One?"

Fredrick gasped quietly, a whisper-like breath through clenched teeth. He felt his face and neck grow cool. His warm flush of a moment ago paled.

"Ah," continued Natty. "I see that you have. In fact, I'm surprised you'd have such a terribly shocked look on your face. Didn't you know him as Dr. Jeremiah Onu?"

"I…."

Natty snorted. And then.

"Ah yes." A deep, calm voice came from the direction of Natty's right flank. "Dr. Jeremiah Onu. What a nice ring it has, wouldn't you say?"

Natty turned toward the voice, his body also partially postured toward Fredrick. The man wore a large, deep hood pulled over his head. He reached up and pulled it away, revealing a smoky mass, dark, indistinct tendrils twisting and turning until they formed a shape, a white-bearded face, silvery glasses, a balding head. He scoffed. "So, if it isn't the man himself," he said. "The one and only 1^1."

"I prefer Jeremiah," he said, glancing toward Fredrick and winking significantly.

Natty scoffed. "I hear you've been busy," he said.

"Oh? I'm flattered that someone of *your* stature would have the time and energy to concern themselves over me."

"Indeed. And it seems like your presence here is not so trivial after all."

Jeremiah smiled gently. "The universe as we know it is trivial. The reason for its existence, none."

"Such nihilistic thoughts don't become you, One."

"Liberating," said Jeremiah. "Not nihilistic. When we are free from the burden of causality, then we are free to do as we wish."

Natty scoffed. "Yet, you are here and not floating aimlessly around the universe."

"I am not yet free from causality."

"And whose fault is that?" A smirk crossed his face, and his eyes grew wide.

"As long as Griddish and all her children still exist, then the universe will never be at peace."

"Peace. Whatever. Sounds like a pretty boring proposition to me."

Fredrick sucked on his cigarette, drawing deeply of the smoke. Fredrick blew into the air, the smoke mixing with warm steam from inside his lungs. He flicked the cigarette across the slick, cobbled alley. It skittered along wet stone and stopped in a shower of sparkles. "It looks like you've found who you're looking for."

Natty turned towards Fredrick, a smirk crossing his face. He pushed his hand through his thick, black hair.

And then, the ground rumbled deeply. Windows rattled in their frames, some shattering and falling to the street in a shower of shards. Lamp posts, which emanated deep, purple LED light, rocked from side to side. Fredrick glanced at Natty and then towards Jeremiah, or One.

Dark tendrils twisted and twined from One's head, and from his feet, like writhing roots, they bore into the ground below. The bitumen beneath his feet split apart and then surged upward, falling again and rolling like waves in a stormy sea.

And then, silence. Fredrick gazed in the direction of One, but he was gone. All that was left was the quiet buzz and pink and blue flicker of fluorescent light, and smudgy, graffitied and tagged walls awash with the milky white light of the planetary ring.

Fredrick glanced at Natty, then surged forward, pushing past him, running until he stood on the ground where, not more than a moment ago, Jeremiah stood. He crouched onto one knee and gazed at the broken street. Those dark tendrils continued to twist and turn, writhing and boring deeper into the ground. A moment later, they stopped, frozen like black stone, and then faded away like steam.

"Jeremiah," mumbled Fredrick. "One." Fredrick stood up, glancing over his shoulder at Natty.

"You can't run away, Varling," shouted Natty, his voice echoing along the dark canyons of the night city. "You can't hide from the Vérkatrae. You know what they did to Var 8. To your home. And now, they're here. One is here. You know what One is, don't you Fredrick? You know, right?"

The voice of Natty faded. Fredrick heard his own heavy pulse pound in his ears, his heart beat heavily in his chest. His breath was raspy, the cold air burnt his throat and his nose. His booted feet slipped on the damp, slick bitumen. *One is a Vérkatros. So why is he here? Why now?*

Fredrick walked quickly along the dark road. He could hear the waves of the sea pound against their steel barriers. He shivered as he felt the dampness of his own sweat under his coat. He glanced up at the planetary ring. It was cold, silent, yet bright, stretching across the horizon like a giant, icy band. He turned onto the walkway of the small bungalow and kicked the door open. He ran in, towards a closed door. He opened it.

"Oh, thank god," he mumbled. He took a deep, sighing breath. On the bed, a nest of messy, black hair dangled over the edge of a pillow. He quietly, on tiptoes, stepped towards it. He paused, gazing down at the sleeping face, eyes closed peacefully, mouth open, and a gentle snore. "I thought they came for you Cyth," he whispered as he reached towards Cythiria's hair and stroked it aside. He looked at those two scars on her forehead, those two red dots that she had ever since she was a child, ever since that day when they fell through the Slipshot and landed here, Var 7, Farth, this strange yet familiar world. *Those* scars.

"Dad," he heard a whisper.

"Yeah, what's up?"

"Did you bring me something to eat?"

Fredrick snorted quietly. "Of course," he said, reaching into his coat pocket, feeling the paper of the sandwich he wrapped for her before he left. "I'll leave it in the kitchen for you."

"Ok," slurred Cythiria, turning away from him onto her side.

Fredrick felt a welling up inside. He sniffled. *I don't know what I'd do if something happened to you, Cyth. I....*

Fredrick stood up, bent over and pulled the quilt over Cythiria's shoulders. He turned and quietly walked out of the room, closed the door silently, and stepped into the kitchen. He took the package out of his pocket and placed it on the table. He smiled. *Whenever you're ready, Cyth.*

CHAPTER 18

Descent

Var 7, Farth, Nissy

In the ring of Rive Amber's gym, Cythiria blinked away the rivulets of sweat that dripped into her eyes. She held her gloved hands close to her face, her chin down, eyes focused. She stepped to the side, pivoting her hips, her shoulders leaning forward. Her breath was choppy, as she blew air through her mouth in small, regular puffs.

She focused on Rive, those dark, glaring eyes, that thin scowl that curled up on one side of her face. She felt the wind of her sparring strikes as they whooshed by her ear, those kicks that flew up the middle barely missing her jaw and nose.

"Step forward. Don't let your opponent chase you. Strike and follow through!" shouted Rive.

Cythiria threw a jab, a hook, a kick. Rive ducked and turned, dancing and pivoting as a blur. Cythiria inhaled quickly through her nose, clenched her teeth, and raised her gloved hands to her face.

The hollow clap of the bell clanged against the windowpane of the front door and echoed through the wide chamber. Cythiria glanced towards it. Her eyes grew wide. And then, she felt herself fall. The back of her head struck the canvas floor of the ring, and the world was awash in a spray of tiny sparkles.

Cythiria lay on her back. The world around her spun, and her stomach turned. She blinked. Above her, a shadow formed and grew close. Those dark, glaring eyes, that thin scowl seemed to fizzle into view.

"Who are you waiting for, Cythiria?" said Rive.

"I…, I'm not…."

"Because there's no one there. There never will be, Cythiria. Only I will be there for you."

Cythiria's stomach turned. She felt her eyes grow damp, her lips tremble. Rive moved close to Cythiria. She could feel her breath on her face, those glaring, piercing eyes stare deeply into her own. She could feel Rive's hands grasp her wrists, pinning her down to the mat. Rive moved closer. Cythiria could feel the warmth of her face against her cheek. "Remember what I told you," Rive whispered, the words slithering into her ear like snakes. "You belong to me."

Cythiria turned her head away. She felt Rive release her grasp of her wrists and stand up. She turned her head and looked up. Rive stood there, nose high, dark glaring eyes, a rising, quivering scowl as if she were about to spit. And then she turned, her feet tapping lightly on the canvas as she glided away.

Who was I waiting for?

After a long, bruising workout at Rive's gym, Cythiria reflected as she walked along the city streets. She glanced up at the deep blue sky. The planetary ring appeared as some long, wispy cloud that seemed to dangle just above the tips of the tall, slender towers of Nissy.

When I turned to look, and then Rive knocked me down, who was I expecting? Because nobody's coming to see me. Especially her. Chelss. I mean, why would she? I certainly wouldn't!

143

Cythiria walked along the old city streets, past the tagged and graffitied walls, the slick, bitumen roads. The *whoosh!* of rushing, busy vehicles slithered through the urban canyons, and the patter and babble of human traffic bubbled up and down along the sidewalks and courtyards where stands and carts of food sellers congregated.

Her stomach gurgled. "Geeze, I'm hungry," she mumbled as she sniffed deeply of the rising scents. *Rive doesn't ever let up.* She slapped her stomach with the flat of her hand. It sounded taut and hollow. She glanced around the courtyard, at the chairs and benches that were scattered about. She looked at one in particular. *That's where I saw HER. And then that guy came over.* She shuddered. She reached up and rubbed the side of her head, which was still sore from Rive's early morning strike. "Worthless!" she mumbled. *Why would I turn my head away from Rive like that? She must think I'm an idiot! As if someone would walk through that door just to see me….*

She pulled her large, deep hood over her head and shoved her hands in her pockets. She continued to walk aimlessly, gazing distractedly at the tall towers and the blinking traffic lights until, before her, stood two square black structures, the school that she once, not long ago, attended.

She stopped and sighed. *Like coming back to this school will change anything…. Why do I even bother? I'm sure she's forgotten me by now.*

The murmur of laughing and chatting voices echoed along the courtyard between the dark buildings of Nissy Public. She glanced at the clusters of students as they stood in groups. Her eyes followed them and then she saw *her*.

Cythiria held her breath. Her heart beat heavily in her chest, and her pulse pounded in her ears. Her neck and cheeks flushed hotly, and her legs trembled. Her stomach fluttered.

"Chelss," she murmured. *Idiot, idiot, idiot. This is the last thing I need right now. She doesn't want to see me anyway. She never wanted to see me. Why would she?*

Cythiria gazed apprehensively towards Chelss, who stood, her back leaning against a wall. Her long, brown hair flowed freely down her shoulders from two ponytails, one on each side of her head. She wore a breezy white shirt and a pair of loose, shiny sweatpants that hung airily from her hips, revealing a slender midriff. Her lips were glossy and red. Her long eyelashes fluttered sleepily as she smiled up at someone who stood over her, a hand pressed up against the wall next to her head.

Cythiria felt a tightness in her chest. She stepped forward and then paused. Her breath shuddered. Her face flushed. "I can't," she mumbled. "I can't do this." *She's happy. She's better off without me around.*

She turned and stepped quickly away, down the sidewalk, through the busy courtyard. She paused at an alley. She stepped in and then leaned her back against the wall. She slid down the wall until she sat on her haunches. She wrapped her arms around her legs and rested her head on her knees, her body quivering as she sobbed.

The train rattled and swayed as it *whooshed!* along the tracks. Cythiria's head wobbled as she dozed. Her head snapped up. She looked around, raising her hand to her mouth to wipe away some fresh drool.

A pink and blue fluorescence pulsed along the dark city streets below, as Cythiria gazed out the window. *How long have I been here? Hours. Back and forth. To where?*

The subway rattled to a pause at her usual stop, the one that would lead her home. The doors hissed open and Cythiria jumped up. She stepped onto the platform, skittered down a stairwell and then jumped the turnstiles. She walked onto the sidewalk, blinking at the pink and blue, fluorescent pulse reflecting off the damp streets, which were bathed in a purple LED glow.

She sniffed the air, which smelled of sea decay. She walked along the edge of the steel barrier that kept Nissy's sea at bay. She jumped onto it, her boots sliding on the damp, corroded surface. She looked at the sky, the bright, milky white ring that just seemed to hover over Nissy's ambitious, blinking cityscape. She felt the rumble of the sea as it pounded angrily against its barrier. "It would be so easy," she mumbled. *So easy to just fall and float away.* She reached towards her forehead, touching the scars on her head. They started to tingle and burn and the sound that echoed through her head was a distant, lonely whistle.

But Rive would be angry with me. She'd look at me with those eyes of hers. She'd scoff and say I was weak. We are not all born with the tools we need to survive. We must forge them ourselves and then hone them. That's what Rive said.

Cythiria smelled deeply of the chilly, night air. She sighed and turned, jumping down onto the road that followed the city's sea walls. She walked until she arrived at the small bungalow that was her home. It was dark inside. Fredrick was still at work. Jillian, on the road, somewhere. She walked to her room and fell prone onto the creaky bed. She buried her face in her pillow and sobbed while tears streamed down her cheeks.

She imagined Chelss next to her. *I only want her with me.* And then she fell to a restless slumber.

A chilly dampness coursed through Cythiria's body. She gasped for breath as her heart pounded in her chest. Her neck and back felt wet with a cold sweat. Her stomach turned as a feeling of panic welled up inside of her. She sat up and gazed wide-eyed into the dark. The scars on her forehead burned. A deep grinding sound echoed through her head, reverberating through her bones.

"Not again," she whispered. "Not this again. I can't do this anymore, I just can't…."

Cythiria stood up and groped in the darkness. She stumbled to the door and pulled it open. She gazed into the living room, at the gentle white light that was cast through the uncurtained window from the planetary ring. Her throat tightened as tears streamed down her cheeks.

She walked to the kitchen. *I can't do this anymore. I just can't. I don't want to be here. I just want to go away, to be free, to feel…relief.* She stumbled to a drawer and pulled it open. She reached in. She felt the cool metal of the blade between her fingers. She grabbed it and then leaned her back against the wall and slid down onto her haunches. The two scars on her forehead pulsed and burned, a warm, crimson rivulet tickled her nose. The grinding sound, like stone on stone, like a hammer striking steel, echoed through her skull.

Her hand trembled as she gazed into the mirrored surface of the blade. It glinted in the icy white light cast by the planetary ring. She saw a reflection of her own dark eyes, her forehead dripping with blood. Her stomach turned and her mouth watered salty. She wanted to heave, to vomit, to expunge, to forget. To forget about Rive. To forget about *her*. About Chelss.

She turned her forearm up. She gazed at the taut muscles, the thin, green veins beneath smooth flesh. She sobbed as tears dripped down her cheeks and splattered on the floor.

She raised the knife with her other hand. She took a deep, quivering breath. And then, she slashed. Once, twice. The blade cut through her flesh. The pain felt good as it quieted the echoes in her head, the pulsing and burning of her forehead. She slashed again and paused, smiling, as the tiled kitchen floor grew dark crimson and slick.

She dropped the blade. It *clanged!* when it struck the hard floor. She smiled. Her body felt light, as if a burden had been lifted from her chest. Her vision blurred and faded. She heard footsteps. They were distant, lonely. She heard a voice. It was urgent, strained. "Cythiria! Cythiria!" it said. "Cythiria! What have you done?"

And then, darkness.

⚘

Natty Mick leaned against a light post, its buzzing, white light cast him in a milky glow. He gazed up at the planetary ring. It was bright tonight, its edges and grooves sharp and clear. Waves slapped against the steel dikes that held back the waters of Nissy Bay. Natty crinkled his nose as the smell of sea decay wafted past him along a chilly, evening breeze.

He took a deep breath and closed his eyes. The world around him grew to an inky blackness as he was absorbed and enmeshed by the Tenddrome. A point of light appeared and then approached.

"You're not gonna like this, Rive," he started.

"And what might that be?"

"Your little *project* might not make it."

Rive sighed with consternation. "And what is that supposed to mean?"

"She tried to off herself, as the Varlings like to say."

Rive paused. "Are you sure about this?"

"I'm standing right outside her house. An ambulance is on the way. But it might be too late." Natty waited. "What are you going to do now, oh great leader, now that your little project is done for?"

Rive sighed deeply. "Perhaps we should see this as an opportunity."

"Opportunity? Opportunity for what?"

"For much needed change. For a new beginning."

"With all your plans hinging on Cythiria being alive, Rive, how do you expect to move forward on the body of a dead Mechanic?"

Rive paused. "I'm returning to Var 7. I'll handle it."

Natty scoffed. "There's one more thing."

"Which is?"

"One. He's quite the pest, you know. Burying himself inside this ridiculous little Var and then showing up at the most inopportune time."

Rive paused. "We need to draw him out and understand his goals."

"Yeah, no shit. Got any suggestions?"

"I'll leave that to you."

The inky blackness faded. Natty blinked at the sudden brightness of the white light that flooded the street upon which he stood, as he returned to Var 7 from the Tenddrome. The city echoed the distant wail of an approaching siren. "Sure thing, your highness," he scoffed. "Whatever you say."

CHAPTER 19

Rushing Home

Var 7, the Deserts of Farth

The cab of the large truck rattled and swayed down a wide freeway. Jillian Crenshaw gazed out the front, bubble shaped window. The sky was a dark blue, and the horizon started to glow from the light of the rising sun.

Stars speckled the skies along this lonely road. The ring sparkled and its lines appeared sharp and bright in the early morning light. A few smaller vehicles whooshed by, quickly leaving the rig to its own solitary ventures.

Jillian yawned. She rolled the window down just a bit, letting a cool, dry breeze fill the cabin, replacing the stale, musty air with a woody, aromatic scent. The arid, desert air was very different from the oceanic dampness of Nissy, its blue bays filled with small boats and grand ships, bobbing and cruising along at all times.

In fact, most of Var 7 was desert, which explained why cities were so large and so few and far between. The burgeoning population of Farth remained clustered in certain areas and did not expand its reach far beyond those, save for a few smaller settlements which were peopled by the more solitary, anarchistic types.

So why did Griddish decide that Var 7 was ok, Jillian wondered, but Var 8 was to be eliminated, "deconstructed," as the Mechanics might say? "I suppose Var 7 knows its place," she mumbled. "Or, it has an understanding of its role in the universe." Unlike the people from Var 8.

The road ahead was straight and steady, surrounded on both sides by tall, dusty mountains. Jillian felt a sense of calm, a steadiness that she never knew on Var 8. On Earth. Perhaps it had something to do with her station there, her class, her place in the world. An unrelenting drive to live up to expectations. A desire, and an ability, to change the world.

That had all disappeared on Farth. Suddenly, Jillian Portentia Crenshaw had no expectations, no hopes, no dreams. No paved path before her.

But she had Cythiria.

"All those dreams I had seem so distant now," she mumbled. Now, life was about survival, not accomplishment. It was about achieving basic things, like food and shelter, and no longer about obtaining the accolades of the people around you, people you didn't even know or care about.

"Which is why Cythiria needs to stay in school." Jillian was insistent on that. It meant that there would be a future for her, where she could exist in a place of privilege. Where she could form a dream and pursue it and people would listen to her and support her.

A chime emanated from the cab's dashboard. Jillian gestured, and a holographic screen flickered on. Fredrick's face appeared. It was a pre-recorded message, since livestreaming was not always possible out here in the isolated areas.

Jillian glanced up at the bright, planetary ring. It was the ring that determined the rules of life on Farth. The planetary ring was everywhere, all the time. It was part of Farthian identity. It was something that everyone adapted to.

In the holographic projection, Fredrick's eyes looked distant, distracted. His lips were curled to a deep frown, his face was haggard, his hair stringy. There were dark circles under his eyes, almost like when he was back in San Francisco, tormented by those Vérkatrae and a certain Mechanic Class Slave by the name of Opal Fremmitty.

Jillian gestured again and the video started to play.

"It's Cythiria." Fredrick sighed and pushed his hair back. "You need to come back as soon as possible. She's…not well."

The video stopped. Jillian felt her stomach turn. Her heart started to pound in her chest. "What the fuck is that supposed to mean? Goddammit, Fredrick! Can't you be more specific?"

She gestured again and the rig accelerated.

"What the hell could have happened to Cythiria?"

CHAPTER 20

A Checkered Past

Griddish, Ashen Fissure, the Dusk Quadrant

"I'm not sure I trust this," said Betel. She looked over the casks of Waftring liquor. "It's all too convenient."

"There you go again, Betel. Always so paranoid."

Betel turned towards Matere, her face rigid, intense. "Nothing happens in Griddish that is not known by the Slaves. That is why the Tenddrome exists. At least, that is why it existed in the beginning. So that Slaves could share information across a vast network of other Slaves. It would make completing tasks easy and efficient and less prone to error. It also meant that every single one of them could easily know what anyone else was doing."

Matere sighed. "That was a long time ago, Betel. Times have changed. Why do you think the Dusk Quadrant was built? So that Slaves could get away from a system that became a burden to them, even if it was only temporary."

Betel shook her head. "That still doesn't protect certain facts from being propagated. Such as these casks of Waftring liquor. There are no secrets in Griddish, my dear Matere Songgaard."

No secrets. Well, there are some secrets that even you aren't aware of, Betel. At least one of those will be the undoing of these Slaves. Or at least, we can hope. It all happened so long ago, back when our world was still at peace and we Engineers were the greatest inventors in the universe....

Matere Songgaard gazed out the window, which shimmered in the gentle, Griddish light, casting a warm glow on his otherwise pale, unshaven face and matted white hair. He pushed up his glasses, which had slid down to the tip of his oily nose, tilting them so that they rested evenly on his head.

An oval-shaped building that looked like swirling clouds rose auspiciously from the Council's quadrant known as Governance. Clusters of Engineer Class Citizens clad in golden yellow and white streamed down the cobbled street named Midriff Stump into the great hall from which they governed the vastness of Griddish.

He shook his head.

His eyes followed rolling, green hills, manicured lawns that extended to the edge of the Council's crystal dome.

"We're sheltered here," he mumbled. *Why do we need a dome in a domed world? It's ridiculous. But not meaningless. It's as if we have something to prove. But what? That we can?*

He sighed deeply as he turned away from the window. He walked to the center of his chamber towards a panel that sat at the middle of the otherwise dim room. From it, a holographic globe turned and fizzled, casting weak electric blue light along the walls and floors of the chamber. He gazed at it, stroking his rough chin with his hand. He removed his hand from his chin and gestured a curving motion. The globe split in half and opened up. Inside, he saw layers that seemed to twirl and flow into each other like water. In some places, dark, inky-looking fluid was chaotic, almost stormy, in others, calm.

The Tenddrome has changed since that day it was created. Evolved, perhaps. What it has become, we just don't know. Still, it is how all Slaves connect to each other. Through the Tenddrome, Slaves manifest their intentions, query their counterparts, initialize Nodes. It is robust, perfect, and impenetrable.

"Impenetrable," mumbled Matere. "But only to us, the Engineer Class Citizens." Matere scoffed bitterly. "And still, if only we could understand it better, then maybe we can make progress."

Progress! Matere scoffed. *Progress towards what goal? What would we gain if we understood the Tenddrome better? Would we be able to control an uncontrollable force? Can the Slaves be controlled? Or the Vérkatrae?*

Matere sighed deeply and rubbed his sandpapery chin with his hand. He turned and walked out of the chamber and down a narrow corridor, his heels *clanging!* distractedly along the hard, metal-tiled floor. He entered an adjacent room and approached a glowing blue light. He stepped up to it and gazed through a window into a coffin-sized chamber. Inside, he saw a face that was crowned by flowing, white hair, a slender, almost wispy body, arms crossed upon a naked chest.

"I cannot access the Tenddrome," mumbled Matere as he gazed at the peaceful, slumbering face. "But you, my friend, can. You have an intimate connection with it, with all Slaves and even the Vérkatrae. Unfortunately, there is only one way that I can have any effect on what the Slaves do there. The work I have done on you, all the tests, all the modifications, can only be introduced to the Tenddrome in one way. Hopefully, it won't be too painful for you. You will live on. Just not today."

⚔

"Not today," mumbled Matere. Matere sighed. *I do have blood on my hands, but I did it for a purpose. To understand the Slaves by infecting them with their own virus.*

"What was that?" said Betel.

Matere sighed. "Nothing, nothing, never mind. For whatever reason these casks of Waftring liquor are here, it doesn't really matter. We need to take advantage of them while we still can. So, let's party it up with the Slaves and see what kind of information we can get from them. At the very least, we can spread a little more chaos among their ranks."

Betel shook her head. "Typical," she spat.

CHAPTER 21

A Moment of Light

Var 7, Farth, Nissy

Cythiria opened her eyes. She squinted at the bright, hospital-yellow light that filled the room from buzzing overhead lamps.

"Ugh," she mumbled. She moved. Her legs, her arms, her body ached. She lifted her arm and gazed at it distractedly. It was bandaged from her hand to her elbow. She turned it. The gauzy wraps crackled, and her skin underneath burned and stung.

She hissed through clenched teeth. "Where am I?" she mumbled.

She heard quiet, pattering footsteps on the tiled floor. "You're awake," came the gentle voice.

She glanced up at Fredrick. The bloodshot, saddened eyes, the pursed brows betrayed the almost forced smile that crossed his face. "Did I…?"

Fredrick nodded. "We're at Nissy General."

"That bad, huh." She looked again at the gauzy wrapping.

"Can I get you anything?"

Cythiria sighed. "How about a new head?"

Fredrick reached towards Cythiria's head and pushed aside a stray lock of black hair, careful not to touch the crossed bandages on her forehead. "Yours is just fine."

"No, it's not."

"How about something a little easier, like a glass of water."

"Sure."

Fredrick turned towards a table and reached for a bottle of water. He twisted the cap and tilted its contents into a glass.

"I asked someone to come by," he said, pushing the glass towards Cythiria.

"For real? Why would you do that? I must look like shit now."

"I don't think this person would mind."

Cythiria heard the light patter of footsteps near the door. She turned her head. Her eyes grew wide. She felt her heart pound in her chest and her neck and face flush.

"Cythiria," came the whispering voice.

"Chelss, I…."

Chelss stepped towards Cythiria, paused at the edge of the bed, and leaned towards her. Cythiria gazed into her hazel-colored eyes. She sniffed. A florid perfume filled the room in her wake. Her long, brown hair was tied to a side ponytail. Her lips were painted pink. She wore a puffy white jacket and baggy jeans.

"Your dad texted me…." Chelss's eyes scanned the bandages on Cythiria's arm.

Cythiria glanced towards Fredrick. "Texted? But how?"

"I rifled through your stuff after the…incident. Your device had three contacts in it. Me, Jillian, and someone named Chelss with a heart emoji next to it. I figured this person was important to you."

Cythiria flushed. "Gawd, how embarrassing."

"Look, I'm sorry about the match," interrupted Chelss.

Cythiria's eyes grew damp. She sniffled. "I was hoping you would come. I wanted to see you."

"You should have texted me."

"I wanted to. I typed out so many messages, but I deleted them before I could build up the courage to send them. I figured you just didn't want to see me anymore. I was afraid that maybe you would confirm that." She sighed. "I guess I wanted to hold on to hope somehow."

"I…your coach…."

"Rive?"

"She told me to stay away from you."

Cythiria tried to sit up. "What?"

The bell echoed a hollow clap on the cracked glass door pane of Rive's gym. Chelss, her hair tied to a pair of ponytails that flowed from either side of her head, paused. She stepped towards the caged ring that sat at the center of the main chamber.

"She's not here," grumbled a low voice.

Chelss jumped and turned towards it. "Is she coming today?"

The woman who faced her glared at Chelss with dark, burning eyes, her upper lip rising to a scowl. She held her nose and chin high. "She's in training."

"Can I see her?"

"Cythiria doesn't need any distractions right now."

"But…" Chelss felt her chest tighten and her stomach turn. "…I…I'm a friend. I just want to see her."

"She doesn't need you. She needs to focus." Rive's face darkened, and her eyes grew spiteful. "People like you will only serve to bring her down."

Tears formed on the corners of Chelss's eyes. Her voice quivered. "Does Cythiria feel the same way?"

"Indeed, she does. She's a loner who depends only on herself. So, I suggest you turn around and don't ever come back here."

Chelss, her eyes wide, turned and ran towards the door, slamming it open as she stepped onto the street. She could hear the hollow clap of the bell behind her. "Why, Cythiria? Do you really want to be all alone? Or is Rive all you need in this world?"

She reached into her pocket and pulled out a device, stroking its surface so that the screen lit up. She flipped through a list of contacts. "Cyth," one of the entries read. Chelss stuffed the device back into her pocket. She sighed deeply and wrapped her arms around her waist. She walked towards the train station, through the turnstiles, and down a dark corridor.

"I wanted you to do well, since you weren't coming to school anymore. I was hoping you found something for yourself. Something that you loved to do. Some dream that you could pursue, even if it was without me."

"Oh, Chelss…." Tears streamed down Cythiria's cheeks. Her nose grew a shade of pink. She sniffled.

"I thought maybe it was best that I just got out of your way. Just like Rive said."

Cythiria sat up and wrapped her arms around Chelss's neck, pulling her close. She sobbed. "You could never be in my way."

Chelss pulled away. "Are you sure? Do you really believe that?"

Cythiria sniffled. "I mean, look at me. It's not like I'm on some path to glory." She smiled through damp, reddening eyes. "Not even Rive Amber can fix something this broken."

Chelss looked up and down Cythiria's body, her eyes pausing at the bandaged arm. "You do look like you are in need of repairs."

Cythiria smiled. "More than repairs. A whole replacement would be in order."

Chelss reached her hand to her eyes and wiped away forming tears.

And then, from seemingly out of nowhere, a loud, angry voice shouted, "Cythiria!"

Cythiria jumped. She glanced toward the sound of the voice. "Jillian…?"

"What did you do?" Jillian shouted. Her red hair was tied into a ponytail under her peaked cap. Her overalls were smudgy and wrinkled, her green eyes blazing like fire. She turned towards Fredrick, a scowl growing on her face as if she were about to spit. "How could you let this happen? I trusted you with her. Were you drunk or something?"

"No," said Fredrick. "I wasn't drunk."

"Then how? How could this happen? How could you have fucked up so bad?"

Fredrick raised his hand and pointed towards the door. Jillian glared at Cythiria, then Chelss, and turned. Fredrick reached out and took hold of Jillian's arm. She tore it away and stepped through the door into the corridor. Fredrick followed behind.

Bickering shouts echoed through the hall.

Cythiria felt the scars on her forehead tingle. She heard a whistle echo in her head. She turned towards Chelss.

"Let's get out of here."

Chelss raised a brow. "Really?"

"I need to get away from them," she said, nodding towards the door. "They're giving me a headache."

"Where'll we go?"

"Who cares? I can't stand this place. I just need to get out of here." She sat up and faced Chelss. "Will you come with me?"

Chelss paused, locking her gaze with Cythiria's. She smiled conspiratorially. "Sure, let's do it."

Cythiria raised her arm and glanced at the gauzy bandages. "I don't suppose these are gonna come off very easily," she said, hooking her finger into the wispy material and pulling it. Cythiria shook her head. "Nope. Doesn't look like it." She jumped down from the bed and her feet slapped on the cool, tiled floor. She shivered. She searched the room and found a paper bag pushed into the corner. She opened it and pulled out a tank top and a pair of baggy sweatpants. "Thanks, dad," she mumbled. She glanced down at the thin gown that she wore and tore it off. "Always looking out for me," she said as she pulled the clothes on. She turned towards Chelss, holding her open, un-bandaged hand towards her. "Ready?"

Chelss smiled and nodded, taking hold of Cythiria's hand. "Um hm."

"Let's go."

Cythiria tip-toed towards the door and slowly pulled it open, peering through the crack into the lobby. She inched her way out and looked to the right and the left. On the left, at the far end, Fredrick and Jillian stood face to face, hands and arms gesticulating. Cythiria heard Jillian's voice as it echoed sharply along the yellowed tiles. She watched as Jillian lifted her arms angrily, her red ponytail swinging from side to side, while Fredrick gestured placating hands.

Cythiria sighed. "I guess it's to the right then."

Cythiria darted into the corridor, Chelss in tow. Their pattering feet echoed along the floors and walls. Cythiria grimaced and ducked her head, glancing back at Fredrick and Jillian, whose heads were turned toward her, mouths agape.

Cythiria and Chelss ran towards a metal door at the end of the dim, narrow corridor. Cythiria kicked, and the door slammed open. She darted forward, running and jumping down a flight of stairs. She could hear the pleading voices of Jillian and Fredrick.

"Cythiria, come back!"

"Where are you going? Don't do this!"

Cythiria continued to run. She felt Chelss's hand in her own, she heard her raspy, labored breath. She looked back at Chelss, glanced at her face, her hazel-colored eyes, the widening smile spreading across her face, baring white teeth. Cythiria felt a warmth, a kind of lightness well up inside of her.

And then she tripped, falling down the stairs, and crashed into the wall. Her head hurt, and her ears rang. She reached her hand to her forehead and touched it with her fingers, which were covered in a crimson dampness that dripped onto her tank top.

    Chelss paused, the smile disappearing from her face. She stepped towards Cythiria, took her head into her own two hands and looked at the wound.

    "It's ok," said Cythiria. "I'm used to it. I'm a fighter."

She stroked her forehead with her hand and wiped it on her tank top, forming a long, crimson smudge. She took Chelss's hand into her own again and continued to jog down the stairs. At the bottom, the two stopped at a closed door. Cythiria kicked it open and the two dashed into a lobby. Cythiria smiled as she looked towards a glass door, and beyond, an open street and blue sky.

    "Almost there," she said between heavy, raspy breaths.

    The pair dashed across the street to the sound of angry horns, into a gray, concrete parking structure. They ran towards a set of stairs and climbed upwards, their pattering feet echoing through the stairwell. The air was dank and oily and smelled of urine. They emerged at the top of the structure, pausing as they gazed towards the deep blue of Nissy Bay, at the clusters of birds that circled and fluttered through the sky, at the small, white boats that sailed randomly in choppy water. Cythiria sniffed the air which smelled of sea decay and flowers. She glanced at Chelss, who also gazed out onto the bay. Her long brown hair had fallen to her shoulders and fluttered in the breeze. Her warm, hazel eyes smiled, as did her lips.

    "Let's leave Nissy," said Cythiria. "Just go somewhere else. Together."

    Chelss nodded.

    Cythiria turned and stepped forward. And then, silence, deep, as if she had been drawn into a vacuum. She gasped as the world around her turned azure. She turned towards Chelss, who stood frozen, her hands reaching towards Cythiria, her hazel-colored eyes looking forward, unmoving. Cythiria ran towards her, reaching out to grasp her, but she was knocked backwards, falling onto her back as she crashed into the blue-tinged dome.

She stood up. She heard echoing steps and a voice. She squinted towards the sound. A black, gaping hole hovered where she looked. She blinked her eyes hard and shook her head, as if trying to make sense of what she was seeing.

CHAPTER 22

Confrontation

Var 7, Farth, Nissy

Natty Mick smirked. He pushed his hand through his thick, black hair, glancing around the city streets. He could hear Nissy's hum, smell the scent of human piss and rotting garbage. He glanced up at the planetary ring, its image light and wispy, like some long cloud in the bright, Nissian daylight.

He frowned disapprovingly.

He glanced around the enclosing, oppressive walls of the buildings around him. Dirty gray, dilapidated, or covered in peeling and tagged and re-tagged graffiti. The streets were damp beneath his feet, the open gutters flushing a stream of dirty water away to the bay.

He scoffed.

He walked over to the center of the empty, cobbled street, and glanced down at a crack that stretched across its surface. He crouched down on one knee, reluctantly lest he soil his otherwise spotless clothes.

It was here that *he* appeared. And then buried himself again. One. Along with that idiot Varling. What was his name? The one who considered himself a daddy to his little girl? Like that could ever happen with a Mechanic Class Slave. Delusion runs strong in the Varling DNA.

"So," he started, talking towards the crack in the cobbled surface. "It looks like you have not disappeared after all. One, 1^1, Dr. Jeremiah Onu, or whatever it is you call yourself. We all thought that you had finally banished yourself to the edges of the universe where you belong. I mean, what concern does a Creator Class Vérkatrae like yourself have of such trifles like the Vars? Still, it's not like you to hide like this. I suppose, in your ancient form, you just can't walk around this place like some normal law-abiding citizen. You would have to change back to one of them, these weak Varlings. To Dr. Jeremiah Onu, professor of ancient philosophy. But then, you couldn't spread chaos across the universe." He paused, focusing on the long crack on the street's surface. He glanced up towards the planetary ring, a distant gaze, as if recalling a memory. "What was it that you said? That Griddish is corrupt? That only through the destruction of everything that Griddish has touched will the universe return to a state of balance? Or some such bullshit.

"Honestly, I can't disagree with you on the former point. Griddish is indeed corrupt. Some of us like it that way. Rive likes it that way. Then she has a reason to tear everything apart and start all over again. It sounds like you two are quite the same in some ways. You have your own agendas that you'll see through until not a single person is left standing."

Natty scoffed. "Whatever. Not like I care all that much anyway. To be honest, Griddish was getting pretty boring up until the war started. Nothing to do but go around the Vars and fix things. A pretty pathetic life, if you ask me."

Natty paused. "In any case, I'm not here to pontificate about the big plans that you brainy types like to concoct. I'm only here to tell you that your plans may be fucked over pretty bad now. It seems like the one that everyone was depending on to bring about your grand apocalypse has gone and killed herself. The little project that Rive Amber was putting so much hope on is finally gone. The little Mechanic Class Slave who would be the new messiah, or whatever bullshit you want to call her, is no more."

Natty stood up. He scoffed. "Which is all for the better, if you ask me. She was pretty worthless, you know. You'll just have to find a new crippled, suffering soul," he said with a mocking tone. "I'm sure there are plenty of options out there. I suppose you'd better get started on your search."

Natty turned and walked back towards the direction from which he came. He paused and glanced over his shoulder, smirked, and continued on.

The ground beneath his feet vibrated and then rumbled. He made a quick pirouette and crouched, his body ready to strike. A wide, burning smile crossed his face.

The ground split, and from the widening crack, smoky tendrils stretched upward and then congealed, forming a dark mound. It morphed, twisting and cracking until it formed the image of a man, his head hooded, his face buried in the shadows of its cowls.

"So, I see the great 1^1 has awakened from his nap," said Natty, smirking. "You really have to slow down on these grand entrances. You'll raise the suspicions of these Varlings. And if you're discovered by them, what will you do? Blow them all out of existence?"

"Well, if it isn't one of our dear Slaves who hails from the enemy of us all, the place that should never have existed in the first place, our one and only Griddish," said 1^1, pulling his hood from his head. "I am flattered that you would come so far just to see me."

"Why don't we cut the crap and get to the point, Jeremiah. You do prefer that name, correct?"

"Indeed. The sound of it rolls off the tongue quite nicely."

"Whatever. So, answer me this. What are you after?"

"After?"

"Your goal?"

"My goal." Jeremiah paused. He gazed up at the light of the planetary ring as if recalling a memory. "I am only here to help a friend."

"And that being?"

"Why, those Varlings who you and your colleague abandoned to this world."

Natty paused. "And what about the Slave?"

"The Slaves shall return to their origins, to the Tenddrome. That is inevitable, and so it does not concern me."

Natty snorted and shook his head. "That's pretty laid back for someone who wants to see the end of the universe."

"Ends and beginning are simply a matter of perspective."

Natty scoffed. "Not this crap again. I swear, you and Rive are starting to sound alike."

"The universe has its own way of resolving its differences, with or without me."

The ground started to rumble, and the street cracked. Jeremiah's body split apart into dark, fibrous tendrils which a moment later, faded to smoke, returning to the ground from which he came.

Natty shook his head. "Pompous ass," he mumbled, and then turned. "As if any of that dribble he just spouted has any meaning to me whatsoever." He scoffed. "Now what am I going to tell Rive?"

CHAPTER 23

Falling into Familiarity

Var 7, Farth, Nissy

Cythiria gazed at the azure-colored dome that enclosed the area around her. The sounds of the world – the winds, birds, the distant slapping of waves, the hum of a living city, were gone, replaced by a deep silence. Cythiria could hear her own breath, the pounding of her own pulse inside her ears.

The silence was broken by a voice. "The time has come, Cythiria," she heard. It was *that* voice, the one that had become so familiar to her recently. The voice that challenged her and assuaged her feelings of isolation, of loss. *To regain what I have lost. That is what she said.*

"Rive?"

From behind a black hole, the dark deformity that was torn open in this space, a figure emerged. It stepped towards her, slowly, confidently, the hollow sound of *clunking!* heels echoing through the silent, empty space.

A moment later, Rive Amber stood before her. She stood straight, her nose held high, her dark eyes burning, a scowl growing on her lips.

"What've you done to Chelss?" said Cythiria.

"It's time to return home, Cythiria."

"What have you done to Chelss!" Cythiria screamed.

Rive stepped forward and struck Cythiria sharply on her jaw with the back of her hand. Cythiria fell backwards, her head striking the ground.

Rive jumped towards the supine Cythiria and pressed her forearm against her throat.

"*Chelss* is the least of your concerns right now," Rive hissed.

Cythiria kicked her leg, knocking Rive to the side. She jumped up, crouched, and raised her fists in front of her face. Her chin tickled. She wiped a crimson rivulet from her skin with the back of her hand.

Rive scowled. "You can't fight me, Cythiria."

"I can and I will," said Cythiria, as she circled.

Rive stepped forward. She planted her feet and then swung a high kick towards Cythiria's head. The strike glanced off Cythiria's forearm. She stumbled to the side.

"You don't belong here, Cythiria."

"What do you mean I don't belong here? I was born here. I've lived here all my life."

Rive scoffed, her upper lip quivering to a snarl. "Is that what you think, Cythiria? Do you really believe you belong here?"

"I've got dad, and mom, and…."

"*Dad* and *mom* are not who you think they are, Cythiria." She spoke, her lips quivering as if she were about to spit.

Cythiria lurched forward. Rive slipped to the side and struck Cythiria on the back of the neck with her elbow. Cythiria stumbled forward, tumbling onto the oily surface. She pulled herself onto her knees, hissing at the stinging pain in her arm. She glanced at the gauzy wraps that were now stained dark crimson.

"Look at you," said Rive. "You can barely keep yourself alive. Why do you think that is Cythiria? Is the pain too much for you? I know, Cythiria. The Vars are like poison to us Mechanics. They slowly strangle us to the point where we can only wish for our own death."

Cythiria stood and stepped backwards. Her limbs felt heavy and numb. Blood trickled from her mouth and down her chin. Her vision sparkled and fizzled. *Vars…Mechanics…what are they?* She lurched forward, leading with a right hook. Rive stepped aside and struck her torso with a heavy knee. Cythiria tumbled to the ground, gasping for breath, her eyes rolling up under their fluttering lids.

Rive paused. "I know how it feels, Cythiria. But *they* don't, those people you call your parents. They can *never* know how you feel. They can never truly help you." Rive's eyes softened, her snarl faded. "But I can." She reached an open hand towards Cythiria.

Cythiria gazed up at Rive. Her head and neck prickled with breaking sweat. She gasped for air. And then, she kicked Rive's hand, turned, and pushed herself up onto her feet. Her arms and legs trembled. Her vision started to fade. She turned towards Rive, stumbled forward, and threw a jab.

And then, she felt an iron grasp, wrenching and twisting as Rive turned her own arm under her back and locked it. She screamed as the tendons on her shoulder stretched and pulled as if they were about to be torn from their bones. She was pushed forward, towards the black hole that hovered in front of her. She gazed into it, into its sheer blackness. She felt it pull at her hair and her skin and her clothes like tiny, plucking fingers. She heard a whisper tickle inside her ear. The words gurgled like warped knots. "I will help you regain what you lost," they said.

What I lost. She turned her head and gazed through the azure dome, at Chelss, who stood frozen in time, her arms reaching forward, still like some ancient statue. Her long, brown hair flowed down her shoulders, her hazel eyes gazed forward, her mouth agape, perhaps captured in the midst of a scream. Cythiria's cheeks grew wet, as tears mixed with blood from the cuts on her face flowed in steady, pink rivulets, dripping onto the oily surface beneath her feet. Her stomach turned, and she sobbed. Her body heaved. "Chelss!" she screamed. "Please, don't leave me. Don't leave me again."

And then, she fell into darkness.

CHAPTER 24

Sudden Loss

Var 7, Farth, Nissy

Chelss held tightly onto Cythiria's hand. She smiled wide, panting as she ran in some direction. She was not sure where she was going. Only, she was with Cythiria. It felt good to run, together, with her. The inside of the school was deadening. The screens, the cold robotic voices, the flashing lights that ran along the floors and walls of the hallways, the machines that she would plug into, wearing those devices on her head, the headphones, the goggles. They would all block her feelings towards the world, towards Nissy. *As if the real world never existed. Or had anything important to say.*

Cythiria's hand was strong, rough. She was a fighter. The blood was caked on Cythiria's forehead. Her fingers were stained crimson. Chelss would patch her up later. Except now, they were together, running somewhere.

"Let's leave Nissy." Those were Cythiria's words just now, as they paused their escape. Chelss felt giddy, a fluttering in her stomach, her neck and face flushed. *But where will we go? Is there anything outside of Nissy, anywhere we can hide? I've never run away before. I wouldn't know how to survive on my own. But Cythiria would know....* Cythiria is a fighter. She knows how to survive. It's part of her being. An instinct.

Cythiria gazed back at her and smiled. Chelss looked into those dark eyes. They were warm, welcoming. Like a home where she could feel safe, protected. Something she never felt before. It was so foreign, so unexpected. *I'm sorry, Cyth. I'm sorry I was so cold to you before. I'm sorry I didn't have faith in you. I just don't understand you, and why you do what you do. And yet,*

I would not want to live without that strange feeling you give me. It's more than safety. It's fullness and presence and….

The sky flashed an azure blue. Chelss's body stopped for a moment, as if she were suddenly immersed in a deep pool of water. She screamed, but no sound was made. And then, her legs weakened, she fell to the ground. Her breath was raspy, her heart pounded in her chest. She looked around. Cythiria was…gone.

She stood up. A feeling of panic, despair filled her core which, a moment ago, was warm with giddiness. "Cythiria," she whispered. "Where did you go?" Her throat tightened. Her eyes grew damp. "Cythiria!" she screamed. "Cythiria!" She heard footsteps behind her. Voices. A strong arm around her chest. "Cythiria!" Her wide eyes groped blindly in all directions. "Cythiria!"

She was pulled to the ground. She started sobbing, her nose wet, tears streaming down her cheek. "It's okay," she heard. It was a voice. A man's voice. Gentle, calming. "It's okay. We'll find her. We'll find Cyth."

Chelss pulled the arm away and stood up. "Get your hands off me!" she screamed. "Don't fucking touch me!" She turned and ran towards the stairwell that delivered her and Cyth to this place and was gone.

Fredrick sighed deeply.

"What'll we do?" said Jillian, as she looked in the direction of Chelss's escape.

Fredrick shook his head. "What *can* we do? When Rive Amber came here, we should've known she had a reason for doing so."

"Is it all over for this place now? Like it was for Earth?"

"I don't know, Jillian." Fredrick glanced around. "Back then, I could sense those Vérkatrae. Now, either they aren't here, or I'm just not able to."

"Is there any way we can get Cythiria back?"

Fredrick's eyes dampened. "She was never ours to begin with, Jillian. We always knew that they would return for her eventually."

"I can't accept that, Fredrick. There must be a way. I won't leave Cythiria in the hands of that monster."

And yet, it was exactly that monster who brought Cythiria back from the brink. Or, maybe she drove her to the brink, and that's really what she wanted. "At least we have one possible lead."

"And who might that be?"

"Dr. Jeremiah Onu."

CHAPTER 25

Home

Griddish, Ashen Fissure, The Bastion

Cythiria opened her eyes. She squinted at the gentle blue light that washed over her. She sniffed the odorless air. A low and generic hum of running equipment filled the space around her. Electric flashes occasionally sparkled as holographic spheres floated in the air before her, turned, and morphed, while insect-like rows of characters skittered nervously up and down them.

She took a deep breath as she lay on her back. The pallet under her body was hard, unmoving. Her ribs ached and her slashed arm throbbed and stung. Her legs were stiff and sore and felt bruised. She lifted her hands and gazed at her arms. The injured one was wrapped in a fresh, white, almost wispy gauze. She touched her face with her hand, stroked the side of her cheek and then her brow. Her fingers groped along the two scars on her forehead. They felt like tiny craters. Her fingers slid over to her temples and then up to the top of her head. Her skin was smooth, shaven. She gasped as she gripped air where hair should otherwise have been.

"What happened to me?" she mumbled as she pushed herself up with her uninjured arm. She groaned and then lay down again.

"I wouldn't try too hard just yet," she heard. The voice was soft, gentle. She glanced towards it. "You've had quite the journey." A man stepped forward and stood next to her as she lay prone on her pallet. His hair was white, his figure slim, his face delicate and reassuring. His soft, gray eyes gazed into her own, gently probing, yet remaining distant. Cythiria felt her body deflate, her tense muscles relinquish their tight grip.

"My name is Benj, Cythiria."

"Ooookay." She felt her neck grow warm. "And how do you know my name?"

Benj smiled gently. "You're the one we've all been waiting for," he said, matter-of-factly.

Cythiria grimaced. "You sure about that? I think you were probably waiting for the wrong bus."

Benj smiled mysteriously. He stepped forward and gazed at Cythiria's forehead. He blinked his eyes quickly and reached for a device that rested on a table next to her. It was made of two sharp prongs connected to a small handle. He blinked again and touched the tips of the two prongs to Cythiria's forehead, pressing them into the tiny, crater-like holes.

The muscles of Cythiria's body contracted, her eyes grew wide, her jaw clenched, her hands rolled into fists. She tried to scream, but her lungs held no breath.

And then, the world morphed. Images twisted and turned into each other. Her stomach turned. Her eyes rolled up into their sockets. The flickering blue light of the chamber faded, enveloping her in an inky blackness.

A face fizzled into view, hollow, scruffy cheeks, silver framed glasses, white, spikey hair. Sharp, penetrating eyes that gazed down at Cythiria, peering into her, groping. She heard a voice, echoing. Words that said, "You will live on."

"What do you mean?"

"You have made a great sacrifice so that they can finally gain access to the Slaves."

"They?"

HOME

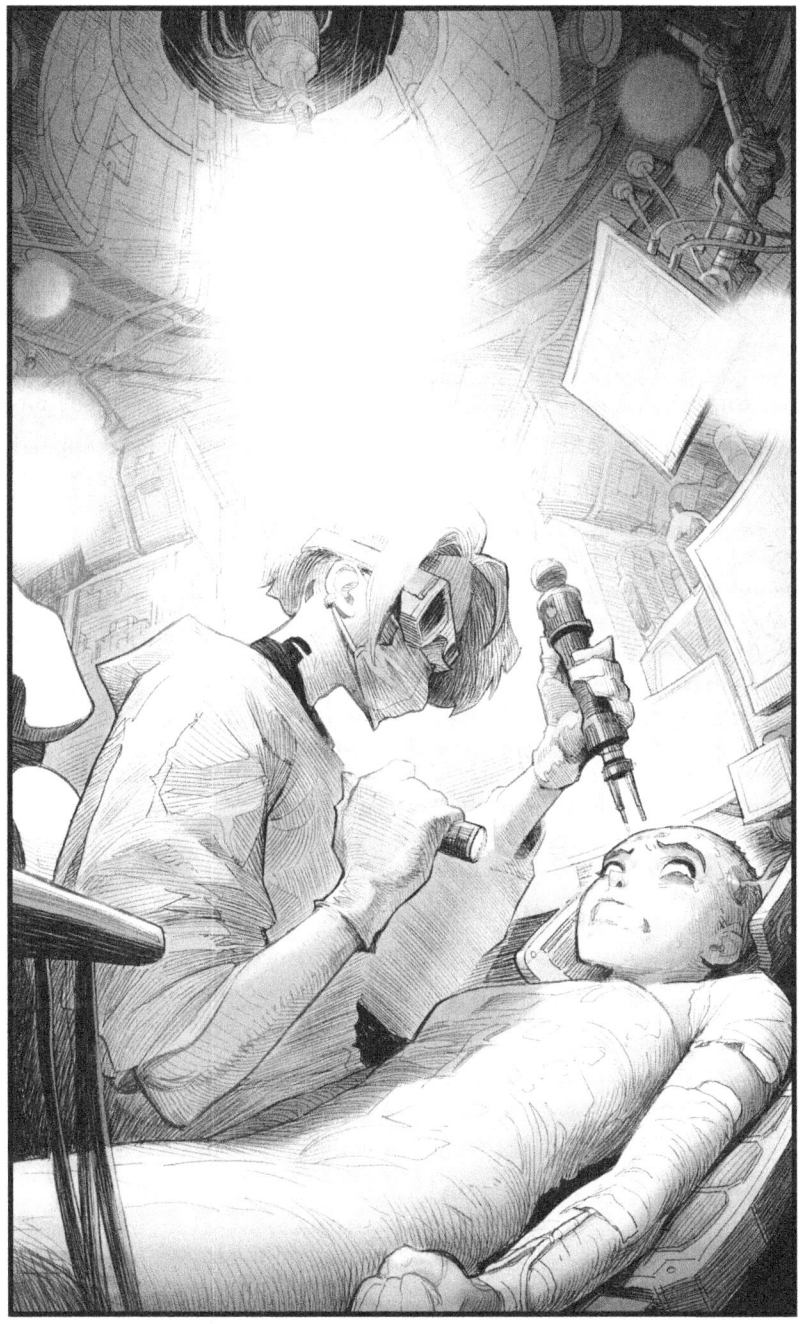

"The Vérkatrae. It is necessary for the continued existence of your kind." The voice paused. "So, you will live on, in one form or another."

"I will live on," mumbled Cythiria. "I.…"

She felt a sharp pain in her chest, numbness that spread through her body. She tried to lift her arms, to kick her legs. She felt her breath slow to a gasping, raspy pace. And then, darkness.

She opened her eyes. She stretched her arms and legs outwards, kicking and thrashing silently. In the distance, a single point of light emerged from the inky blackness. And then, another, and another, until they multiplied into vast and intricately intertwined clusters, forming a sphere that seemed to grow eternally in all directions.

Cythiria sniffed. An odor, perhaps, filled the space around her. Cool, wispy breezes like smoky tendrils wrapped themselves around her, pierced her body, and flowed through her veins. *These…creatures…cannot access the Tenddrome's core. They can only reside within its perimeter, like a moon that orbits a planet.* She held her hand out as the smoky wisps entwined themselves around her limbs and then fizzled away. *These are…Vérkatrae? But, what are Vérkatrae? Somehow, they are familiar to me.*

She felt herself pulled towards the sphere, towards the clusters of lights. She laughed as she plunged into them, as they danced around her body and cast cool, white light upon her weakened frame. And then, her body scattered, as if it had been torn into millions of pieces, each one itself morphing into its own point of illumination.

The darkness faded. That gentle face gazed down at her, those penetrating yet distant eyes, the soft smile. "Welcome back, Cythiria."

"The Tenddrome," she muttered. "I saw the Tenddrome. And the Vérkatrae.…"

"Ah, yes, it looks like you are already recovering some of your memories."

"My…memories…?"

"Indeed. You've had quite the journey, my dear Mechanic Class Slave."

"Slave?"

"More will come to you as time passes."

Cythiria heard footsteps. They were certain, solid, confident.

"I see Cythiria has awakened," came the voice.

"Rive…." Rive Amber glanced down at Cythiria. Her gaze was soft. "Why…why did you bring me here?"

Rive paused. "I promised I would help you regain what you lost."

"Where is…*she*? Where is Chelss?"

"The world you left is no longer your concern." She paused. "You won't be missed."

Cythiria pushed herself onto her side, turning her back to Rive. She started to sob, as tears streamed down her cheek and splashed and puddled onto the hard pallet beneath her. "I don't belong here," she mumbled. The image of Chelss, as she stood on the outside of a translucent, azure wall, frozen, her arms stretched towards the Mechanic Class Slave. "I just want to go home."

Cythiria felt an almost airy touch on her arm, a gentle stroke. "You *are* home," came the soft, nurturing words of Rive Amber. And then, a shuffle, followed by the solid, confident clicks! of her heels as she turned and walked away.

CHAPTER 26

Questions

Var7, Farth, Nissy

Where did you go, Cythiria?

Chelss leaned against the wall of the classroom, gazing out the window onto the school's central courtyard. Clusters of students skittered and milled among the dark walls of the building, flashes of directional lights illuminating like lightning strikes beneath their feet. Chelss's hazel eyes moved towards the morning orange and blue-green firmament. She gazed at the gentle, white ring through tall, thin, spiky towers that stretched relentlessly towards the sky. She sighed.

Where did you go, Cythiria?

The rattle and scrape of feet and the babble and murmur of voices broke her from her reverie.

"Please proceed to your assigned workstations," rang the gentle, robotic voice, as it echoed flatly through the classroom. Chelss grit her teeth. She reached for her backpack and slung it onto her shoulders.

"Fuck this," she mumbled as she trudged towards the classroom door, kicking it open. She stepped into the dark corridor, the flash of directional lights under her feet pointing behind her.

"Student number 15988, Chelsea Brimwater, please proceed to your classroom," echoed the voice along the hall, sounding in her own ears as if its source hovered at her side.

"That's Chelss to you, bitch," she shouted. She stomped down the corridor and into the courtyard, her quick stride rushing her past the black, blocky buildings that made up the campus. She paused and sniffed the cool, morning air. Her ears pricked at the sound of electric cars as they hummed and rattled by. She gazed up at the ring, past the blinking towers. She snorted, a smirk crossing her face and terminating in a crooked smile.

She dashed across the street towards the subway. She paused at the turnstile, grabbed each side with her hands and kicked her feet into the air. *Just like Cyth would do.* She bound up the stairs onto the platform as the train whooshed into the station and stopped. She paused. The doors hissed open, and she bound in. She grasped the handrail as she glared at the floor of the train, her hazel-colored eyes shifting, lips pursed.

I never trusted people.

The subway train rocked side to side as it squealed over its steel tracks. Cool, white lights flickered with each lurch of the car. Chelss sat and glared at the floor, ignoring the upbeat jingles and the colorful animations of advertised products that blared at her.

I didn't trust Cythiria either. But, it's not like I didn't have my reasons.

༄

"Chelsea! Where's my Chelsea?" shouted the man as he fumbled in the dark, his words slurred, the steps stumbling and uncertain. "Where did you go?"

Chelss heard a bang on the door to her room as she pulled up her covers. Her body quivered, and her stomach turned. Her arms and legs were taut like wound coils, as if they were preparing to spring at any moment on their own. Her ears pricked up at the sound of her door opening.

She heard the man stumble in, cursing as he tripped over stray furniture or pieces of clothing. She felt his body fall heavily onto her bed next to her. The springs squealed under the weight. She could hear heavy breathing.

She felt the covers pulled down to her shoulders, and her face was exposed to the cool, night air in her room. She could smell alcohol infused breath and stale sweat. She gripped the top of the quilt, her hands holding fast.

She felt a finger stroke her cheek. "Chelsea, you're so beautiful," she heard, the words slurred and mumbled. "You can have whatever you want. Just say it. Plenty of men will give you anything you ask for."

Chelss closed her eyes tight. The smell of the alcohol was strong, the rough hand was large and clumsy. The stench of old sweat filled the space around her.

"You do that, then maybe I don't have to work so hard. Think of your dad, for once. I brought you into this world. Don't be such a selfish little bitch." His words were growing angry. He ground his teeth. His body, next to hers, stirred. "It's because of you that your mom left me, the bitch. I hate her." His voice grew calm, sorrowful. He began to sob. "You don't want dad to hate you too, do you? I love you, Chelsea, so just do your dad this favor. It's only once, and it's real money. Better than the money I make out there fixing and moving shit around for people. Fucking bosses don't pay me enough. I have a family to feed, too. I got a kid. A beautiful girl. A girl that everyone loves."

Chelss felt her throat tighten, tears squeezing from her clenched eyes. *Go away, go away, go away. Leave me alone!*

"Come on, Chelsea. Your dad is getting old. He can't work like he used to." She felt a hand on her chest. It moved down to her leg. "He's not a young man anymore."

Chelss felt her heart pound in her chest. She shuddered at the drag and stroke of the clumsy, groping hand on her body.

And then, she jumped up and stood next to the bed. The man looked at her through bleary, bloodshot eyes. He staggered onto his feet and stumbled forward, wrapping his arms around her waist. She fell to the ground and kicked him in the face, again and again until he relinquished his grasp. She stood up and ran towards the door, out into the hallway. Come back here you little bitch!" she heard, the voice bellowing, the words slurred. And then a mournful wail, followed by whimpering.

She paused. Her ears pricked up at the sound of his cries. She stumbled down a rickety set of stairs, into a narrow hallway. She paused, glancing up at the framed photos of her mother and father. The pictures were old, from a time that seemed so long ago.

Chelss walked to the front door, opened it, and stepped onto the wet, bitumen surface of the street. She glanced up at the planetary ring. It was bright, cold, mirthless. The pale blue and white street lights flickered and buzzed. She could hear the hum of Nissy all around her. She stepped forward and paused, glancing over her shoulder at the door behind her. She turned her head and faced forward, and walked.

The morning light woke Chelss up from her sleep. She rose from her bed and stretched, yawning and scratching as she did so. She gazed out the window. The planetary ring was bright this morning, its ridges sharp and certain, perhaps even confident.

Her body jumped at the sound of a knock on her door. It slowly creaked open.

"Hey, um, I'm sorry," came the gravelly voice from a face that peered around the slightly ajar door. "I didn't mean…."

"It's fine," said Chelss.

"Look, I was drunk, and I…."

"Forget it."

She heard the door creak and close quietly as it clicked into place. She sighed as she pulled her knees close to her chest. *Always the same thing.* She felt her throat tighten and her stomach turn, and tears well up inside of her. She swallowed hard.

"Fuck it," she mumbled. "I don't have time for this bullshit. I'm not gonna cry for him or anyone else. Not now, not ever."

I wanted to leave that place. I didn't want to be around him. Every day was a threat to me. But I had no choice. Where would I go, here in Nissy? How would I survive on my own? Chelss sighed as the subway car rocked and squealed. The rhythmic flash of white lights was hypnotic. "I'm sorry, Cyth. I'm sorry I didn't trust you. It's just that, I didn't know *how* to trust you." She paused. A slight smile slipped across her otherwise stoic face. "I will find you, Cyth. I won't give up. Not now. Not ever."

QUESTIONS

CHAPTER 27

Convalescence

Griddish, Ashen Fissure, The Bastion

Cythiria sat up from her pallet. She sniffed the clean, filtered air. She glanced around the small room. The walls were washed in flickering blue and white as a holographic sphere emerged into the center of the chamber.

She heard the solid, confident click of Rive Amber's steps echo from an unseen corridor. She recognized those steps immediately, their beat and pace unique to her. Cythiria's body stiffened, and her chest tightened. She stood up. The room started to spin and pulse and the two scars on her forehead throbbed and stung.

Rive stepped up to the pallet and glared down at Cythiria. "We are leaving."

Cythiria clenched her jaw. "Leaving? To where?"

"Your home, Sanguine Heap."

"My…home?" She looked up at Rive, her large eyes growing wet with tears. "My home? A home that I haven't even seen? How can that be a home to me? How?" Tears streamed down Cythiria's cheeks.

Rive crouched down and gazed into Cythiria's eyes. "You can't go back to Var 7. Not now. Not ever."

"But why?" Cythiria's lips quivered. "Why can't I go back home?"

Rive paused. "You don't belong there," she said, her voice soft, almost like a whisper. "The Vars, they have a way of slowly killing us. Soon, Var 7 would have killed you. In fact, it almost did."

"I don't care," said Cythiria through wet sniffles. "It doesn't matter to me. So what if I die there? Does it even matter? Why can't you just leave me alone? Does anyone even care?"

"I care," said Rive. "Griddish cares."

Cythiria rubbed her nose with her hand. "I just…."

Rive stood up. She held her hand towards Cythiria. "Let's go."

Cythiria took Rive's hand and slowly stood. She stepped forward, lightly. She glanced around the chamber, at the man named Benj whose cool, gray eyes followed her, a gentle, reassuring smile crossing his face.

Cythiria sighed as she followed Rive. Out the chamber, and down a long corridor awash in gentle blue light. Buzzing, electric torches were mounted on the walls, casting flickering shadows and emitting a gentle, burning scent.

 The two turned, entering a wide chamber. Cythiria glanced around the shimmering, featureless, metallic walls and the tubes that wound their way along them. She looked up at the distant, glassy ceiling. They stepped forward and before them, the wall seemed to split in two, silently, as a gentle white light flooded the giant chamber.

Rive stepped first and Cythiria followed, into the world of Griddish. Cythiria paused, squinting and holding her hand above her eyes. She took a deep breath, sniffing the cool, humid air which smelled of grass.

In the distance, a cluster of tall spike-shaped buildings reached towards the white sky. They looked broken, abandoned, eerie, a desolate cityscape that had been burnt and crushed by some unseen monster. Wide, green plains led to the cityscape among clumps of short, rolling hills. A cool breeze hissed through the grass, wafting a florid scent towards Cythiria. She smelled deeply. Beyond, along the horizon, and in clusters, thin, needle-like towers stretched upwards. Countless, they littered the view wherever Cythiria's eyes followed. She gazed towards Rive, who looked upon her with sidelong glances.

"Eventually, it will all become apparent to you."

Rive stepped forward, towards a pair of machines. But not quite machines. Their bodies were flat, their bulbous eyes jutting forward from their streamline shape. A pair of antennae turned and swiped momentarily and then was still. They rested in the grass, their spidery legs turned up inside their chassis, as if in a slumber, waiting.

Rive paused, blinked her eyes, and mounted the first machine. Cythiria paused before the other, touching its body with her hand. The metallic skin was warm, soft, confusing to the touch, like no texture she had ever felt before. The machine rose, its bulbous eyes turning towards Cythiria. Cythiria stepped back.

"What is it?" she said.

"A Vérkatros," said Rive. "Transport Class."

"A Vérkatros," mumbled Cythiria.

"Do you remember them?"

"I…." She looked at the one who sat before her, her eyes glancing along its body. Its warm, soft yet metallic skin shimmered a blue and then yellow color, flashing momentarily, and then quieting to a deep green. "Why the colors?" she mumbled as she gazed wide-eyed at the machines.

"Colors?" said Rive, tilting her head to one side.

"The colors? What do they mean?"

Rive paused. "You've been through a lot, Cythiria. You'll need time to adjust to your new surroundings."

"But I…."

"Let's go."

Cythiria mounted the Vérkatros. She sat on the back. A moment later, the machine shuddered and then rose from the ground. It turned and then lurched forward, hissing along the grassy plains. The cool, fragrant air of Griddish brushed against Cythiria's face.

She glanced down at the back of the Vérkatros and stroked the warm, soft skin. It was smooth, like touching the metal surface of a car, or a cool windowpane. At the same time, it was soft, as if membranes had been pulled and stretched over some solid object, while also having their own pulse and rhythm, a shudder, a kind of sway.

The colors were muted now. Every so often, Cythiria would see a flash of green, or dull yellow. It was as if the colors would flow through the Vérkatros' skin, grow and shrink, spread out and contract and shimmer, quickly like waves or blotches of spilt ink.

She glanced at Rive's Vérkatros. That one was larger than hers. Its skin was a flat, almost muddy gray, not flashing colors like the one she rode. Its stride, the rhythm by which it hovered across the grassy plains, was more steady, confident, perhaps more informed, as if it had been here much longer and had a clearer vision about where it was going, and what it was doing.

As if it were alive.

Alive.

"Are you alive?" she said, returning her gaze to the Vérkatros upon which she was mounted. "Do you have feelings, like, the way people have feelings?" She looked down upon its back. It flashed yellow, then orange, and returned to green and then gray. "Do you understand what I am saying? How could you? You're just a machine." Cythiria paused. "And yet…."

Cythiria glanced to her side, at rows upon rows of rolling green hills, enrobed in twisting and tangled greenery, shrubs, and scrubby brush. Among the hills, clusters of those needle-like towers stretched towards the sky. Or was it a sky? Its light was gentle, diffused, as if it had no single source. It was different from the sky in Nissy, the deep blue and sometimes red firmament. It didn't have that planetary ring that stretched across it and dove down into the horizon as if it were a giant, white snake. It cast its own cool light, sometimes illuminating the night streets with an icy, ghostly glow. But only if there were no clouds in the sky. Only on the clearest of nights when the stars would shudder and pulse as if they were about to explode.

There were no stars here. Not yet anyway. Not until night came. If it would ever come. Just flat, soft light. Infuriating, in a way, in that it was so calming, almost boring.

Cythiria sighed. She could feel her chest tighten and her eyes dampen. She sniffled and her nose turned a gentle shade of pink. She thought about *her*, about Chelss. How she came to the hospital. How Cythiria felt her heart pound in her chest when she saw those hazel-colored eyes again. They were cool, maybe even cold, sometimes. *At least, they were when I first met her.* She chuckled. *I think she hated me at first. Her lips were pressed to a judgmental frown, and she held her nose in the air.* Cythiria smiled. *That's Chelss for you.*

Will I ever return to Nissy? Will I ever see her again? Or dad? Or Jillian?

Cythiria sighed deeply. Her body still hurt. Her arm was still wrapped in a light gauze, and it stung when she turned it or lifted it. *If only I had done the job properly. If only….*

"We're almost there," she heard from Rive. Her voice, as usual, was strong yet calm, authoritative. The kind that no one would dare to question. *Why does she even want me here? What good can I do in a place like this? It would be better off if no one interfered. If they would just leave me alone. Just let me go. Let me leave.*

It was hard to tell how time passed in the never changing light. The dark walls of Sanguine Heap rose from the green plains. The walls themselves were black, and they formed a large rectangular structure. At each corner and in the center stood a tower. Atop the central tower, a glassy dome.

The two approached a large gate, which opened before them. They passed under an arch, upon which was carved in bas relief, images of people she didn't know, nor care about. Inside the gate, a large courtyard was filled with people. They stood in formations, or they sparred with each other, using weapons that looked like whips, whose thongs were made of light and whistled as they cut the air. Others swung around lassos, whose loops had spikes that caught onto objects, and wouldn't let go.

The Vérkatrae paused. Cythiria glanced down at the back of the one she was mounted on. She stroked the warm, smooth skin. The colors morphed into orange and red. She felt her body tighten, grow tense, as if the colors themselves spoke to her, or conveyed some kind of private message.

She swung her leg over the edge of the Vérkatros and landed on the ground, her heel falling to a solid *crunch!* on gravelly soil.

"So, this is the one you spent so much time on," she heard. She glanced towards the voice. A man, with thick, dark hair and a smirk that crossed his face, stepped toward her. He scowled and stepped around her, pausing behind her. He snorted. Cythiria shuddered. "Not much of a specimen if you ask me," he grumbled towards Rive.

"She will be," said Rive, matter-of-factly.

"And her training?"

"A Bestiar, like the rest of us, Natty."

Natty scoffed and then rolled his eyes. "Whatever. Frankly, we have more pressing problems right now."

"Such as?"

"The Engineers. They're pushing the boundaries now. Even with the Vérkatrae at our disposal, we can't seem to finish them off."

"We need time."

"We don't have time, Rive," said Natty, his lip curling as if he were about to spit.

Rive sighed and then stepped forward. "Come," she said, glancing momentarily at Cythiria with glaring, yet drooping, tired eyes.

Cythiria followed Rive into the central building of Sanguine Heap. Its entry corridor was dark and smelled of must. Upon the walls were mounted electric torches that buzzed and hummed. The corridor opened to a wide chamber. Its walls were rusty, corroded. Cythiria glanced up. From the top, which seemed so far away, streamed light from a glassy dome. The sound of wing flaps echoed along the walls as large bird-like creatures crossed just below the dome, living among the rafters.

Cythiria shuddered. The echoing sound of rhythmic chants filled the chamber, the clash of booted feet upon stone, the whistle and crackle of whips, the groans and cries of people struck down. The room seemed to pulse and spin. Cythiria followed Rive, through another dark corridor, into a chamber that was filled with rows of pallets set one next to the other.

"Stay here," said Rive. "For now." She turned towards Cythiria. Her eyes softened. They seemed almost wet, as if tears started to form. A gentle, subtle smile rose from the corners of her mouth. "I'll be back, I promise. I said I would help you to regain what you lost. I won't forget that." She raised her hand and placed it on Cythiria's shoulder. "Not ever." She turned and walked out of the chamber, her heels clicking a steady, confident beat until she was gone, and the room grew silent again.

Cythiria's eyes snapped open. She sat up from her hard pallet and glanced around the wide chamber. She squinted into the darkness, her eyes following the empty pallets, arranged throughout the chamber in neat rows.

She sniffed the stale, musky air. She took a deep breath and stood. Her back ached, and her arm tingled as the wispy gauze took on a crimson color. Cythiria reached to her forehead and groped the two scars with her fingers. They felt like tiny holes now, like sockets to which one could apply a plug, or a cable. *Maybe they can tether me to the Tenddrome.* She snorted and turned towards a dark corridor. She stepped forward, her stumbling, uncertain steps shuffling a hesitating echo.

She paused at the entry to the corridor, peering into the dark and along the dank walls which were speckled with buzzing, electric torches. A cool, dry breeze wafted from the corridor, carrying the sounds of distant, echoing voices, groans, screams, and rhythmic chants. She shuddered and wrapped her arms around her waist.

She followed the corridor to the main, central chamber. She gazed upwards towards the distant dome, as gentle white light streamed and illuminated the floor below. Her stomach turned, and she felt lightheaded.

She walked towards the main gate, gazing cautiously into the courtyard as she exited the dark halls of Sanguine Heap. Bestiars stood regaled in clothing that looked military, like heavy boots, cargo pants, tool belts that held various equipment, like those laser whips, known as the Plaxis Strands, Twutches, and Capsas. She heard chants, clashing metal, and pained groans.

She glanced towards rows of awaiting Vérkatrae, their bodies still, quiet, as if in slumber, awaiting perhaps to be awakened. Some were very large, perhaps the size of a hundred Bestiars. Others, the size of a single Bestiar. Still others were small, canine-like, slithering close to the ground as if stalking some unseen prey.

Cythiria sighed. And then, something caught her eyes.

It was a flash at first. A kind of shimmering glow that waved and rippled an array of colors. It was blue at first, then green, yellow and red, and then returning to green as some pulsing light. She walked towards the flashing colors and paused.

"It's you," she said, as she stepped close to the Vérkatros that rested on its chassis, its legs curled up underneath it. It turned its streamlined body towards Cythiria and gazed at her through glassy, bulbous eyes. Expressionless, it seemed, maybe vacuous, yet, feeling. "You're the one who brought me here at first. I…."

She reached up and touched the Vérkatros on its head, gently. Its surface was warm, smooth, and hard. Like metal, but also like skin.

"Do you have a name?" She paused, glancing around the courtyard. "You're not like the others, I don't think. You're smaller. You can barely even carry me around, yet you did. Am I heavy?" Cythiria snorted. "I don't see how I could be. Not since being here." She rubbed the Vérkatros' body, more vigorously this time. Its skin flashed orange and then red and returned to green, yellow, and then gray. "And those colors. Why do you change color so often? The others don't. They always stay the same. But you're different." She smiled sadly and then sighed. "Are you trying to express your feelings? I wish I could express mine. Right now, I just feel kinda numb. Like, I don't know why I'm here. Only that Rive, who took care of me back in Nissy, she brought me here." Cythiria's voice cracked, and her eyes grew damp. "And she took me away from someone. Someone who cared about me." The colors of the Vérkatros flashed yellow and then red and returned to gray. "I…don't think I'll ever see her again. I just don't know…."

Cythiria turned and leaned her back up against the side of the Vérkatros. She slid down and sat on her haunches. She pulled her knees close to her chest and wrapped her arms around her shins. Tears streamed down her cheeks. "I can't do this anymore. I just want to go away. I want to be left alone. I don't belong here." She felt the Vérkatros' skin grow warm, and it started to vibrate a steady, soothing hum. Cythiria lifted her chin and gazed up at the bulbous eyes of the Vérkatros. She stood up, rubbed her wet, sniffly nose, which had grown a shade of pink, and wiped away the tears from her eyes and cheeks.

"I don't know if you have a name, but I'm going to name you." The Vérkatros' skin flashed orange, then red. She paused, gazing up towards the sky and pursing her lips. She lifted her forefinger to her chin. "I'm going to name you Blinky." The Vérkatros vibrated and flashed, its colors bright red and pink. Cythiria chuckled. "You know, because you blink your colors so much, kinda like a neon sign back in Nissy. In fact, to make it official, I'm going to give you a ribbon." She glanced around the courtyard and then down at her shirt. She pulled at the edge until she was able to tear away a small strip. She jogged to a burnt and blackened part of the courtyard, picked up a stone, and rubbed it into the strip. She jogged back to Blinky and held it up to his bulbous eyes. "See? It has your name on it." She looked over Blinky's body and reached for one of his flicking antennae. She tied the ragged ribbon onto the antenna, double and then triple knotting it. "It won't fall off. And if anyone asks, you can just say you're Blinky."

Blinky flashed red and pink, then yellow and gray. The twinkle in his bulbous eyes faded, and then he was still, motionless. Cythiria tilted her head. "Blinky? Are you ok?"

"Consorting with Vérks?" she heard behind her. She jumped at the sound of the voice. She turned to face its owner.

"Rive, I…."

With her nose high, Rive Amber glared at Cythiria, her dark eyes burning. "The Vérkatrae are a necessary evil, Cythiria. Someday, Griddish will no longer need them. And then, we can all live in peace."

Cythiria's face grew warm, and her neck flushed. "But I was talking to him…."

"Vérkatrae don't talk, Cythiria." She paused. Her eyes softened, as did her voice. "You've been away for a long time, Cythiria. You've forgotten many things. Perhaps, those memories will return to you. Until then, you will have much to learn about Griddish."

Cythiria sighed. "Griddish," she mumbled. *What is Griddish? And what part of me belongs here?*

"Come," said Rive, turning away. She glanced backwards over her shoulder towards Cythiria. "We have a lot of work ahead of us." And then she stepped forward, her stride solid, rhythmic, confident, as always.

CHAPTER 28

To Begin the Quest

Var7, Farth, Nissy

The gray-colored hospital building rose from the grassy hills like broken teeth. Chelss paused as she waited at an intersection. Sirens echoed in the distance, wailing as they announced their arrival to the emergency driveway. Clusters of people lumbered along the sidewalks and near the doors, some toted around in robotic wheelchairs. Children ran and laughed on the green grass, along the edges of fountains, and through the always whooshing glass doors.

Chelss shuddered as she recalled that day. Cythiria lay on her bed, her arm wrapped in bandages, her black hair matted against her oily face. Cythiria's dark eyes brightened as Chelss stepped cautiously into the room, and her face and neck flushed. Her face always flushed. Chelss snorted. *Always so awkward. A real weirdo….* A gentle smile spread across Chelss's face as she recalled those large, blinking eyes. Unbelieving. As if they had seen a ghost. Chelss felt her stomach turn just a bit, a feeling of warmth and comfort spread through her chest. *I didn't know, Cyth. Rive told me to stay away. Otherwise, maybe I would have trusted you more.*

Chelss shook her head and squeezed her eyes shut, as if trying to cast away the memory of that day. She walked up a grassy hill until she arrived at the front door, which whooshed open as she approached. She stopped, gazing into the dark corridor. A man looked up at her and smirked, winking once, and then returned his attention to his desk. Chelss turned and looked towards a building. It was open, with built-in layers, a city garage. Cars paused and whooshed onto the adjacent street, and from the street to the inside, shooting down dark, echoing, concrete slots.

Chelss walked towards the building, pausing as she stepped inside. She glanced around the dank, gray interior, sniffing. A subtle smell of oil and urine wafted along the breezy, underground corridor. She walked towards a bent and rusty metal door and kicked it open. She stepped inside a narrow stairwell that swirled upwards. The stench of urine attacked her senses now. She coughed and reached towards her face, covering her nose and mouth with her hand. She trudged up the stairs until she arrived at the top. She kicked the door open and stepped onto a potholed, concrete surface. She looked around, turning towards Nissy Bay and gazing at the choppy, blue water. Tiny ships sailed along, leaving white streaks in their wake. Clouds of birds turned and swirled in the air, squawking and screeching a cacophonous collection of wails. The planetary ring, which looked like one long, continuous cloud, seemed to dive into the blue water along the horizon.

Chelss turned towards the concrete platform, her eyes shifting among the parked cars that were scattered about. She sniffed the air, which still smelled slightly of burning metal, only it was cold and stale now. Undetectable, most likely, had it not been experienced before.

Chelss stepped forward. She remembered the moment when Cythiria disappeared suddenly, gone in the time that it took for one heartbeat or a single breath. She recalled Cythiria and someone else, maybe twenty feet away. Another person, tall and slim like her, her stance strong and confident. She wanted to shout, to warn Cythiria. And then, the blue flash and a translucent wall that seemed to descend just in front of her, separating her from Cythiria. A moment later, Cythiria was gone.

I looked for you, Cythiria. I looked everywhere. But you were gone. I couldn't believe you would just disappear like this. Until….

Chelss walked along the cracked and pocked concrete platform. She gazed at the ground, her eyes shifting along the driveway, between the parked cars. And then, she stopped.

Her eyes caught sight of a black smudge on the ground. It was as wide as two cars side-by-side. She crouched down and gazed into it. She stroked the surface with her finger, which was now covered in soot. She sniffed it. Her eyes grew wide.

"That's it," she said, her voice tense with excitement. "That's the smell." She stood up. "So, it was here that Cythiria disappeared," she mumbled. "Somehow…." She glanced around. "Without any traces. No clothes. No… remains." Her voice cracked, and her eyes dampened. "Nothing."

She walked to the edge of the platform, gazing over a concrete barrier. The hospital building stood just across a street. From here, she could see the front door, and people milling about on the lawn and along the curbs of the driveway. She walked along the barrier to a corner and looked around. She glanced down.

"Hello," she said, squatting. A scratched and dented blue, metal tube jutted up from the surface. Cracked concrete enrobed its base. Chelss touched it and then poked it. It wobbled like a loose tooth. She stood up, turned, and jogged towards the other corner. There was another. She ran to another corner, and then the last one. Both had the same blue colored tube buried into the concrete. She paused, pursing her lips as she gazed upon the odd-looking device in front of her. She poked it and then grabbed at its nail-like head. She yanked and twisted, her face flushing pink, her breath growing short and raspy. Until finally, it dislodged. She tumbled backwards. Laying on her back, she held the device up with both her hands. It looked like a spike, and it had a sleeve along its shaft, with eye-like objects that encircled its base.

Chelss stood up. She took the pack off her shoulder, opened it, and thrust the device into it. She glanced around suspiciously, pulled the pack onto her shoulder, and ran towards the stairwell, down the winding stairs, and onto the street. Minutes later, she stood in the subway station, hugging the pack in her arms, her breath short, hazel-colored eyes wide, a smudgy, crimson smile crossing her face, her brown ponytails disheveled.

"I'm coming for you, Cyth," she whispered between breaths. "I'll find you. I promise."

CHAPTER 29

A Discovery

Griddish, Ashen Fissure, the Dusk Quadrant

Natty Mick hovered his Vérkatros to a stop. He sat on the ridge of a deep, grassy depression. In the center, a gateway rose. It stood upon a platform, and from it, emitted a warm yellow and red light. High in the sky, above the gateway, canopies floated, casting shadows on the area immediate to the portal.

"Fucking Rive and her patrols," he grumbled. *Useless work. She should tell someone else to do it. As if anyone would be up to anything at the Dusk Quadrant.*

The Dusk Quadrant. The place where Slaves came to forget. Or, perhaps disconnect. To be rid of the Tenddrome only long enough to see one's near end, and then return to the world of the lucid.

Natty scoffed. He was about to send the command to his Vérkatros to turn, except a tiny movement captured his attention. He saw a pair of figures step out of the glowing portal. He paused and gazed down into the depression, watching them with a hawkish eye. He slithered off his mount and sat on the edge of the grassy ridge.

"Well, *those* two look familiar."

The figures faced each other, exchanged some words, and gazed towards the sky. They sat on the edge of the platform.

"What are they up to? And even more important, why are Matere and Betel here? At the Dusk Quadrant?"

Matere stood, extended his hand, and helped Betel up. They turned and stepped back into the portal.

Natty stood. "If I don't find out what they're up to, Rive's gonna have questions," he grumbled. "And I really don't want to deal with that. She's just gonna end up giving me more work. *Natty, go do this thing, Natty go follow that person…,*" he said with a mocking tone. "As if I don't already have enough to do."

Natty gazed down into the depression, took a deep breath, and jumped. His feet slipped out from under him, and he rolled and tumbled to the bottom, landing face down in a deep patch of grass. "Fuck!" he shouted as he stood up. He gazed down at his grass stained clothed and brushed away stray blades with his hands. He sighed and then walked towards the portal that led to the Dusk Quadrant.

He stepped onto the platform and paused. He could feel the pull of the Dusk Quadrant on his body, a creeping tingling and numbness that started with his fingers and toes and made their way to his legs and arms. His vision glitched, distorting the objects around him. He took a deep breath and stepped in.

The world around him grew silent, as if he had been sucked into a vacuum. And then, he heard breathing, steady, rhythmic, surrounding and enclosing him as if the Dusk Quadrant itself had its own body, its own heart and lungs.

He stepped forward, down a long, narrow corridor. The air around him smelled heavy, spicy, like that of cinnamon. Waftring. He knew what it was, all Slaves knew what Waftring was. To his left, in a wide, open space – he didn't know how wide – he could hear the rhythmic slap of water on stone. Perhaps a vast body of water. In the sky, he could see glowing orbs like moons or planets, and beyond, innumerable points of light like stars.

He pushed forward until he arrived at a large, open gate. He stepped through. His eyes followed the figures of Matere and Betel as they stepped in and out of a wide chamber. He didn't have a clear view of them. His vision was slowly fading, replaced by colors and morphing shapes. Even through such glitchy, blurred vision, it was their movements, their forms that he recognized. He blinked hard as he watched the two figures walk back and forth, carrying objects. Maybe boxes, or crates. His body grew heavy, languid, as if he were standing in a pool of viscous oil. His breath was shallow, his hearing muffled and watery.

He turned away from the two figures and staggered along the long corridor, its dim walls lit weakly by light from red-colored torches. He felt his stomach turn, his heart pound inside his chest. He blinked again. *The Tenddrome will save me from this.* But the Tenddrome could not be called forth.

He stumbled through the corridor, his hands and body pressed against its walls. He saw other Slaves. Some passed by him, but they looked like faceless auras of light. Or, perhaps ghosts. It was the Varlings who believed in ghosts, not Natty, not the Slaves.

In the distance, Natty saw a point of white light. He reached towards it, his heavy, numbing legs barely following the orders that he gave to them, to move forward, to escape this place.

The light grew larger and brighter. He could feel a cool, moist breeze brush against his face. He tumbled out of a wide gateway onto a stony surface. He squinted, in spite of the canopies that floated in the sky above him.

Natty breathed heavily, and sweat poured from his forehead and neck, drenching his thick, black hair. He sat up and turned onto his hands and knees and heaved. He sat back on his haunches and took a deep breath. He closed his eyes.

A moment later, the area around him plunged into darkness. A light flickered in front of him, morphing into a figure.

"You called?" came the voice. It was Rive Amber's.

"I…."

"It seems you have experienced something unexpected."

"The…Dusk Quadrant."

"Ah yes, the place where Slaves go to forget. And what is it you wish to forget, my dear Natty Mick?"

Natty shook his head, as if to try to cast away a kind of dullness that overtook his mind and body. "It's *those* two?"

"And who might *they* be?"

"Matere and Betel."

Rive paused. "What of them?"

"I saw them loitering around the gateway." His sharper senses started to return to him, but his head ached and his eyes burned. "So, I followed them into the Dusk Quadrant."

"That's awfully obliging of you," said Rive, a tone of irony in her voice. "What got into you all of a sudden? This is not the Natty Mick I know!"

Fuck off, Rive. "They seem to have settled there."

"I suppose they have good reason to. The Council is obliterated, burned to the ground, a shell of its former self. They have nowhere to go, nowhere to call home, since they decided to return to Griddish from Var 8. The Slaves, with their reduced faculties inside the Dusk Quadrant, would not recognize them as anything different from anyone else. It's amazing to me that *you* even noticed them."

"A moment later, and I might not have recognized myself." He paused. "They were carrying…crates around."

"Ah, so they found my stash of Waftring liquor."

"*Your* stash?"

"Indeed."

"But why?"

"Why not?"

Natty hesitated. "I don't understand."

"When you give an opportunity to Matere and Betel, they will almost certainly turn that into disaster."

"As if we don't have enough to deal with."

"Yes, but their disaster is of a special kind. Perhaps classy is the word. One that makes things happen. A catalyst, you could say."

"But why Waftring liquor?"

Rive snorted. "Because Slaves love their Waftring liquor."

Natty sighed deeply. "I don't understand you, Rive. First, the war. Then that little brat from Var 7. And now Matere and Betel with more Waftring liquor than they can handle. None of this makes sense."

"It doesn't need to make sense, Natty. You see, Griddish needs change. What other way to bring about change than to enhance our own suffering? Bend a rigid object enough and it will snap. I've simply given Matere hope.

Now let's see what he does with it. I'm certain it will be quite gruesome." Natty could feel the smirk behind Rive's words. "When you've recovered, I'll need you to return to Var 7."

"What for this time?"

"I don't want the Slipshot to be reopened from there."

"As if it could."

"Unfortunately, upon leaving with Cythiria, I left some traces behind."

"Traces?"

"Perispikes."

"And you want me to do *what* about your own carelessness?"

"Fix it."

"Great," he grumbled. The darkness faded and the light of Griddish washed over Natty. He squinted at the sudden brightness of the sky. *Pretty fucked up, that's what you are Rive. This isn't going to end well.*

He stood up, wobbled for a moment on weakened legs, and looked up from inside the depression to his awaiting Vérkatros atop the ridge.

"Shit. How the hell am I gonna get back up there now?"

CHAPTER 30

A Visit

Var 7, Farth, Nissy

The train rattled to a stop. The door *whooshed!* open. Chelss pulled on the straps of the backpack as she jumped onto the platform. Her breath was quick and raspy and her heart beat heavily in her chest.

She bound down the stairs and through the turnstile, hopping over the gate as Cythiria had done many times before, smiling warmly as she recalled the times they ran together. She paused at the street, glancing up towards the bright white of the ring, which cast its own ghostly glow onto the damp, night streets of Nissy. Small, electric cars hummed and clattered by. Across the street, mounted upon the otherwise dark walls of the surrounding buildings, flickering pink and blue lights reflected upon the slick, wet surface of the roads.

She sniffed the air. It smelled cool and humid. She sighed. She ran across the street, among the passing cars that barely slowed before her as she advanced towards a narrow, cobbled alley, unlit save for the glow of the planetary ring and a few weak, buzzing LED lights overhead. The lights themselves cast a purple tinge on the walls and along the damp cobbles of the alley.

She entered the alley and stopped at a rusty, steel door. She tried to calm her raspy breath, as the chill of the night air burned her throat and her lungs.

She tugged at the shoulder strap. She could feel the heavy weight of the spike that she carried with her. It clanged, lightly, among the other objects in the pack, her tablet computer, her headset that she used to connect to her workstation. A few miscellaneous objects. She shuddered and pulled her jacket close to her body, clenching her jaw to silence her rattling teeth.

She gazed at the dented, steel door. The sounds of voices murmured and bubbled from inside. She sniffed the air. A warm smell of fresh bread and smoke wafted along a dry, gentle breeze and then faded. She felt her stomach grumble and her mouth water. She swallowed hard and licked her lips, which started to chafe and crack in the chilly night air.

She jumped as the steel door crashed open. She looked towards it. A man waved and then turned, walking into the alley towards the street and the train station. Chelss dashed forward.

"Fredrick!" she shouted hoarsely. The man turned towards her.

"Chelss…."

Chelss stepped towards him and paused. She looked into his tired, drooping, bloodshot eyes. A frown curled downwards along the corners of his mouth. His face was scruffy, unshaven. His hair disheveled. His back slumped. His hands were thrust into the pockets of his jacket.

"I…." Her voice cracked. Fredrick frowned deeply and glanced towards the milky-white planetary ring, his blue eyes flickering in the ghostly white light. "I'm sorry I didn't come to see you, after Cyth disappeared. I just…."

Fredrick sighed deeply. "Do you know what happened to Cyth?"

Chelss shook her head. Her long, brown ponytails brushed against her shoulders. "A moment, she and I were together. And then, she was gone." Her eyes dampened and she sniffled.

"I'm sorry, Chelss," he said, his breath infused with alcohol, his words ever so slightly slurred. "I'm not much help." His voice cracked. "I've looked for her ever since that day, but…."

Chelss pulled the pack off her shoulder and let it fall with a heavy, metallic clang onto the cobbled surface of the alley. She opened it up, reached in and took hold of the spike-looking object. She held it up for Fredrick to see. Her hazel eyes began to burn, her lips pressed to thin lines, her brow pursed.

Fredrick looked at the object. His eyes grew wide. He looked at Chelss, holding her gaze with his own.

"Where did you get that?" he said, with forced calm as his voice started to shake.

"I found it near the hospital. In the parking lot."

He glanced at the spike, then Chelss. He paused.

"Tell me." Chelss's voice was thin, tense. "What is it?"

Fredrick sighed and looked down at the damp cobbles of the alley. "It's nothing," he said. "You should go home. It's cold out here."

"Bullshit!" shouted Chelss. "I'm not going home. I want to know what this is. If you won't tell me, then I'll find someone else. I'll keep looking until I figure out what happened to Cyth!" Chelss's hazel eyes were wide, burning. Her lips quivered, her hand, which held the object, trembled.

"Cyth," mumbled Fredrick. "That's what I used to call her." Fredrick sighed. His gaze softened as he looked into Chelss's eyes. "Look, what you're up against, the place where that thing came from," he said, as he nodded towards the spike-shaped object, "Is bigger than anything you or I can handle alone. You'll never be able to reach Cyth again, not if that had anything to do with it."

Chelss clenched her teeth. "I don't care. I want to know what happened to her."

Fredrick sighed deeply. His eyes softened and a tiny, gentle smile crossed his face. "I guess I knew this day would come someday." He paused, glancing suspiciously at the object in her hand. "If that's involved, it also means that Cyth is probably still alive."

Chelss let out a deep sigh, as if she were holding her breath, waiting for the words that she was preparing herself to hear. A slight smile curled up on the corner of her mouth. Her body relaxed and her hands stopped trembling, her eyes drooped. She wanted to sit down on the curb of the alley and deflate.

"But what I don't know," continued Fredrick, "Is whether or not she decided to go on her own." He paused. "She…may not want to be here anymore, Chelss." His voice cracked. "I know she had a hard time with things."

"I don't believe that. Not after we ran off from the hospital. She was fighting to stay alive. She…." Her body grew tense. "She wanted us to be together."

Fredrick shook his head. He rubbed his rough chin with his hand as he gazed up at the milky, bright light of the planetary ring. He sighed. "Then I guess we have no choice." Fredrick smiled gently, his eyes brightening as he gazed at Chelss. "Cyth was lucky to meet you. But getting her back will probably be life threatening." He paused. "I don't suppose you'll give up on finding her?"

Chelss shook her head.

"Then I suppose I should tell you what's going on, as far as I know."

⁂

Natty Mick scoffed. A puff of steam poured from his nose in the chilly night air. He glanced at the two figures who stood in the alley, their weak shadows cast by the bright light of the planetary ring. The wet, cobbled surface of the street glistened with the deep purple of LED lights. "So, they've found out Rive's little secret," he mumbled. *Not that they can do anything with it. They would need to access the Tenddrome, after all, just to initialize the Perispikes.* Natty paused. *Still, that didn't stop them last time. Last time, he and that red head had Matere and Betel.* Natty sighed deeply. "Fucking Rive always making our lives harder. Why can't she just take care of things herself?" *Disillusioned bitch. Going on and on about Cythiria and how that little twit is going to be the future of all of us Slaves. As if that's going to happen. She can't even get access to the Tenddrome. That's basic stuff for us. And yet, she can't do it.*

Natty shook his head. *At least one individual will want to know what's going on. And it isn't Rive. Nope. I'm thinking a specific Creator Class Vérkatros would be interested in this information.*

CHAPTER 31

Adapting

Griddish, Ashen Fissure, Sanguine Heap

Rive Amber stood behind Cythiria. With one hand, she grasped Cythiria's wrist, with the other, her hip. Cythiria felt Rive's body press against her back, whispering instructions that tickled the inside of her ear. Cythiria shuddered, the hair on the back of her neck rose, goose bumps formed on her arms.

"Hold the base of the Plaxis in your hand. Relax your fingers, don't grip so tight," said Rive, as she stroked Cythiria's fingers with her own. "Remember, you are not like other Nodes. You haven't accessed the Tenddrome as yet. You can't send commands directly to your devices as other Mechanics do. Instead, turn your wrist to ignite it. This Plaxis Strand has been modified for you, so be cautious." She paused. "Your survival will depend on your ability to utilize your body properly."

Utilize my body properly. My body. It's…weak now.

Cythiria flicked her wrist. The Plaxis did not ignite.

"Do it again," commanded Rive.

Cythiria flicked.

"Again."

Again, she flicked.

"Again."

Cythiria's neck and back grew damp with sweat. Her breath was raspy and ragged. She grimaced. Her hand and wrist and arm started to ache.

She flicked again.

A plasmic arc shot from the end of the Plaxis Strand and licked the ground in front of her. The smell of burning metal wafted through the air. A tittering, tinny whistle echoed along the stone surface of the courtyard. A wide, toothy smile spread across Cythiria's face. She laughed, an almost bell-like chime.

"I did it!" she shouted. She glanced at the handle of the Plaxis, her eyes following the electric arcs. She held it as far away from her body as she could, her head turned shyly away, as if the arcs would turn and strike her face.

Rive gazed at Cythiria. Her eyes were soft, her mouth curled to a tiny grin. "I knew you could do it, Cythiria."

Cythiria felt her neck flush and her cheeks grow warm.

"You have to become comfortable with your Plaxis Strand, Cythiria," said Rive, her dark eyes now glaring, a thin scowl rising on her lips. "It's the only weapon that will save you when it comes time to fight."

The smile on Cythiria's face faded, and her face grew a shade of pale. "When will I fight?"

Rive paused. "Soon." She glanced towards the sky, towards the dome that covered Griddish. A thunderous clap echoed along the walls of Sanguine Heap, and along the apex of the dome, flashes of rainbow colors rippled through gently lit skies. "If you don't, then this may be the end of Griddish, the end of our world." She returned her gaze to Cythiria. "Perhaps it would be better that way. But for now, this life is all we have. Griddish, the Tenddrome, is our only manner of survival."

"Except for me," said Cythiria, a tone of apprehension in her voice. "I can't access the Tenddrome. But I can survive without it."

"The Tenddrome is always part of you, even though you do not see it now. It envelops you, forms you, changes you. You are a Node within the Tenddrome. As such, you are a Node connected to every other Slave that exists and has existed and will ever exist in our world. There is no future and past in the Tenddrome. There is only that which exists."

That which exists. Cythiria gazed at the flickering Plaxis Strand, its tinny, whistling arcs that burned the surface of the ground which it touched. *Do I exist? I…am barely alive. I never wanted to exist, never asked to. Yet….*

Rive turned. She paused, glancing over her shoulder, her dark eyes piercing. "Keep practicing. Don't stop. Ever."

Cythiria stared at a ceiling shrouded in darkness. She turned her supine body. The pallet creaked under her weight, its hard surface pressing against her shoulder, her ribs, her thigh.

She sighed. The chamber hummed with the rhythm of sleeping Bestiars, the snores and groans blending into a steady, beating drone. The air smelled dank and musty, with an occasional waft of musk from the sweating bodies that filled the chamber's rows.

Cythiria's stomach turned. She reached her hand towards her neck, touching it, stroking it with slender fingers. She stroked her cheek, and then her head, which was now covered with a thick mane.

Her chest tightened and ached. She saw, in the darkness, the hazel-colored eyes of Chelss as they gazed at her coolly, judgmentally, her long eyelashes curling to tiny wisps, her slim fingers stroking a wayward lock of brown hair behind her ear. She imagined red-painted lips curling down to a gentle frown.

Cythiria touched her forehead, her fingers stroking two tiny scars, like cool craters that once burned hot, but had now settled.

Cythiria sighed.

The Tenddrome. I still can't access the Tenddrome. Everyone around me can, without any problem. Why did Rive bring me back here? What use can I be? If a Slave is made by their connection to the Tenddrome, then what good am I? I wish she would just leave me alone. She wouldn't even notice if I was gone.

"But the way she looked at me," Cythiria mumbled. She felt her throat tighten. She swallowed hard.

Chelss. Do you even know that I'm gone? Do you care? Did you ever like me? I mean, why would you like someone who is so useless? I'm sure you're with someone else now. That guy maybe. The one you hung out with when we were both in Nissy.

Cythiria sniffled. Warm rivulets flowed down her cheeks and dripped silently onto the hard pallet. Her body heaved and trembled as she sobbed. "Why did you bring me here, Rive?" she whispered. "Why? Can't you just leave me be? Let me go?" She clenched her teeth and wrapped her arms around her own body. "Just let me go…."

The crack of clashing arms and rhythmic shouts and chants echoed along the stone walls of Sanguine Heap's inner courtyard. Cythiria watched as squads of Bestiars cheered, or stood to attention, while their leaders barked orders at grapplers who sparred mercilessly with each other.

Cythiria gazed up at the cool, gentle light of Griddish's dome. Her chest started to ache as she thought about the warm starlight of Farth, Var 7. Or the bright ring that lit the night in a wash of ghostly white luminescence.

She thought about the tall, thin towers that stretched towards the sky, the blinking lights, the flashing neon pink and blue that reflected off damp, cobbled street surfaces. She thought about Dad's kitchen. It was always warm inside and smelled of spice and wood smoke and old oil. She would walk in, make herself at home. The people who worked there, in their grimy, gray or yellow aprons, hairnets and scarves, would ask her about her day, about her fights, her training, her work at the gym. School. Especially tree trunks. She giggled. *Tree trunks.* And Dad would bring her warm morsels that he would cook up just for her. She would slink back to a dark corner, nibble, and doze off while she sat on open boxes of half empty cans, produce, flour, or bottles of mysterious colored fluids that smelled of tomato and pepper.

The way home would be cold, the subway harsh and clattery. But Dad was there. Some days, he would just carry her home, even after his long day at the restaurant.

Cythiria felt her throat tighten and her eyes grow damp. She sniffled and rubbed her nose, which grew to a brighter shade of pink.

She wiped her eyes with the back of her hand and took a deep breath. She flicked her hand. The Plaxis Strand whistled and buzzed to a long, licking arc. She lifted her arm, swung and whipped while the tongue-tips of plasmic arcs danced along the cobbled surface beneath her feet. She smiled. The Plaxis was more natural now. It suited her. She could feel its weight, its balance, even though she could still not connect with the Tenddrome. She could not command it the way other Slaves did.

"Maybe one day," she mumbled. She flicked the Plaxis, shutting it off as its electric arcs retracted to its base. She sighed and glanced around.

And then *he* caught her eye.

She smiled wide, her dark eyes brightening. She jogged and then stopped before the Vérkatros that stood before her. She gazed into his large eyes and glanced along his brightly flashing skin, a skin that was somehow metallic yet soft and warm. She saw yellow at first, then red, then orange.

"Blinky," she said, touching his wide, streamline body with her hand. She glanced at the flicking antennae on his head, at the little ribbon that was still tied to one of them, the name "Blinky" scratched onto it. "I see you kept my little gift." She paused. "I'm happy that you like it."

The Vérkatros, Blinky, retracted his legs, his chassis resting lightly on the surface of the cobbled courtyard. Cythiria sat and leaned her back against his body. She sighed as she gazed at the gentle light that emanated from the dome. "I don't know what to do, Blinky. I just want to go home. I don't know why Rive brought me back here. I feel so useless, like my life means nothing. I can barely survive here on my own." She paused. "But I don't really have anything back home either. I just feel like I can't really live, you know? That, there's always something inside my head, that it just won't leave me alone." She started to sniffle, and tears streamed down her cheeks. "I don't belong anywhere, Blinky. I…just can't go on anymore."

Blinky's legs extruded from beneath his chassis, as he stood up. Cythiria stood next to him. "I'm sorry if I depressed you. Are you leaving already?"

Blinky turned and leaned his body towards Cythiria. His skin flashed yellow and then orange and then grassy green. Cythiria grabbed onto Blinky's side and pulled herself up onto his back. "Is this what you want, Blinky?" Blinky turned. A gentle hum, and his legs retracted underneath his chassis as he rose quietly from the surface and started to hover. He whooshed forward, through the dark, stone archway that marked the gate of Sanguine Heap.

He hovered onto a wide, grassy plain. Cythiria felt a cool breeze brush against her hair and her face. She shivered. She glanced at the broken cityscape of Ashen Fissure, the tall, cracked and crumbling spikes that stretched weakly towards the dome. She heard the occasional, distant pop and crackle, the sounds of war and weapons. Above her, she heard deep, echoing crashes followed by waves of rainbow light, a sign, she had been told, that something struck the outer dome of Griddish. A meteor, perhaps. Cythiria smiled at the splashes and waves of color, as if this potentially deadly event were designed by a happy, optimistic artist who took joy in an unknown future.

She glanced along the horizon of Griddish, if Griddish could be said to have a horizon. It wasn't like Farth here. This place was flat, a wide, endless disk that somehow strayed aimlessly through space. Yet, that horizon was littered with tall, slim Slipshot Silos. Endless rows and clusters of Silos as if they themselves could constitute a forest of trees. And each Silo, linked to some distant world. Like Farth.

What are those other worlds like? Are they like Farth? Are they still alive? Or have they died long ago?

Blinky continued to move forward, hovering and swaying lithely. Cythiria chuckled. *That's all I know. Farth. Nothing else. I don't understand much about the world.*

A single, solitary Silo seemed to rise from the disk's surface. Blinky pushed forward and then paused at the edge of a wide, round platform. He extruded his legs and came to a gentle stop.

"Where are we?" said Cythiria as she gazed towards the Silo. It was quiet here. The platform was empty. She could hear the breeze rustle through the short, grassy hills that surrounded the Silo.

She jumped down. The ground beneath her boots was soft. She stepped onto the platform. Its surface echoed a tinny, metallic *click!* She glanced at

Blinky. His skin flashed yellow and green, a moment of purple, and then cool gray. She took a deep breath and walked towards the center of the platform, towards a dark blotch that appeared stained into the metal cobbles. On each side, rows of black Transposal posts formed a circle before the tall, slender Silo. She glanced up towards its apex, where she saw a dark portal.

She continued to walk, her boots echoing their tinny clicks until she stopped at the point where the black posts converged. She sniffed the air, which smelled of stale, burnt metal. She shivered, and her stomach turned.

"What is this place?"

"Your way back to…them," came a voice.

Cythiria turned to face the voice. "Rive…."

Rive Amber stepped onto the platform, her solid, confident stride echoing along the metal-tiled surface. Her lips curled downwards to a frown, quivering slightly as if she were about to spit. Her dark eyes glared sharply as she walked toward Cythiria.

Rive stepped up to Cythiria and paused. Her glare softened, and her brow pursed. "That is the way back to Nissy."

"Nissy…." Cythiria turned to face the Slipshot Silo.

"Why are you here, Cythiria?" said Rive, her face hardening. Cythiria glanced towards Blinky and then returned her gaze to Rive. "I see," said Rive. "The Vérkatros has brought you here." Rive paused. "If you wish to return to *them* Cythiria, I have no way of stopping you."

Cythiria's eyes dampened, and she sniffled. "I don't belong here, Rive. I'm so useless. I can't even use the Tenddrome."

"Do you think you belong to Var 7? What do you have there, Cythiria?"

"I have friends. I have a family."

"Family," Rive scoffed. Her lips quivered to a sneer. "And what did you gain from that, Cythiria? When I brought you here, you could barely keep yourself alive."

Cythiria's throat tightened, and tears streamed down her cheek. "I tried, Rive. I tried so hard," she sobbed.

Rive stepped close to Cythiria. She could feel the warmth of her body, a slight, steady breath on her cheek. Rive placed her hand gently on Cythiria's shoulder. "The Vars have a way of slowly killing us, Cythiria. Only the strong can survive for very long."

"But I'll be strong. I'll work hard…." She gazed into Rive' eyes, her own dark pools quivering, pleading.

"Cythiria, there will be a time and a place for everything. You belong here, in Griddish, with me. Only I can help you discover what you've lost." She paused. "If you wish to return to Var 7, then I will not stop you." Rive turned. She glanced over her shoulder at Cythiria. "But whatever you do, commit yourself to that path, and do not waver." She reached into her pocket and, with a sweeping motion of her arm, threw a pair of Capsas onto the platform. They bounced and clattered along the surface, stopping in front of Cythiria. She gazed at them, those tiny, egg-shaped devices, their smooth surface reflecting the gentle, Griddish daylight.

Rive stepped forward, her slow, steady gait, her solid step echoing a tinny tap along the metal-tiled surface of the Slipshot Silo's platform.

Cythiria fell to her knees and sobbed. Tears streamed down her cheek and splashed silently onto the platform's surface. "I don't know what to do," she mumbled between sobs. She felt a gentle nudge at her shoulder. She glanced at Blinky, who stood next to her, his skin flashing a deep red and purple color. "If I go back, I'll only hurt people. Like Chelss and dad and Jillian. They'd be better off without me. I'm sure Chelss has found someone else she likes better by now. Why would she even like someone like me, who cries like this and is so worthless?" She pressed her body against Blinky and gazed into his wide, almost airy eyes. "I guess Rive is right. She's all I got now."

CHAPTER 32

Waftring Liquor

Griddish, Ashen Fissure, the Dusk Quadrant

Matere pushed a chair against a table. He stepped back and crossed his arms, gazing over the chamber. In the center, a long table was surrounded by twenty chairs on either side, and one at the head, one at the base. Along the walls, which were now colored a deep blue, divans and chaise lounges were placed, and next to them, short, square tables.

Above, attached to a distant ceiling, hung a blue chandelier, and from it emanated a gentle glow from plasmic torches.

The air smelled of spice, like cinnamon, from Waftring liquor.

"Not bad, aye?" said Matere.

Betel reluctantly nodded her head.

"It's even better than Temple Pizza, if I do say so myself."

"That's not saying much."

"And it was even cheaper to start up. With all that free Waftring liquor, I'd say we did a pretty good job of it."

"Are you done patting yourself on the back?"

"Not quite." He paused.

"Well then?"

"Furnishing is great, too. Can't believe we were able to scavenge all this stuff."

"So, what's the plan, my brilliant Engineer Class Citizen?" The tone of Betel's voice was drenched in sarcasm.

"Bring in the Slaves."

"And?"

"And give them lots of Waftring."

"So?"

"So that they will reveal a thing or two about what they're currently up to."

"That could take time, Matere."

"And so, we must be strategic. Get the right people in, and we'll soon be at the heart of this Slave-driven war."

Betel sighed. "And how do you plan on doing that?"

"Oh, my dear *former* great Councilwoman," he said, smirking as he turned towards her. He could hear the sound of grinding dentine from Betel's clenched jaw. "Every great plan starts with a tiny first step."

"You and your platitudes."

He turned towards the door. A young Mechanic Class Slave poked her head in. Her eyes were bleary, and a crooked, toothy smile crossed her face.

"What's going on in here?" she slurred and then giggled.

Matere rushed forward and met her at the entry. "Please, come in." He escorted her to the closest chair, pulled it out, and motioned for her to take a seat. "I'll be right back," he said, rushing off towards the storage room behind the chamber.

"She's just a kid," grumbled Betel through clenched teeth, taking hold of Matere's arm and stopping him as he was about to rush by.

He looked at her through his silver-framed spectacles. "Hardly. The Slaves are ageless, damn near immortal."

"What do you plan to do with her, Matere?"

"Simply provide her a drink."

"You know that's their addiction, right?"

He glanced back at the Mechanic, who looked around the room through groping, unfocused eyes.

"I'm simply going to give her a taste of what we have to offer and then ask her to come with her friends next time."

Betel shook her head. "I don't like this, Matere. It sounds like you want to pimp out that young Mechanic so you can have your way with the Slaves. We're supposed to be better than this."

Matere scoffed. "Better? And how did you come to the conclusion that Engineer Class Citizens are all such model beings? How is it possible that they – that we -- can be better than anyone else, after all that's happened?"

Betel sighed deeply. "The reason we left Griddish in the first place, way back when we landed on Var 8, was to change the way things are done in Griddish. That was what you told me, and that was what convinced me to leave the Council and join you on your quest to save the world."

Mater looked into Betel's cool, gray eyes. "Is that the only reason?"

Betel hesitated, and then looked away. "Yes."

"That was before this war started. How many have died so far, both Engineer *and* Slave? And even more, where is this whole thing going? What is the ultimate outcome of Griddish? Total annihilation? Led by the very Slaves who depend on this world for their own survival? They're not like us, Betel. They can't just escape to some Var and live there. We saw that with Opal on Var 8. They slowly deteriorate if they don't have a connection to their Tenddrome. The absence of that connection to their world and to each other slowly rots away their minds until they reach a state of such utter and complete darkness that their only hope is suicide. The Slaves are not well, Betel." Matere nodded his head towards the young Mechanic, whose head was lolling about as she clumsily hummed some unknown song. "At least, if we can get inside, somehow, maybe we can turn the tide. Maybe we can stop this path to self-destruction. Because if Griddish dies, what will happen to the Vars? Will they even be able to survive on their own?"

Betel sighed deeply. "So, I'll ask you again, Matere. What's your plan?"

Matere paused. "Slaves were fortunate enough to be able to take comfort in one another. At least, the early Engineers were kind enough to grant them that when they designed them."

"I don't like where this is going, Matere."

"Let's make this place a little club where lonely Slaves can get to know each other, and take comfort in each other's embrace when the Tenddrome is not looking."

"So that you can expose them at one of the most vulnerable times in their lives?"

"No, not expose, Betel. Disrupt. Because that's what this war needs right now."

Betel paused. She shook her head. "Fine, Matere. Do what you need to do." She lifted her finger and pointed it at Matere's nose. "But don't you dare go any further than you have to. Don't play with their minds, Matere."

Matere took hold of Betel's arm and gazed into her cool, gray eyes. And then, he dashed towards the back storage room, returning to the waiting Mechanic Class Slave with a glass of Waftring liquor.

CHAPTER 33

Explanations

Var 7, Farth, Nissy

Natty Mick glanced up at the wispy planetary ring. In the bright sun of a Nissian day, it appeared as a long, streaky cloud that reached across the sky, plunging in the blue waters of Nissy Bay.

He glanced down at the crack in the cobbled street, smirking as he pushed his hand through his thick, black hair.

"You're getting more and more predictable the older you get," he said, stroking his chin with his fingers, gazing skyward as if recalling a memory. "At least on Var 8, you would hang out in better places. Now, you seem to enjoy burying yourself in holes."

Natty's ears pricked up at the echoing tap of slow, measured footsteps. He made a quick pirouette, his eyes settling on a tall, slim figure whose bald head gleamed in the brightness of the sunny day. He held a sagging, brown bag in one hand. He reached inside of it with the other, grabbing a handful of its contents, and scattering it onto the cobbled surface of the street. A flock of birds fluttered, landed, and pecked at the items, squawking and flapping as they bickered with each other over their heavenly arrival of tasty seeds.

"Although one could take great comfort in living a solitary, private life," came the deep, calm voice, "Sometimes it's worth it to put that aside momentarily and enjoy the arrival of a beautiful day such as today, don't you think?"

Natty grit his teeth, scowling. He scoffed. "So, it looks like the great 1[1] has finally ascended to the surface, and exposed himself for all to see."

233

"I'm glad you noticed, though I don't know if I should be."

Natty snorted. "Noticing you is the last thing on my mind."

"And yet, you are here. Your words belie your stated intentions."

Natty scoffed. "As if. But now that you are homeless, stuck here in Var 7 like those other idiot Varlings – what were their names? -- finding you has become a bit of a chore. I really hate shouting into random holes in the ground, now that you decided to become one with the soil, or whatever it is you're doing. Gone are the days when I can just strut down to the local university and ask for some weirdo professor of philosophy."

Jeremiah smiled. "Well, then, I suppose we should celebrate your success. You've managed to find what was simply hiding in plain sight."

"Yeah, sure." Natty smirked. "But you see, there's one thing about you that bugs me. And that's the Tenddrome. You always reside somewhere within the Tenddrome. You may be hard to find, but you are there, nonetheless."

Jeremiah reached into his bag and tossed another handful of seeds. More birds arrived, bickering louder this time as they pecked at the tiny morsels. "It is not possible to be in two places at the same time. Either I am here, or I am somewhere else."

Natty smirked. "Ever the philosopher, Dr. Jeremiah Onu."

"I'm flattered that you would pay such heed to a lowly individual such as myself."

Natty laughed. "Not this bullshit again. I swear, you and your fake humility is galling sometimes."

"So then why seek me out? I can't imagine how I could be of any assistance to you."

Natty paused. He smirked and then pushed his hand through his thick, black hair. "All I really want to do is tell you something that might be of interest to you."

A wry smile crossed Jeremiah's face. "So then, perhaps you have discovered the true reason for our existence in this world?"

Natty snorted. "Hardly. It's more about that Varling that you so handily befriended on this miserable planet."

Jeremiah tossed another handful of seeds onto the ground. "Fredrick? Why, he is just one of my dear friends from long ago."

"Sure, he is. The thing is, there's this girl who found one of our Perispikes."

"So, what of it? I can't help it if you Slaves are so careless in your work."

"And she met with Fredrick." Natty paused, as a crooked, toothy smile crossed his face. He stepped closer to Jeremiah. "You see, she's looking for one Cythiria Crenshaw. Does that name sound familiar to you?"

"I know many people."

"And this girl has love in her eyes. You know what that means, don't you?"

"Love is what makes the world go around, as they say."

"It means, she's not gonna be easily stopped. If she's talking to Fredrick, she's going to find out that there's more to Cythiria's disappearance than meets the eye." Natty stepped closer to Jeremiah, crouching down while holding his hands to his knees. "The problem is, she can't initialize the Perispike on her own. She needs someone who has access to the Tenddrome to do that." Natty stood up and sighed with exaggeration. "Can you imagine if another Varling shows up in Griddish? How will they take it? Chaos could ensue. You know how these Varlings can be a catalyst to violence." Natty paused. He stretched and sighed and sniffed deeply of the city air. "I thought you'd like to know, considering how you're somehow always keeping tabs on things." He paused. "Oh, and how you say the only way to fix all the problems in the universe is to end Griddish and its Vars once and for all? Looks like this could be your big chance." Natty smirked and pushed his hand through his thick, black hair. He glanced at the scattering of seeds on the street, and the hopping and chirping birds who pecked at them. "You know, those little shits are like cockroaches with feathers. Real vermin. Don't know why you want to encourage them. Anyway, that's none of my business." Natty turned and started to step away. "Good luck with whatever it is you're up to." He waved as he walked along the street, turned a corner, and was gone.

"Well, that should get him pretty worked up," Natty mumbled as he strolled along the street, its adjacent buildings graffitied and tagged. *Rive is putting too much hope on her little project, Cythiria. She's going to bring us all down. So, let's let the Varlings figure out how to get that stupid little Mechanic back here. Once that's done, I'll assemble some Vérks, and we can finally end this Var once and for all. Good riddance!*

CHAPTER 34

First Mission

Griddish, Ashen Fissure, Sanguine Heap

The smell of burning metal wafted through the inner courtyard of Sanguine Heap. Cythiria raised her arm and sliced downward, the Plaxis Strand hissing and whistling through the air, its tips licking the cobbled surface like a plasmic whip.

"Center your stance," came a confident bark from behind her. She turned her head to face Rive, who gazed upon her with an upheld chin and a scowl that crossed her face. Her upper lip quivered, and she looked as if she were about to spit. "Your power comes from your hips, not your arms."

Cythiria let the whip of the Plaxis Strand fall by her side, as she spread her feet and straightened her posture. She lifted her arm and flicked her wrist, adding velocity to her whip by pivoting her hips with each strike. The sharp whistles of splitting air, the choking smell of burning metal, filled the courtyard. Cythiria felt a prickling sensation on her neck and back as she started to break a sweat in the emanating heat of her ignited Plaxis Strand.

"Very good," said Rive. "Keep practicing with your core. You will improve over time."

Cythiria felt her neck and cheeks grow warm. "I...will improve?"

Rive turned. "Come with me," she said, and stepped forward.

Cythiria flicked her wrist. The Plaxi retracted. She walked behind Rive, her steps in stride with the Bestiar Class Slave. The two walked through the gate, under the carven arch, and into the dark corridors of Sanguine Heap.

Upon the walls were mounted buzzing electric torches that cast a weak, blue light throughout the halls. A few steps later, the flat corridor turned into one with stairs and inclines. Cythiria gazed out the slim windows as she passed them, at the distant hills, and the innumerable Slipshot Silos that littered the landscape.

The two emerged from a narrow passage onto Sanguine Heap's roof. Cythiria glanced around the dark walls that looked like they were smudged with grime and yellow-red rust. In the center, a rotund dome rose from the roof, allowing the gentle Griddish light to flow into the depths below, casting colorful shimmers onto the floor and along the walls within.

Cythiria glanced up at the sky, at the gentle white light that did not ever waver, that was never displaced by the silence and dark of night. She heard a distant crack! and rumble! as a shimmering wave of rainbow colors danced in the sky, perhaps caused by the strike of a meteor outside the dome.

She sniffed the air which smelled of burning grass and moldy decay. She crinkled her nose and walked towards Rive, who waited next to a corner tower that overlooked a wide, rolling plain. To her left, she could see the tall, white spikes that were once the towers of Ashen Fissure, jutting upwards from the ground like broken teeth.

She sidled up to Rive, who gazed distractedly into the distance. The once green plains were now a shade of brown. Far-off, echoing *pops!* rolled along the surface and among the ramparts of Sanguine Heap.

Rive sighed deeply. "We can't survive much longer," she said. Her eyes were distant, drooping, bloodshot. Her lips turned to a frown. She turned to face Cythiria. She gazed at Cythiria's face, her eyes sweeping from the two scars on her forehead to her eyes, nose, chin. She raised her hand and touched Cythiria's face, her fore and middle fingers stroking her cheek. Cythiria's neck and face grew warm, her heart started to beat rapidly in her chest.

"You've grown, Cythiria," said Rive, her eyes softening and growing distant. "Since I first saw you on Var 7, I knew. But I've been always watching over you, ever since the day you left Griddish."

"I…."

"You are a beautiful woman, now."

"No, I…."

"And you belong to us Slaves. You belong to me."

Cythiria felt her stomach turn. Her legs and feet started to tremble. Her breath grew short. "No, Rive, I don't believe you. I know you're lying to me. I'm useless here. I can't do anything. I can't even survive on my own."

Rive smiled gently. "Your mastery of the Plaxis Strand has grown."

"I only know the basics. I would be worthless in a fight. I…."

"Cythiria, I need you to do something for me."

Cythiria looked into Rive's eyes, brow raised. "You need me to do something?"

"I…." Rive looked away. Her voice cracked. She sighed quickly. "There are people out there who don't want us to succeed."

"Succeed at what, Rive?"

"They don't want us to determine our own future. They'd prefer we stay where we are, that we continue to do our work with the Slipshot and the Vars. They don't know that we're tired, Cythiria. We want change. We want to be free from the burdens that we've borne for so long." She paused and turned to face Cythiria. "In many ways, I envy you Cythiria."

Cythiria raised a brow. "Envy me?"

"Because you cannot access the Tenddrome, you are free from it. You are not determined by its designs. You are not oppressed by its ancient rules. Most Slaves, if they were freed from the Tenddrome today, would despair. The Tenddrome is a place of safety, of comfort. Like a cocoon that wraps itself around you, and at the same time, chokes your life away. But you eventually emerged outside of its oppressive grasp. You've had to survive on your own, without its guidance, even though your entire being was designed to work only within its confines." Rive paused. "I know it was painful for you. I saw that in you, in your eyes, your loneliness, your isolation. *Those Varlings*," a scowl rose on Rive's lips, "Your so-called Varling parents, they don't understand you. Not the way I do."

Cythiria's voice cracked. "But without them, without Dad and Mom, I don't know what I would have done. I…."

Rive placed her hand on Cythiria's shoulder. "I'm depending on you, Cythiria."

"Depending on me for what? I don't understand what you want from me."

Rive looked towards the brown, grassy meadows, along the horizon, as her eyes flitted across endless clusters of Slipshot Silos. "Your blindness is our advantage."

"Blindness?"

"I…want you to kill someone."

Cythiria's face grew pale, her gaze distant, eyes wide. "Kill…?"

"A man named Matere Songgaard."

CHAPTER 35

Making Plans

Var 7, Farth, Nissy

Chelss gazed out the window of the train car as it rattled along the track, swaying from side to side, hurtling through Nissy on above-ground tracks. Neon pink and blue lights flashed through the windows as the car passed above busy intersections filled with clusters of people walking and milling around night time markets. In the sky, the milky white planetary ring cast a bright tinge along the edges and surfaces of the towers that made up Nissy.

"I have to know why Cyth was taken away," she mumbled.

The train car was empty, except for her, Fredrick, Jillian, and a few sleeping or drunken bodies that were draped about the benches. Chelss gazed down at the backpack that lay on the ground between her feet. The top flap was folded over, revealing inside the blue-gray metal spike that was the Perispike. She sighed deeply and then kicked the bag, which rattled a metallic ting among the other stuff inside.

In the chilly, rattling car, she pulled her jacket close to her body. She glanced sidelong at Fredrick. He was slumped over, his shoulders bent forward as if he were carrying a heavy burden on his shoulders. His hood was pulled up onto his head, but his face revealed itself to her. She could see, in the flickering blue and pink light, distant, tired, bloodshot eyes, dark circles, drooping lids. His face was rough, stubbly, his expression worn. He shook his head, as the corners of his mouth turned to a deeper frown, his thoughts, perhaps, trying to shake them away, banish them to some dark closet deep inside his mind.

Jillian gazed into the distance, her nose and chin held high, her jaw set, the corner of her mouth curved down to a frown. Her brow was furrowed and her green eyes were soft, gentle, nurturing. To Chelss, her expression seemed like an act of sheer willpower, a contradiction in itself. She tugged at the brim of her cap, crossed her legs and arms, and shifted in her seat.

Chelss felt her stomach turn. *Where did Cythiria go? Why would she leave? Or, why was she taken?*

Fredrick sighed. He turned towards Chelss for a moment and then looked away.

"Um," started Chelss, "I just want to thank you."

Fredrick glanced at Chelss. "Thank me? For what?"

"For finding me when Cyth was in trouble."

"Oh, that." Fredrick sniffed, and his eyes seemed to grow damp. "It wasn't too hard. Cyth, she's not the most social of butterflies."

Chelss smiled. "I suppose not."

"Cyth only seems to be in one of three places at any given time. She's either at school, at home, or at Rive's gym. And school was even off the table, since she started with Rive."

"And you were okay with that?"

"In some ways, it eases my worry. She's predictable." He paused as he sat back on the chair and glanced at Jillian, who cast him a disapproving gaze. He looked out the window, his gaze distant and reminiscing. He rubbed his scratchy chin with his hand. "But Cyth, she's her own person. And then the… attempt she made on her own life. It's so hard to make the right decision when so much is on the line." He looked at Chelss with his tired, drooping eyes. "Honestly, I didn't know what to do." He sighed. "I still don't."

"Rive Amber," mumbled Chelss. Her upper lip curled to a scowl and trembled. "She told me to stay away from Cyth. She said Cyth had other things to deal with." She paused. "Do you know what those other things were?"

Fredrick shrugged. "I wish I knew myself. I assume Rive was preparing her for something."

"For what?"

"I guess she wants her back in Griddish."

"Griddish," said Chelss, under her breath. "There's so much I don't know."

Fredrick forced a smile. "Consider yourself lucky." Fredrick paused. "I'm sure you'll learn more as you delve deeper into what that thing in your bag does," he said, nodding towards the Perispike. "To be honest, I don't know much either."

Chelss pulled her jacket closer to her body and wrapped her arms around her own waist. "I know I'm not the most likable person," she said. "I can be kinda cold sometimes."

"Nonsense," said Fredrick, turning his head and smiling at Chelss. "I like you. Otherwise, I wouldn't go through all this trouble."

"You'd be the only one."

"Cyth likes you."

"Maybe."

"She does. I can tell. There's no doubt about it in my mind."

Chelss smiled. She felt her chest tighten and her neck and face grow warm. "She's very lucky to have someone like you."

"I'm sure she'd disagree with that assessment." He glanced at Jillian, whose mouth curled to a subtle smile, a twinkle in her green eyes. Fredrick felt a kind of lightness inside his core.

"No, I can tell. She's a real daddy's girl."

"You think so?" Fredrick laughed. "I'm not so sure."

Chelss paused. "I'm not close to my parents. My dad was away a lot. And when he wasn't, he liked to drink and fight, especially with my mom. Mom was always working, mostly temporary and part time gigs. I think it's hard for me to find friends. I always push them away. I didn't really have someone I could depend on all that much, someone I could trust. My mother tried her best, but she had other worries. Eventually she left." She snorted gently. "Except for boys. They like me, especially if they're trying to get laid. I guess they look at me as some kind of conquest."

Fredrick sighed.

"At least they would give me attention. That was something I craved, I guess, even though I hated them." Chelss sighed. "But Cyth was different. She was always so persistent. She would never stop trying to get close. I think I really needed that." Chelss sniffed. "She was someone who was so honest about her own feelings, even if they were incredibly raw and painful." Her voice cracked. She lifted her hand and dabbed the sides of her eyes with her forefinger. "I just hope I can see her again."

Fredrick smiled warmly. "I promise, we'll find her. One way or another, we will."

The train rattled and squealed, its inner LED lights flashing off and on as it whooshed! into a curve.

And then.

A figure appeared at the opposite end of the train, hooded, its long flaps waving with the rocking rhythm of the car. It moved towards the trio. Fredrick's body stiffened as he cast his arm in front of Chelss. Jillian sat forward and glared.

The figure paused and then pulled its hood down. "Well, Mr. Munchen, Ms. Crenshaw, it certainly is good to see you again."

"Dr. Onu?" said Fredrick. He and Jillian exchanged glances.

CHAPTER 36

Blood and Seduction

Griddish, Ashen Fissure, Sanguine Heap

Cythiria gazed across the brown and yellow plains from atop the Fortress of Sanguine Heap. She heard the strange words of Rive Amber as she stood next to her, and her stomach turned.

Who is Matere Songgaard?

"Matere Songgaard is spreading discontent among our people," said Rive. She gazed at Cythiria, her eyes sharp, yet pleading. Her lip grew to a quivering scowl. "He seduces Slaves, promising them comfort. Currently he operates out of the Dusk Quadrant."

"The Dusk Quadrant…," said Cythiria.

Rive made a quick pirouette. Cythiria followed. The two walked along the ramparts and turned down a dark, narrow corridor, which emptied into a small chamber. Rive paused in front of a glimmering, holographic projection. She stood aside and motioned for Cythiria to stand next to her. Cythiria stepped up and looked into the glimmering field of light. A moment later, she could see her own reflection. She glanced away and then returned her gaze to herself, looking up and down the reflected image of her own body. Her hair had returned to its previous thick, dark locks. Her body was strong, confident, like that of a fighter. It was even stronger now, stronger than it had been when she was in Nissy, when she would spar with Rive Amber.

But still, there are those scars. She glanced down at the crisscrossed scars on her arm. She turned her attention to her face. *And those eyes. They're different now. I'm not a child anymore.* She glanced at the scars on her forehead, those two tiny craters that she received as a child when she first arrived on Var 7. *But still, I don't belong here, not if I can't access the Tenddrome. I'll always be alone, always isolated from everyone else.* She thought about Chelss, about her long, brown hair, her cool, hazel-colored eyes.

Cythiria's ears pricked up at the sound of shuffling feet behind her. On either side, a Mechanic Class Slave stepped up. Cythiria felt hands on her body, which clenched and stiffened at their invasive touch. She glanced at Rive Amber, who returned a reassuring nod. She relaxed. Her clothes were pulled off piece by piece, until her body stood bare in front of the holographic reflection. She felt a damp chill as a moldy-smelling breeze wafted through the chamber from the twisting depths of Sanguine Heap. She shivered as she wrapped her arms around her chest and waist.

Rive gazed upon the Mechanic Class Slave. "You're beautiful, Cythiria."

Cythiria felt her neck and face grow warm. "No, I'm not. I...."

She felt new clothes pulled over her head, clothes that squeezed and pressed against her body. She felt herself pushed down onto a chair. Fingers pulled at her hair, poked her face, scratched her eyes and lips. She looked into the reflective surface of the holographic projection, and then looked away for a brief moment. She returned her gaze to those eyes that looked back at her. Eyes that were hollow, tired, and strange, unfamiliar. *Those are not my eyes. That is not my face.*

She saw the reflection of Rive as she stepped towards her. She felt her face move close to her own. She heard a whisper, she felt it in her ear, as if the words themselves had grown their own legs and were crawling deep inside. "You *are* beautiful, Cythiria. Use that to your advantage. That, and your blindness."

My blindness.

Cythiria stood on the cobbled surface of the inner courtyard of Sanguine Heap. She pulled her arms close to her body as Bestiar Class Slaves strolled by and gazed at her with their probing eyes. Sharp glances that moved up and down her body. She shivered as she looked towards the outer gate.

A Vérkatros appeared, stepping towards her with its long, spidery legs, its streamline body tilting from side to side, its antennae flicking seemingly random patterns. "Blinky," she said, a wide smile crossing her face. She jogged towards the Vérkatros, whose skin flashed orange and red, and pressed her body against his, spreading her arms across his body. "Blinky, I'm so happy you came." She stepped back and gazed into his round, airy eyes and grimaced. She started to sniffle and sob. "I'm so scared, Blinky. My heart is beating so fast. Rive wants me to…." She lifted her hands to her eyes and wiped away forming tears. "I feel sick. I don't want to do this, Blinky. I don't know if I can. I…."

Blinky's skin grew warm, the shimmering colors morphing to purple and blue. He retracted his legs, allowing his chassis to rest on the courtyard's surface. Cythiria sighed deeply and stood up. "I suppose there's nothing I can do. Rive is depending on me. She says it's very important that I…kill that man. A man I don't even know. She said he's an abomination, a problem to us Slaves. I don't know why she hates him so much. But I have to do what Rive asks of me. She was there when I nearly…." Cythiria looked down and gazed at the crisscrossed scars on the inside of her forearm. "She saved me. I owe her my life." She looked into Blinky's round eyes. "Can you help me, Blinky? Can you be there for me?" She gazed at the small purple ribbon, which was still tied to one of his antennae. It was ragged, and its color faded. It fluttered in the cool, gentle breeze that blew through the inner courtyard. Cythiria's throat tightened, her lips quivered, and tears streamed in slim rivulets down her cheek. She swallowed hard and then faced Blinky.

She pulled herself up onto his back. His body shuddered and then rose. He turned and lurched forward, through the courtyard and under the gate. They *whooshed!* across dry, hissing grass, the cool, moist Griddish air whipping through Cythiria's short, dark hair. To one side, the ruins of Ashen Fissure jutted upwards towards the dome's inner apex.

Binky pressed forward, hovering upon the plains until they reached a depression. Blinky hovered to a stop. Cythiria paused. She held her breath for a moment. She could feel the heavy beat of her heart in her chest. She dismounted from Blinky's back, stroking his warm, shimmering skin with her hand.

"Is this it?" said Cythiria, as she gazed into the depression. From where she stood, the grass covered plains descended in a steep slope. At the bottom, a gateway, from which emerged bodies that seemed to swerve randomly as they walked. Above, canopies floated in the air, staggered in step-like fashion, and casting deeper levels of shadow the closer one got to the gateway.

Cythiria held her arms around her waist and shuddered. She turned towards Blinky. "I guess I have to go now. Could you wait for me, Blinky? Could you wait until I return?" The Vérkatros' skin shimmered red and orange, morphing into blue and purple. "Are you scared like me, Blinky? Those colors, do they mean you're afraid? Because I am." She held her hand up. "Look, I'm trembling like a leaf."

She stretched her arms upon Blinky's body and sighed deeply. She stood straight, sniffling and wiping her eyes with the back of her hands. She unzipped her jacket, letting it fall onto the grass. She bent over and pulled off her boots, then her pants that fit like loose, airy overalls. She gazed down at her own body, her slender arms and legs. She felt her short hair brush against her neck in the cool breeze. She felt tight clothes press against her body. She smelled a spicy perfume waft from her shoulders.

She gazed towards the distant gateway. She stepped forward, her feet turning and twisting on the rugged, grassy surface, walking and sliding unsteadily until she reached the bottom of the depression. She stepped onto a tiled surface. Her boots echoed a tinny tap as she walked towards the yellow and red illuminated gateway. A man stepped out and staggered towards her, his eyes glassy and bloodshot. He gazed at her a moment, smiled, and then staggered away. Cythiria felt her heart skip and jump in her chest.

She passed others, Slaves of various classes, she assumed. Maybe they were like her. A Mechanic Class Slave. Or, since Rive started leading them, a Bestiar. *There's no one like me. I'm the only one here who can't access the Tenddrome. I don't belong here.* These Slaves looked tired, their bodies bent and worn. They glanced at Cythiria as she passed by, momentarily, and then, they returned to their own, internal worlds.

Cythiria took a deep breath. She stepped towards the gateway, pausing at the tall arch upon whose stone surfaces were carved patterns in bas relief. She gazed into the gateway. Its portal glowed invitingly. Cythiria stood straight and stroked her clothes, as if to banish away any wrinkles. She lifted her head and pointed her nose stoically forward. She took another deep breath, mumbling, "Here we go," as she stepped into the portal.

Dark, inky blackness enveloped Cythiria. Her chest tightened and her breath grew raspy. She stepped forward, groping and clawing the air in front of her. She sniffed. The air smelled of spice, like cinnamon. Her body grew heavy, numb, her muscles that had been tight and sinewy, felt relaxed, almost rubbery.

The darkness faded and was replaced by a deep, red glow. The wide corridor was warm, its walls hidden in the deep shadows that clung to its fringes. Cythiria stepped forward. Before her, she could hear the slap of water against stone. She paused and peered into the dark void that was perhaps a lake or a sea. The air smelled fragrant, joyful. She looked up. A dark sky was illuminated by a large, white orb, and dots of light like stars were scattered about, sparkling and twirling in a rhythmic dance.

Along the shore of the water, she could see people who were sitting, talking, embracing. She could hear giggles, moans, and chattering.

She turned and walked down the corridor. A man paused and gazed at her, his bleary eyes moving up and down her body. He smirked, as a crooked smile crossed his face. Cythiria felt her neck and face grow warm, her chest and stomach tighten. Her body started to tingle. She stepped backwards, pressing her back against the wall of the corridor. She lifted her hand and touched her neck and ear. The man stepped towards her, his groping eyes gazing into hers. He stepped closer. Cythiria felt her body tremble.

She let out a quick breath and then bit her lip. "No," she whispered. *I must do what Rive has sent me to do. I must find…him.* She stepped aside, slipping under the outstretched arm of the man. She ran down the corridor and paused, glancing behind her, as she fell onto her hands and knees. Her chest heaved, her breath grew ragged, her body felt warm and tingling. *What is this place? Why am I feeling like this?*

"In the Dusk Quadrant, all Slaves are equal, and each Slave is isolated from the Tenddrome." She recalled Rive's words. "Each Slave is equally blind. But you, Cythiria, have been blind nearly your entire life. That is why you have the advantage."

Blind my entire life.

Cythiria stood up and continued down the corridor. She could hear voices, laughing, fighting, bickering. She continued to walk, the heels of her shoes clicking along the stone cobbled surface, echoing sharply along the shadowed walls.

She paused, following a cluster of echoing voices, until she arrived at a wide, round gateway whose latticed frame was colored a deep red. She stepped in, pausing as she lifted her hand to her nose. That smell, the spicy aroma of cinnamon was strong here. Through the gateway was a wide chamber, and in the center, a table. Around the table, chairs, with people seated, drinking elegant glasses of yellow-colored liquid.

She glanced around. Mechanic Class Slaves gazed languidly as they sat at the center table, some, their heads resting on their crossed arms. Others were drinking Waftring, talking, smiling, touching each other.

Cythiria's eyes glanced along the walls of the chamber, at the divan and sofas that were filled with people. Some leaned into each other, embracing.

"Care to sit?" one asked, as she looked up at Cythiria, her hollow eyes bleary, unfocused, distant. Cythiria shook her head.

And then, she saw *him*. Her heart started to pound in her chest. Her legs trembled as if they would turn and dash away on their own. Her neck flushed and prickled at the breaking of a new sweat.

Yes, it was him. It was Matere Songgaard. She recalled the images of him, the ones that had been shown to her by Rive. His disheveled hair was gray, his cheek and chin rough and unshaven. His arm was a tangle of wiry tendrils, blue, metallic. Like that of a machine, or a robot, or even a Vérkatros.

She reached for her Plaxis Strand, pulling it out and flicking her wrist so that it lit up the room in a cool, blue light. She could hear gasps, some shouts and screams, shuffling feet, falling chairs as it licked the floors with its plasmic arc, emitting a sharp, tinny whistle.

The man named Matere Songgaard turned his head to face her. His body followed. A smile crossed his face.

"So, you've finally awakened, I see. I knew it would happen one day, Cythiria."

Cythiria paused. "How do you know my name?"

"Oh, I know you quite well." He paused. "I suppose my dear friend Rive Amber has sent you?"

"I…." She gripped her Plaxis, and her hand trembled.

"Under what pretense, may I ask? I suppose she says that I am corrupting you Slaves? That would be so typical of her." He took a step towards her. "Yes, yes, Rive and I go way back. Although I wouldn't exactly call us friends. No, maybe 'frenemies' is the right word. I can hear her now. 'That man is taking my children away from me. The same children that I send to the slaughter on a daily basis.'"

"Shut up!" screamed Cythiria.

Matere took another step forward. "Even Slaves need hope. And sometimes hope means removing themselves from what binds them to their world." He paused. "Did you ever wonder why Slaves love their Waftring so much? I have. I've come to the conclusion that it fulfills a very specific desire. Do you know what this is, Cythiria?"

Cythiria shook her head.

"It's the desire for death, Cythiria. For non-existence, if only for a very short time. So, in the end, Rive Amber is really just fulfilling a very important need, but on a grand, dramatic scale, which is, honestly, so typical of her."

Matere took another step closer to Cythiria.

"I can see you're scared, Cythiria. I can see it in your body. You're shaking. You can barely stand here, you just want to run away, don't you, Cythiria?

Why is that? Are you puzzled by what you see? Frightened by your very first act of murder? Do you wonder how it is that I know you so well? That I know your name? Your face? Well, you see," he reached his hand towards his trousers. "You are my invention." He pulled out a Plaxis Strand, igniting it and slashing, and then quickly striking Cythiria on the shoulder.

Cythiria screamed and stumbled backwards. From her shoulder and chest flowed a deep crimson. "But how?"

"How?" Matere slashed again, missing Cythiria as she stepped to the side. "Don't you think it's a little strange how you perceive the world? Did you ever wonder why you saw things the way you did?"

"I…." Blood dripped from her chest onto the floor below. Her vision blurred and her body grew numb.

"Did you ever think that it was strange the way you saw the Vérkatrae? You do see them differently, don't you?" Matere slashed again, striking Cythiria on her chest.

Cythiria groaned, falling onto one knee. She could smell the rusty scent of the blood, mixed with smell of Waftring spice. Her breath grew short. *Blinky. You. Your skin. The colors.*

"You're just a product of my experiments, Cythiria. Before you were even born, I created you…."

Created….

Was I…created?

By this Engineer?

"Do you remember?" came Matere's voice. The sound of his voice was close to her ears, echoing whispers that seeped into her skull. She felt a wide, strong hand grasp her throat. She reached up and grabbed hold of his forearm. The skin was hard, yet soft and warm. Like Blinky's skin. Like the skin of all the Vérkatrae. She could see that face. The gray hair, the silver-framed glasses. And then, the flash of a memory.

"I couldn't move or breathe. The air around me was chilly. It was dark at first. When I woke up, I can't remember if I could see or not. Not the real world, not a place of things and people. I tried to move my arms, to reach out and touch the world around me. I knew then that I was inside something. A box. Or, a tube, maybe. I could feel it press against me, squeeze my body.

"I was still. My body didn't have the rhythms that it did before. No regular breathing. No heartbeat. Just complete stillness. Only total silence.

"And then, a light appeared. I could see an image, blurred at first. A head, maybe, looking through a window. I could see steam fill that box that I lay in. I could hear a hissing sound. A thump, a muffled voice. Words. Words that became clearer for a moment and then faded in and out like some ocean wave. I felt a shock deep inside my body, a pain so intense that I wanted to scream. That I just wanted to die.

"And then I was still again. Darkness surrounded me. The darkness was thick and heavy, weighing down my arms and legs and pressing against my chest. I saw points of light. Single, bright points, like needle pricks. And then more appeared. So many that they seemed to light the entire space around me. And they cast a warmth that made me feel comforted, like I was home. I felt…light. As if I had a burden that was removed from me.

"And then, my body burst apart, into many points of light. How could I see this? How could I feel it? I had no body left, no eyes that could see. And yet, I felt that I belonged to something. Something so large that I could never fathom its depth. I was a part of that, now. Like I've never been before.

"But still, something was wrong. Something that ate away at my soul. My soul. As if that ever really existed. It was something strange. Something new.

"And then, the world was dark again. And I was me again, whatever that means. I saw through eyes. I listened to whispers from the Tenddrome. I learned from other Nodes. Like all Slaves do. But something was different about me. I didn't know what it was back then. I still don't know what it is about me. A type of lens, maybe. A view of the world."

She paused, choking not just from the hand grasped around her neck, but from a welling deep within.

"Blinky," she whispered. *It was you. You were the one I saw differently. You were my connection to the Tenddrome, and the Vérkatrae. They all said Slaves cannot really understand the Vérkatrae, because there is nothing about the Vérkatrae that can be understood. But you're different, Blinky. Or maybe, I'm different.*

Cythiria stood up, her body slumped, whistling plasmic arcs licking the floor from her ignited Plaxis Strand. The scent of burning blood and metal filled the chamber. Cythiria felt her stomach turn, nearly gagging and heaving as she gripped her chest and shoulder with her free arm.

"I don't care," she grumbled hoarsely. "I don't care about any of that." She stood straight, sharp pain coursing through her body, blood dripping from her wounds. *It's ok. Blood means nothing. Rive taught me that. She taught me to be strong, to fight back. To gain what I lost. I see that now.* Cythiria coughed. She could taste the rusty aroma of blood in her mouth. "I don't care about any of that." She bound forward, raising her arm, striking. Matere stepped to one side, turning his back to Cythiria. She pivoted, striking as he fell forward, slashing his back with her hissing, whistling Plaxis. He tumbled to the ground and lay still. Cythiria dropped her Plaxis and fell to her knees. She glanced at Matere's body. Her vision blurred. She fell forward. The chamber started to spin. And then darkness.

Cythiria felt her own body rise as it was lifted and placed on a hard surface. She opened her eyes. "Blinky?" She gazed into his round, airy eyes. His skin flashed deep purple, then red, then gray. She felt a cool breeze against her face, brushing through her short hair. She looked up at the white sky, and she squinted at the gentle light. "Blinky, you came for me." She tried to move her body, which felt lifeless and numb. She felt a welling sensation in her chest, her throat tightening. Tears streamed down her cheeks and splashed silently onto the surface of the Vérkatros, of Blinky. "I'm so sorry, Blinky. I didn't mean to…. But you came for me. I'm…happy." She sniffled and sobbed. "Tell Rive that I did what she wanted me to do. Tell her that I'm grateful for her. I finally gained what I lost." And then, the world faded to darkness.

Cythiria felt herself cradled in strong arms, her body rocked by a steady gait. She opened her eyes. "Rive…."

Rive looked down at her. "I'm sorry, Cythiria. I didn't want to…."

"Blinky saved me."

"Blinky?"

"The Vérkatros. He saved me."

Rive shook her head. "Vérks can't save anyone, Cythiria. They are just machines."

"No, Blinky is not just a machine. Please, Rive, take care of Blinky. He is my…friend."

Rive glanced over her shoulder at the resting, gray colored Vérkatros. "Vérkatrae are not our friends, Cythiria. They are simply there to carry out tasks."

Cythiria started to sob. "No, Blinky is my friend. Please, take care of him."

Rive sighed. "Ok, Cythiria. I'll take care of Blinky." Rive scowled as she carried Cythiria into the inner courtyard of Sanguine Heap.

Rive Amber walked along a corridor within Sanguine Heap. The dark shadows were punctuated by the electric blue hum of occasional plasmic torches that were mounted to its walls. She sniffed the dank, humid air, the smell of rust and corrosion that seemed to permeate every corner, every crack of her fortress.

She emerged onto the roof. She walked to the edge, her heels clicking firm and steady. She gazed through steel ramparts at the distant horizon, the clusters of Slipshot Silos that littered the landscape as they shot towards the inner apex of the dome. She gazed across the plains towards the distant ruins of the Council of Engineer Class Citizens. She recalled that moment, it seemed like ages ago, when the Vérkatrae bound across the now burnt plains and brought destruction to the Council. An act of declared war, one that she was able to broker with the Vérkatrae. The Mechanics did not control the Vérkatrae. No, the Mechanics could only hope that they held similar goals. At least for now.

Rive scoffed. "What must they think of us now?" *The Engineer Class Citizens were once so mighty, so arrogant. And now, they hide like rats.*

No matter. Griddish will soon be ours. Then we can change the course of this world. We can rid ourselves of the Slipshot, the Tenddrome. Even the Vérkatrae. We will determine our own futures and let the Vars rot on their own, for all I care.

Rive sighed deeply. The air smelled like smoke and decay. *Cythiria did well. Because of her, we can now bring this situation to a final conclusion. We can push Griddish to the brink. And when we do, that is when change can occur.*

Rive turned, her nose high, jaw clenched, her hands gripped tightly behind her back. A quivering scowl grew upon her face. "So," she said. "Let us begin."

CHAPTER 37

A New Arrival

Griddish, Ashen Fissure, The Bastion

The war has devastated our world.

Judith Merlon stood before a holographic projection. Lines of characters scurried within a three-dimensional sphere, casting a nervous blue flashing light upon the mirror-like floors and walls of the chamber.

Judith sighed, breathing deeply of the filtered air. Long, snaking tubes ran along the walls and ceiling and set an almost rhythmic, breathing pulse to the structure known as The Bastion.

Judith tilted her head as she gazed at the flashing holographic projection, the stream of characters and the color patches that morphed and turned in front of her eyes.

"We can't continue this," she mumbled. She closed her eyes for a moment. The image of a pair of color patches, set one above the other, pivoted upon a vertical axis.

The infrastructure is at its limit.

The data was clear. System failures had become more common. The Griddish ecosystem, the network of Nodes that tied all of reality together, was brittle.

Judith sighed, her brow pursed. "If this continues, there will no longer be a Griddish."

She stood up and paced the floor in front of her workstation. Surely, she was not the only one who noticed the trends. The analysis would have been shared among all the Admin Class Slaves. After all, it was their job to make sure that the Griddish systems operated with the utmost efficiency. All the Slipshot Silos, all the devices that were attached to them, that managed them, all the Vérkatrae, all the Slaves, even the dome itself, they were all connected to each other, dependent on each other. If one Node within the network were to fail, there would be errors that would need to be fixed. The Mechanics would do that. But if many Nodes were to fail all at the same time, there would be a series of cascading failures that would result in a catastrophe that Griddish itself had never before witnessed, not even in its eons of existence.

The Slaves were at war with the Engineers. At least, in the past, they had worked together. But no more. "There must be something we can do," mumbled Judith. "Or, something I can do."

She sighed deeply, as she wrapped her arms around her waist. "But what could a technician like me do?" Admins Class Slaves, after all, were designed to monitor things. To make recommendations and provide maintenance specifications to the Mechanics. "The Mechanics. How fortunate they are to be free to move about in this world, and travel to the Vars."

Judith turned and skittered through the corridor, the silvery, almost glass-like walls reflecting a steady, blue light throughout. She turned and walked towards a door, pausing as it opened before her. She stepped in.

A figure stood hunched over a panel that was set in the middle of the chamber. Judith stepped forward, her uncertain footfalls pattering nervously, her breath quick.

"I was wondering when you would appear." The figure turned towards Judith.

"Benj, I…."

He stood tall. His lithe body was slender, almost delicate. His hair was white. He gazed at Judith, his gentle, gray eyes locking onto hers. A nearly indiscernible smile crossed his face.

Judith glanced away. "Always probing, huh, Benj?"

Benj smiled a bit more widely. He lifted his arms and placed his hands on her shoulders, barely touching them while he held an arm-length's distance. "Of course not. I am simply available to you when you need me."

Judith felt her neck and cheeks grow warm. She lifted her hands to cover the latter. "Sure, you are."

He let his arms fall to his side. "So, what brings you here in such a hurry?"

Judith pouted. "As if you don't know."

"Now, why would I?"

"Cuz you know everything about everyone."

"I only know what you choose to share with me." He paused. "So far, you've shared nothing about your current state of mind."

Judith sighed deeply. "God, Benj, you're such a pain sometimes."

Benj smiled. "Am I? I don't wish to be. Not to you, Judith."

Judith snorted. "I'm sure you enjoy it."

"As a Psyche Class Slave, my duty is to help whenever I am needed."

Judith shook her head. She lifted her hand and waved it from side to side. "As if. I know you say that to all the Slaves."

"Only to you, my dear."

"Liar," she mumbled.

"So," started Benj, his voice steady, gentle, "What brings you to my chamber in such a hurry?"

Judith paused. "I want to do something, Benj."

"I think you have plenty to do already, my dear Admin. It seems you and your ilk are quite busy these days."

"I want to do more."

"More?" Benj raised his brows as he gazed at Judith with calm yet probing gray eyes.

"I've always envied the Mechanics. I mean, they are always so awesome, going around in the field, traveling to the Vars, and all."

Benj smiled mysteriously. "I hardly think you have the constitution to take on the role of a Mechanic."

"What's that supposed to mean, Benj?" pouted Judith.

"Your slight frame, your light skin, your pale eyes, those are things that are easily broken in the field."

Judith sighed. "I just…can't stand sitting around while this war tears our world apart."

"So, then, what would you suggest?"

"I want to join the war," she said. Her voice was tense, excited. A bright smile crossed her face, her eyes distant, as if she were looking into the future.

Benj paused. "I have to say, you would be the first Admin to cross over to the side of the Mechanics. This is *their* war, after all. Are you sure they'd even accept someone like you?"

"Someone like me? That's mean, Benj."

"If you haven't noticed, you're not like the Mechanics. Not in any way whatsoever. In fact, Admins and Mechanics are known to be antagonistic towards one another. But even more importantly, are you willing to face the prospect of death? There's a certain probability that you'd get killed, especially someone who has never been trained in combat their whole life."

She hesitated. "I can learn, Benj."

Benj gazed into her eyes. She looked at him and then glanced away, casting her gaze to the floor. "Is there more to it than that?" he said.

Judith's neck and cheeks grew warm. "What do you mean?"

"I think you know what I mean."

Judith sighed. "I want to try to end this war, Benj. Even if I can't do much, maybe I can have some kind of an effect. Even if it's tiny, insignificant, it's better than what I'm doing here, which is looking at a bunch of data that pretty much tells us that we're all royally screwed."

Natty smiled. "'Royally screwed.' Your use of Varling colloquialisms is quite humorous."

"I've been studying."

"I'm sure you have." Benj paused. "You being such a fan of the Mechanics and the Vars. Well, if your mind is determined in this path you have chosen for yourself, then who am I to stop you?"

Judith smiled, and her eyes brightened. "What about The Bastion? Surely this building will not let me go," she said, her hands held up as her eyes skittered along the glassy, shimmering walls.

"Systems are made to be fooled. The Bastion is not a prison, Judith. But I understand your point. We all have our place in this world, and we should be content with that. At least, that's how we were supposed to be designed." He turned and glanced Judith up and down. "Some of us, at least." He sighed gently. "Just leave it to me."

Judith stepped forward and put her arms around his waist, pulling him close. "Thanks, Benj. I knew I could rely on you."

Benj took Judith's arms and gently pushed them away. "So, what is your plan?"

"Go to Sanguine Heap."

"Ah, the home of our dear friend Rive Amber."

Judith sighed. "I want to do this, Benj, but I won't lie to you. I'm scared."

"The future can be scary sometimes."

She stepped towards Benj again and pushed her body against his, laying her head on his chest. Benj wrapped his arms around her this time. She started to sniffle, and her eyes grew damp. "You want to go with me?"

"Oh, I am of no use to someone like Rive Amber. Other than repairing her broken Slaves, that is."

"Doesn't have use for a sissy boy like you in the battlefield," she said, laughing through teary eyes. She pulled away. "Fine," she said. She lifted her hand and rubbed her nose, which grew a shade of pink. "Thanks a lot, Mr. Unreliable."

"It is always my pleasure."

"What do I even bring with me to Sanguine Heap?" Judith glanced around her small living chamber. She sat on the pallet that was her bed, sighed quickly and then stood up. She walked a few steps towards an enclosure. She blinked quickly, and a door *whooshed!* open. She glanced inside at the contents of the closet. Mostly light-colored clothes designed for Admins, delicate, almost airy. *Do Mechanics even dress like this?* Not likely. She shook her head and pulled out a few items, a green-striped jacket, a top and some shorts, and pulled them on. She took out a few more items and tossed them onto her sleeping pallet. She stepped one foot into the closet and groped around in a pile of items that lay on the floor, producing a backpack with an attached container for fluids. "It's important to stay hydrated," she muttered. She lifted it up triumphantly, a wide smile crossing her face, and stepped towards her sleeping pallet, upon which she plunked herself down and sighed. She picked up the clothes, turning them in her hand, feeling the fabric between her fingers, gazing at the shimmering, almost holographic colors. She shook her head and stuffed them one at a time into the pack. She stood up, glanced around the room and quickly stepped towards a countertop. She blinked. A projected image of her own face was cast into the space in front of her. She gazed at the image that looked back at her, especially the almost airy, blue eyes. "Will I even survive out there?" she mumbled as she touched her cheek with her hand. *I'm not equipped for doing the job of Mechanics. I'd be wasting their time.* She paused, shook her head, and turned. She quickly grabbed the backpack and walked towards the door of the small chamber. She paused, glanced over her shoulder, and blinked once. The door opened and she stepped into the corridor.

She sighed. Her stomach turned at the sound of the hollow taps of her feet on the floor. She moved more quickly, as the blue electric torches mounted on the wall sped by.

She entered a large chamber. She glanced around at the towering gate that stood closed before her. Her eyes followed the featureless, shimmering walls, the white tubes that ran along the high ceiling and corners. She smelled deeply of the clean, filtered air. "Welp, this is it," she mumbled, pouting slightly. "I guess Benj is not going to see me off. Too bad. I can never really get close to him. He's so…distant."

She turned and walked towards the gate whose surface was smooth and featureless. She blinked and it parted from the center along an invisible seam, pausing at the point in which it provided a gap wide enough for Judith to walk through. *Looks like Benj got it all arranged. The Bastion won't even miss me.* She stepped through the gate and into the outer courtyard. She paused, glancing along the distant horizon, the gentle green hills, the clusters of Slipshot Silos stretching towards the inner apex of the dome like slender needles. She smelled the fragrant air. She stepped along the metal-tiled surface of the courtyard, cringing just a bit at the hollow tap of her quick feet. She paused at a resting Vérkatros, blinked once, and then mounted. A moment later, the Vérkatros hovered and lurched forward. The cool, Griddish wind brushed against her face and through her hair, while the grassy plains of Ashen Fissure rushed beneath the hovering Vérkatros.

"Well, here we go," she mumbled. She glanced over her shoulder at The Bastion, its smooth, shimmering walls stretching towards the inner apex of the dome. She sighed. *I may never see this place again.* She shook her head. *Imagine me going off to Sanguine Heap. I've barely been outside my own room, let alone roaming around in the wild.*

Judith turned her gaze forward. The wide plains, which had once been a deep color of verdant, were now a shade of brown. "The systems are definitely failing," she mumbled. *Unless we can intervene and reverse the process of degradation, I don't know what the future will be for us.*

CHAPTER 38

An Appeal

Var 7, Farth, Nissy

"Dr. Onu," said Fredrick, looking up at the figure, his silver-bearded face and bald head revealed after he pulled down his hood. The train rocked and clattered as it hurled along the tracks of the subway, the steady, repetitive pulse of fluorescent light casting a thin haze of whiteness on the car's interior.

"Mr. Munchen. I thought we had an agreement."

"An agreement?"

"Outside of the classroom, you may call me Jeremiah." He paused. "It has a nicer ring to it, wouldn't you agree?"

Fredrick glanced sidelong at Jillian, who stood up and faced Jeremiah, her green eyes burning, a scowl crossing her face, her red hair seeming to be an even brighter shade of red.

"You son of a bitch," she hissed.

Jeremiah smiled gently. "Why such anger, my dear Ms. Crenshaw?"

"Don't give me that crap!" she said louder this time. "You know fucking well what you did. You had this whole thing planned, didn't you!"

"Jillian…," whispered Fredrick, pleadingly.

"Shut up, Fredrick," she hissed. She returned her attention to Jeremiah. "If it weren't for you, we wouldn't be in this mess right now. You acted like you were our friend, but this is what you really wanted. You wanted to see the end of Earth. And now you want to take Cythiria away from us." She stepped closer to Jeremiah, glaring at him with sharp, angry eyes. "What are you really after? The destruction of Farth, too?"

Jeremiah paused. "A single individual cannot hold such power over life and death."

"Is that so?" said Jillian, her voice filled with derision.

"Jillian…," pleaded Fredrick, again.

"Indeed," said Jeremiah. "That power lies in the hands of Griddish."

"Even for a Vérkatros like yourself?" Jeremiah stood silent, a look of apprehension on his face. "Don't act so surprised," continued Jillian. "The Vérkatrae were the ones that ended Earth as we know it. They are the ones who forced us here to Farth. And Cythiria has had nothing but problems since she arrived. That's awfully cruel of you, don't you think? Abandoning a child to a place where she can never fit in, where she'll always be ostracized, just because she can barely survive here." Jillian's face was flushed, her lips spreading to a full scowl. "So now what?"

Chelss, who sat quietly next to Fredrick a moment ago, stood up and faced Jeremiah. "I'm looking for Cythiria!" she shouted.

Fredrick stood up and glared at Jillian for a brief moment and returned his attention to Jeremiah. "We need to initialize a Perispike," he said.

"And why would you want to do that?"

"So that we can return to Griddish."

"Griddish is the curse of all that exists in the universe," said Jeremiah. "Why would you want to return to such a place?"

"Because Cythiria is there," said Chelss.

Jeremiah paused. "What makes you so certain?"

Chelss opened her bag, revealing the scratched and dented spike. "She found this where Cythiria disappeared," said Fredrick, nodding towards the Perispike and then glancing at Jillian. He sighed. "I think Rive Amber took her back to Griddish." He paused. "I was going to give up on Cyth. I figured she'd be better off in Griddish, because she could never really adjust to her life in Nissy. She was always in survival mode, always on the edge. I always thought it was a matter of time, that I had no right to interfere. But then I met Chelss, and I realized that I do have a right to interfere. Cyth belongs with us, and we need to do everything we can to get her back."

"Are you sure that's what she wants?" said Jeremiah. He looked at Fredrick and then Jillian.

"It's what I want," said Jillian.

Fredrick sighed. "I don't know if that's what Cythiria wants. But at least she should know that we're here for her. That she shouldn't feel lonely, because someone does care about her. That's why we need to initialize the Perispike. We need to get to Griddish."

"And once you are there, what will you do?"

Fredrick glanced at Chelss and held her gaze momentarily. "I figure someone will find us."

Jeremiah smiled. "That is hardly a strategy."

"Well, it's the best I got." Fredrick stood up, holding his stance despite the rock and sway of the train. "And I know one thing: Only someone who has access to the Tenddrome can initialize the Perispike."

Jeremiah paused, his gaze growing distant for a brief moment. "Preparations have to be made," he said, his eyes now sharp and focused. "Be ready for me."

He pulled up his hood and turned. A moment later, the train whooshed to a stop. The doors hissed and rattled open, and he was gone.

Fredrick sighed deeply. He turned towards Chelss. "I guess we have to wait," he said.

Chelss clenched her teeth, her eyes sharp, challenging. "I don't want to wait. I want to go after Cyth now." She looked at Jillian.

"Me too," agreed Jillian.

"For now, it's out of our hands," said Fredrick.

"Can you trust this Jeremiah person?" asked Chelss.

Fredrick paused. "Yes…and no."

CHAPTER 39

An Introduction, A Beginning

Griddish, Ashen Fissure, Sanguine Heap

The dark walls of Sanguine Heap rose from the brown and yellow grass of the Ashen Plains. Judith shuddered as she gazed at the rust-smudged ramparts that stood atop the sheer, cliff-like surface. She blinked, transmitting a Tenddrome request for the Vérkatros to stop as they approached the outer courtyard.

Judith dismounted the Vérkatros. She looked around the quiet, empty courtyard. She stepped forward as her heels clicked on the cobbled surface. She passed under the courtyard's main archway, gazing at the twisting, stone-carved figures captured in bas-relief. She walked forward, into the inner courtyard, glancing across clusters of broken rods and devices that collected themselves into ankle-high piles of junk. "Awfully messy, aren't they," she mumbled. She pulled her green and white jacket close to her body, hunching her shoulders as if she were trying to shrink into herself. *You'd think they'd be better at keeping things organized, since they oversee the maintenance of Griddish and the Vars.*

Judith sighed and stepped towards a tall gate, which was shut. She closed her eyes and issued a request.

"Arriving, please acknowledge."

"Name?"

"Judith Merlon."

"Class?"

"Admin."

"Station?"

Judith rolled her eyes. *Why so many questions? As if they care. The way this place is organized, you'd think they let anything slide.* "The Bastion, Section III, Systems Analyst."

The ground beneath Judith's feet rumbled and vibrated, followed by the creaking and squealing of rusty hinges. The gate spread apart from its center seam, revealing a dark corridor inside.

"Well, that was easy," she mumbled. "I didn't sense any queries from the Tenddrome. These Mechanics must be sloppy. Or, they're sneaky like Benj." Judith smiled at the thought of Benj, his cool, gray, probing eyes.

She shook her head as if to cast away her rising thoughts. She glanced over her shoulder, across the empty courtyard, and then peered into the corridor. She sniffed. The air smelled of must and dampness. She stepped in. The gate creaked and ground to a close behind her. Judith squinted. The halls were illuminated by a weak blue light from torches mounted upon the walls. She followed them, pulling her arms closer to her body as a chilly, damp breeze blew through the corridor.

She entered the main chamber. She could hear distant chants echoing along the floor and walls, sounding harsh and militaristic, like people striking in rhythm or the clashing of trained weapons to a grim and driving beat. She heard the flap of a bird's wings above her. She looked up and gazed at the skylight, which cast the gentle, white light of Griddish onto the floor below. It seemed so far away from her that her stomach turned as she looked up. She saw the dark bodies of birds as they flew among the rafters and perched along the edge of the skylight.

"So, I'm guessing you're here to drop off a spec," barked a voice. It was strong, confident, sharp.

"I…." Judith glanced at the owner of the voice. She was young, like her, and taller. Her body looked strong, her arms and midsection, which were exposed, chiseled. Her stance was solid, centered, athletic. On her forehead, two small dots ran perpendicular to the bridge of her nose. "No, I want to join," she stammered.

"Join what?"

"Your group?"

"My group?"

"Yes, join your military."

"You're kidding, right?"

"No," said Judith, her voice filled with a sudden sternness. "I'm serious. Is there someone here I can talk to?"

Cythiria scoffed. "I guess Rive would be pretty desperate if she picked up a nerd like you to fight in her war."

"What's that supposed to mean?" whined Judith.

The girl walked up to her, sighed, and lifted her forefinger to her chin. She raised her brow and looked up and down Judith's body. She grimaced. "I don't know, there's really not much to work with here."

"Hey!" shouted Judith, feeling her neck and cheeks grow warm, as she stared at the two dots on this girl's forehead. They looked like scars or maybe…burns. "That's kinda rude, don't you think?"

She scoffed. "That's nothing. Wait till you meet the others. You're gonna think I'm nice compared to them." She paused. A slight smile rose on the corner of her mouth as she watched Judith lower her head, glancing nervously from side to side. "I'm Cythiria," she said.

"Judith."

"Just Judith?"

"Merlon."

"And you're from The Bastion?"

"Yes."

"And you're here because you want to join Rive's army?"

"Yes." Judith pouted.

Cythiria paused. "You *do* know who Rive Amber is, don't you?"

"Of course."

"And you still came?"

"Well, I…um, yeah."

Cythiria smirked. "You know, you might still have a chance to get out. I mean, a scrawny thing like yourself probably won't survive here."

Judith clenched her teeth. "No way," she said, gazing sharply into Cythiria's eyes. "I decided to come, and so here I'll stay."

Cythiria rolled her eyes. She sighed dramatically. "Suit yourself. Don't say I didn't warn you."

The two stood before each other. Cythiria smiled a crooked smirk as she looked down on Judith. Judith looked up at Cythiria, her lips curled to a pouting frown, her blue eyes sharp and stubborn, her jaw clenched and pulsing.

The sound of chanting voices echoing through the corridors broke their deadlocked glare.

"Well, that's not good," started Cythiria.

"What's not good?"

"The Bestiars are coming, no doubt to assemble. If you think I'm a problem, just wait until they show up. One look at a nerdy brat like you and it's over."

Judith glanced down at her clothes, and then at Cythiria, her eyes quivering. "What should I do?"

Cythiria took hold of Judith's hand. "Let's go." She turned and dragged Judith towards a door at the far end of the chamber, stomping forward and then kicking it open. She entered a dark room that smelled of mold, Judith stumbling behind.

"Owww, you're hurting me," Judith whined, as she reached forward and took hold of Cythiria's hand, pulling at her fingers to release her grasp.

"Not until you get changed." Cythiria pulled Judith towards a squat table. "Take them off," she barked.

"Take what off?"

"Your nerd clothes."

"My what?"

"Just do it!"

Judith sighed deeply. She reached her hands down to the bottom of her green-striped jacket and pulled it up over her head. She glanced at Cythiria, who watched her as she undressed. "Do you mind?"

Cythiria rolled her eyes. "It's not like you're all that much to look at," she said, glancing up and down her body.

Judith clicked her tongue. "Could you at least give me a little privacy?"

"Privacy?" shouted Cythiria. "Here?" She lifted her arms and glanced around the chamber. "Where the hell do you think you're going to find privacy?"

Judith sighed quickly. "Fine." Judith pulled the jacket off her arms and lifted it up, looking it up and down. She turned it and placed it on the table, pulling it so that it lay flat upon the surface. She pulled the sleeve down and over, folding it in half, and then from top to bottom, in half again.

"Oh, for fuck's sake," grumbled Cythiria.

"Whaaaat!" whined Judith.

"Can you just hurry up?"

Judith pulled her shorts down around her ankles, and then each leg over her shoes. She lifted the shorts up and folded them in her arms from top to bottom and then placed them gently upon the table. She reached for the jacket and stacked it on top of the shorts. She looked up at Cythiria, her blue eyes large, her lips pouting.

"I can't believe you wore clothes like that all the way here. Like, what were you thinking?" Cythiria sighed and then lifted her finger to her chin and glanced from Judith's head to her feet and back to her head. "You *really* aren't all that much to look at, you know."

"You keep saying that! What's that supposed to mean, anyway?" she cried.

"Kinda scrawny, aren't you?" Cythiria reached forward and poked Judith in her ribs.

"Ow! What'd you do that for?"

"Not sure what Rive is gonna think when she sees you." She poked Judith in the chest.

Judith's lips quivered. Tears formed in her eyes and rolled down her cheeks in slim rivulets. "All you've done is criticize me since I got here. I don't know what I ever did to you, or what I did to deserve this treatment. I came here because I wanted to help. So, if you don't like me, or the way I look, maybe it's better I just leave and get out of your life once and for all. Because it seems like you hate me and would rather have me gone." Judith wrapped her arms around her body and started to sob.

Cythiria sighed. She stepped towards a thin door and pulled it open. She reached in and yanked out a dark colored garment. She returned to the table and tossed the garment onto its surface. "Put that on. It's the smallest size we have."

Judith glanced mournfully towards Cythiria.

"Come on, we don't have much time," pressed Cythiria.

Judith reached towards the garments and separated them. She picked up a pair of loose-fitting, brown colored trousers. She pulled them on, pulling the belt to its smallest size. She reached for the shirt, which was a black colored tank top, and pulled it on. Cythiria shook her head. "They're kinda loose. Well, not much we can do about it. If you survive, you'll be filling them out in no time."

"If I survive," mumbled Judith.

"Just stick with me. I'll make sure you do."

Judith glanced up at Cythiria, frowning. "Really?" she said, a tone of skepticism in her voice.

"Really. I promise." Cythiria smiled gently and then took Judith by the hand, pulling her out of the inner chamber and into the main one. They pushed through groups of sweaty, smudgy bodies, the assembled Bestiar Class Slaves. The chamber echoed with the din of shouting, swearing voices. "Just do what I do," whispered Cythiria. "Don't try to stand out."

Judith glanced around. A heavy smell of musk wafted through the chamber. She coughed and covered her mouth and nose with her hand.

A heavy, solid *thunk!* like the sound of booted footfalls echoed through the chamber. The shouting Bestiars grew silent, stepping into regimental formation. Cythiria stood tall, nodding towards Judith. "Just like me," she whispered. Judith threw back her shoulders and lifted her chin. Her round face and slender neck, her narrow shoulders and her arched back, along with her exaggerated stance, appeared almost child-like. Cythiria chuckled as she gazed upon Judith, her laugh settling to a gentle smile.

"My Bestiars," began a deep and confident voice. Its owner glared at the soldiers, nose and chin high, mouth rising to a near quivering scowl.

"It's Rive Amber," whispered Judith.

"The one and only," mumbled Cythiria.

"She looks…taller."

"Oh, you haven't seen the worst yet."

"What's that supposed to mean?"

"You'll find out." Judith glanced at Cythiria, her eyes wide with fear. "Don't worry about it," said Cythiria. "Just try to blend in."

Judith returned her attention to Rive. "Blend in," she mumbled. "As if."

"We've come a long way," continued Rive, "Since the days when we were mere Mechanic Class Slaves. We lived according to the rules of those who did not understand us. The Engineers, who sought only their own comfort and benefit, while we bore the burden of the Slipshot." Rive placed her hands behind her back and paced slowly, deliberately from side to side. "But that has all changed now. Now, while we fight here, in the fortress of Sanguine Heap, we are poised to change this world. No longer will we be subjected to the whims of the Engineers. No longer will we be the purveyors of tragedy to the Vars. No longer will we depend on the dark designs of the Vérkatrae. Instead, we will determine our own future. We will decide who we will be, and what shall become of us. And we will do this with your strength. My elite Bestiars, you are the future of Griddish. *You* will be the purveyors of change. You will usher in a new era of war, and as a result, a new era of peace."

The Bestiars chanted, striking the ground in rhythm with weapons and boots. Rive glanced at the collection of Bestiars and paused.

"Uh, oh," whispered Cythiria.

"What?"

"She noticed you?"

"Who?"

"Rive."

"What!" said Judith. She looked pleadingly towards Cythiria. "What should I do?"

"Just mind your business. Don't look back at her."

Judith turned her head and gazed distantly towards the walls and ceiling, opposite Rive Amber's burning glare. She heard the steady *thunk!* of boots. And then….

"So, what have we here?" she heard.

Judith swallowed hard and looked towards the owner of the voice. She held her breath while her heart pounded in her chest and her beating pulse throbbed inside her ears.

Rive Amber circled Judith, pausing as she stood behind her. Judith felt Rive's eyes move over her body. She shuddered. "You're not much, are you?" said Rive. Her voice was close to her ear.

Geeze! What's with these people! First Cythiria. Now her.

"What's your name?"

"Judith Merlon," she said, her voice unsteady, quiet.

"I see." Rive stepped back. "What is your class?"

"Admin. Section III, Systems Analyst, The Bastion."

"Interesting," purred Rive. "Cythiria!" she shouted.

"Yes, Rive."

Cythiria calls her by her first name? What kind of a relationship do they have?

"Can you vouch for this…*person*?" Rive's lip curled to a snarl. Her dark eyes grew sharp and penetrating.

"Yes, I can."

"Well, let's see what she can do then." A crooked smile spread across Rive's face. "Judith Merlon!" she shouted. "Prepare to defend yourself!"

"What!" Judith's eyes grew wide. She cast a pleading glance towards Cythiria, who stepped forward while the surrounding Bestiars stepped back, providing space for the pair.

Cythiria lifted her hand, placing them in front of her face, in a defensive, centered stance.

"Look, I…."

"Just lift your hands!" hissed Cythiria. "Do as I do."

Judith lifted her hands and held them awkwardly near her chin, balling them into tiny fists.

"Keep your body low."

Judith squatted.

"Not that low!"

Judith stood.

"Chin down!"

Judith jutted her chin forward, craning her neck.

"Oh, for fuck's sake," grumbled Cythiria. "You look ridiculous."

"Whaaaat! I did what you told me to do," grumbled Judith back.

"Ok, circle."

Judith spun around.

"Not *that* kind of circle. Just stay opposite me at all times." The two circled. Judith, unused to her new Bestiar Class clothes, stumbled over her boots. "Now jab."

"What?"

"Like this." Cythiria threw a jab that just missed Judith's left cheek. She could feel the wind of Cythiria's clenched fist *whoosh!* next to her ear.

"Geeze, that was close."

"Next time it'll land if you don't defend yourself better. Now, jab!"

Judith threw an awkward, crooked punch, releasing a high-pitched squeal as she did so. The surrounding Bestiars chuckled.

"Better?"

"No. Not if you want to impress Rive."

"Why would I want to impress Rive?"

Judith and Cythiria circled. Cythiria lurched forward. A moment later, she stood next to Judith, swung her arm, and landed an elbow solidly on Judith's temple. Judith wobbled and then tumbled onto the floor. Cythiria turned towards Rive, scowling.

"That was hardly fair," said Cythiria.

"Fair?" Rive scoffed. Her lip quivered as if she were about to spit. "War is not fair. Survival is not fair." She turned to face the gathered Bestiars. "The moment you insist on fairness is the moment that you have lost the battle. No one will grant you fairness. Ever."

"Yes!" shouted the Bestiars in unison.

Rive turned and glared at the supine Judith. "Deal with her," she grunted. A quick pirouette, and she returned to the dark corridor from which she emerged.

Judith's head throbbed as she pressed a wet cloth against her temple. She threw her arms over the edge of the large vat, splashing warm, steaming water onto the stone surface below. She sighed. "My head hurts," she grunted. "My whole body hurts." She pushed against the edge of the vat and let herself float on her back. She gazed up at the dark ceiling, the brown walls with the rust-colored streaks. She sniffed the humid, moldy air. Her nose twitched.

What am I even doing here? Like these Bestiars would ever have any use for someone like Judith Merlon. They were all so into their own thing. The war and violence and the military stuff. It's not what Judith expected. "I've never seen such passionate people," she mumbled. Admins were dedicated, true, but not as fired up and fervent as these Bestiars. "I guess I've got Benj, while Cythiria has Rive Amber. That makes a huge difference."

Judith sighed deeply. Her ears pricked up as she heard the slap of bare feet on the floor. She pulled her legs and arms close to her body and pushed her back against the wall of the vat. From the dim corner of the bath chamber, she emerged.

"Hey," said Cythiria.

"Hey," said Judith, glancing down at the surface of the water.

"Look, I'm sorry about that. I thought we should probably end it in the least painful way possible."

Judith snorted. "It's fine. I know I'm not very good at all this fighting stuff."

"Mind if I get in?"

"Sure."

Cythiria pulled her shirt over her head, sniffed it, and grimaced. She balled it up with two hands and tossed it carelessly into the corner. She bent over and took hold of her trouser cuffs, pulling off one pants leg at a time. She held them up, glanced up and down, clicked her tongue, and then threw them into the corner next to the crumpled shirt. She stretched her arms up and groaned. Judith glanced over Cythiria's body, her muscular arms and shoulders, her well-defined abs. Her eyes paused on the jagged seams that crossed her torso, starting at the shoulder and ending at the waist. Cythiria glanced at Judith and smirked. Judith felt her neck and face flush. She looked away.

Cythiria stepped into the vat. Her body sunk waist deep into the water. She splashed the warm fluid onto her chest and shoulders and then sat, sinking neck deep. She sighed deeply. A satisfied smile spread across her face, her eyes drooping as if she were about to sleep.

"You're lucky you came today," she said. "We don't get baths like this all the time. In fact, it's pretty rare around here."

"You call this lucky?" scoffed Judith. She reached her hand up and pressed the cloth against her forehead.

"I really am sorry," said Cythiria, moving closer to Judith, her voice quiet, almost whispering, and gentle.

"It's ok. Really."

"I mean, you probably came out better off in the end, anyway?"

"Oh?" said Judith. "How so?"

"Well, Rive respects you now."

"Respects me? I was knocked out cold."

"Yeah, but you took the hit. That means a lot to Rive."

Judith shook her head. "You people are crazy," she mumbled.

Cythiria chuckled. "Yeah. Mechanics are like that. Real pieces of work. Especially Rive."

"You sound like you're close to her."

"Yeah." Cythiria gazed into the dark corners of the bath chamber. "Me and Rive, we go way back."

"Oh?"

"Ancient history."

"I see." Judith paused. "And the scars?" she said, nodding towards Cythiria's shoulders and chest through the splashing bath water.

Cythiria smirked. "A gift from an old friend."

"Sounds like a pretty terrible old friend."

"I got nothing but terrible old friends," said Cythiria. She glanced at Judith. A crooked smile crossed her face. Her sharp, cunning, almost playful eyes locked onto Judith's.

"I…I'm sorry to hear that." She pulled her arms and legs closer to her body. She felt her face grow warm and her heart thump heavily inside her chest.

Cythiria moved next to Judith. Judith's body tightened as she felt Cythiria's skin brush against hers. Cythiria turned towards Judith. "But maybe we can be friends."

Judith swallowed hard. "Um…sure."

"Don't sound so enthusiastic."

"Well, I mean, we just met."

"Indeed, we did."

"And…I'm grateful that you helped me so much."

"Just stick with me and I'll make sure you get out of this situation alive."

Judith smiled. "Really?" She felt her body relax and her chest grow warm.

"Yes, really." Cythiria lifted her hand and placed it on Judith's shoulder. "I promise."

Judith sighed deeply. "Ok."

"Ok?"

"I mean, we can be friends."

Cythiria stood up. She placed her hands on her hips, her steaming, naked body covered with rivulets of water. "Great!" she nearly shouted. "I got so much to show you."

Judith grimaced. "Uh, ok." *That's what I'm afraid of.*

CHAPTER 40

A Meeting

Griddish, Ashen Fissure, the Council of Engineer Class Citizens

Matere glared across the burnt yellow hills towards Ashen Fissure. He glanced at the shattered ruins of the city, the clusters of Slipshot Silos that littered the horizon. He sniffed the cool breeze that wafted through the broken windows of the former Council of Engineer Class Citizens, its deep corridors dark and damp, its walls cracked and crumbling.

He sighed as he turned and limped to a panel that stood in the center of the chamber. He heard the patter of light footsteps as they echoed along the empty halls.

"Your wounds are improving," said Betel as she stepped into the chamber, "Since your rather unfortunate encounter with that Mechanic Class Slave. At least you're standing now. If only I had been there to back you up."

"It's not anyone's fault except mine," he grumbled, his breath short. "I was careless." He glanced down at his arm, at the coils that twisted and twined and throbbed. "And this arm is acting up lately."

Betel stepped next to him. She took hold of his hand and pulled his arm towards her, looking intently at its coiled surface and the shimmering colors that cast an almost illusionary glow to its surface. "Perhaps the Vérkatrae are upset."

Matere scoffed. "Can they be? Are they even capable of emotion?"

"Well, that is the big question, isn't it," echoed a voice from the chamber's entrance. Matere and Betel turned towards it. "Do you think you can answer it, my dear Engineer Class Citizen?" purred the voice.

"Rive Amber," said Matere, his lip curling to a snarl. His breath grew short and his body warm. Betel stepped in front of Matere, her body centered, feet spread apart. She lifted her hands in defense.

"What a warm welcome," said Rive as she stepped into the chamber, her heeled boots clicking with steady confidence. "You're quite the woman, Betel, defending your man with your own body like that. You'd think, from your terrible attitude, that I was the enemy here."

"And you're not?" grumbled Betel.

Rive snorted. "Of course not. I'm just a simple public servant who only asks for peace in the world."

"Peacemakers are not murderers," said Matere.

"Oh?" Rive's eyes widened, and a crooked smile crossed her face. "And how else does one achieve peace, my dear Engineer Class Citizen?" Her voice was tinged with spite. She paused and lifted her hand, waving dismissively towards Matere. "Besides, what makes you think I'm a murderer? I've done nothing wrong."

"You're the one who sent that Mechanic Class Slave after me."

Rive laughed. "Cythiria? That girl is so often misunderstood."

"Her intentions were *quite* clear," said Matere. He reached up and pulled his shirt down from the collar. Deep, red streaks crossed his otherwise sheet-white skin.

"Awww, did the crazy little girl hurt you Matere?" said Rive, mockingly.

"You have eyes. You can see for yourself."

Rive scoffed. "Well, what's between the two of you is none of my business, really. Cythiria can be quite the jealous type." She turned her head and winked at Betel, whose lip curled to a snarl. "Such venom. Well, I don't want to waste your time. I mean," she cast an exaggerated glance around the chamber, "I'm sure you're very busy people."

"Quite."

"I'm just here to pass on a little information."

"As if we would trust you," grumbled Betel.

"Well, well, don't we have a chip on our shoulder, my most esteemed Councilwoman." Rive smirked and bowed shallowly.

"*Former* Councilwoman," said Betel.

"Seeing as how there is hardly a council left, your point is rather irrelevant, isn't it."

Betel grit her teeth and spread her stance, balling her hands into fists.

"Can you just get to the point, Rive?" sighed Matere.

"Any ruin my fun?" Rive glanced between Betel and Matere and then back to Matere again. She let out an exaggerated sigh. "Fiiiineeeee. Well, if you haven't noticed, there's a few minor characters in this drama who want to bring Cythiria back to Var 7."

"That might be a good thing," grumbled Matere. "Besides, that's none of my business."

"Even when 1^1 is involved?" Matere and Betel exchanged sharp glances. "Just as I thought," smirked Rive.

"And how do you know this?" said Betel.

"I know many things. It's kind of my job these days."

"And you expect us to believe you?"

Rive shrugged her shoulders. "Suit yourself. It doesn't really matter to me one way or the other."

"So why come here then?" said Matere.

Rive pouted mockingly. "I'm only trying to be helpful, Matere. You're such a boor sometimes." She glanced at Matere and then Betel. "Well, I do believe I have worn out my welcome." She turned and stepped toward the entry of the chamber, through the corridor. Within moments, she stood outside the ruins of Development, of the former Council of Engineer Class Citizens.

She sniffed the air. "It stinks here," she mumbled. *It won't be so easy getting Cythiria back to Var 7, now that Matere has been put on notice. And with 1^1 involved, that could finally mean the end of Farth, or whatever those filthy Varlings call it. And then we Slaves will finally be freed from our former selves.*

Rive paused. "So, where is Natty? I have a little task for him on Var 7."

CHAPTER 41

Growing Close

Griddish, Ashen Fissure, Sanguine Heap

"Use your wrist." The plasmic arcs shot from the tip of the Plaxis Strand and licked the surface of the courtyard, cutting the air with a sharp, whistling howl. "Just like that."

Judith straightened her body, lifted her arm, took a deep breath, and held it. She struck in a downward motion. The Plaxis Strand fell from her hand and tumbled onto the cobbled surface, click-clacking to a stop nearly twelve feet away.

Cythiria raised her brow, grimaced, and then let out a raucous laugh.

"Heyyyy," complained Judith. "It's not funny. I coulda hurt myself." She felt her neck and cheeks flush.

"You'll never hurt yourself from a stray Plaxis Strand. They're aware of their place in the Tenddrome. Once they're separated from their Slave, they'll shut down." Cythiria paused. "At least for *normal* Slaves, unlike me."

Judith paused. "Oh, Cyth, you're normal." She clenched her teeth. "Except that you're a real *jerk* sometimes, you know?"

Cythiria jogged over to the Plaxis Strand and picked it up. She walked towards Judith, and then paused in front of her. She reached down and took Judith's hand into her own, turned it upward, and placed the Plaxis Strand into the palm of her hand, gazing mischievously into Judith's light-colored eyes. "Don't lose it next time."

Judith sighed deeply. "Easier said than done. I'm not a fighter like you. I can't do all those fancy athletic maneuvers. It just doesn't suit me very well."

"Then you better get used to it, especially if you want to get on Rive's good side."

Judith clicked her tongue. "Why in the hell would I want to be on *her* good side? Like that's going to get me anything."

"Times are changing in Griddish. You need to be on the right side of history."

Judith scoffed. "Geeze, you and Benj. You're both the same."

"Benj?" said Cythiria. She tilted her head and her eyes grew wide.

Judith felt her neck and cheeks flush. "Oh, just some guy I know."

"Guy?" pressed Cythiria.

"Yeah, a fellow Admin. We kinda grew up together, you know?"

"I don't." Cythiria paused. "Is he *special* to you?"

Judith snorted. "Goodness no. He's just a friend, that's all."

"I see," said Cythiria.

"Anyway," said Judith, looking past Cythiria and nodding. "It looks like you're needed."

Cythiria turned and looked in the direction of Judith's nod. "Blinky!" she shouted. She ran towards the Vérkatros, which stood at the edge of the courtyard. She pressed her body against him and spread her arms across his body. She turned towards Judith and waved her over.

Judith frowned and shrugged her shoulders. With a light, pattering step she walked up to Cythiria and gazed upon Blinky.

"He's my friend," said Cythiria. "He's glad to see me. See his colors? The orange and red mean he's happy."

Judith snorted. "Well, I guess I was wrong about you, Cythiria."

"Wrong? Why?"

"I said you were normal, but now I'm not so sure."

"Awww," whined Cythiria. "Why?"

"A Vérkatros for a friend? Everyone knows Slaves can't be friends with Vérkatrae, Cythiria."

"Can so. I even named him, and I made him a ribbon. See?" Cythiria nodded toward the ragged, purple shred of fabric that fluttered from his flicking antenna.

"Ok, so now I think you're just weird."

"It's ok to be weird sometimes. I think *you're* weirder than me."

"At least I don't see things like colors that aren't there."

Cythiria sighed deeply. "So, you don't see them either," she said, her face darkening, her eyes growing sad. "I was hoping…."

"Hoping what, Cythiria?"

Cythiria turned away. "Never mind." She paused and turned back towards Judith. A wide, almost forced, smile crossed her face. "How about we go for a ride?"

Judith raised her brow. "On that?"

"Yep," said Cythiria cheerily.

"To where?"

"I don't know. Just around."

Judith shook her head. "We're in a war."

"More like a skirmish."

"It might not be safe."

"Come onnnnnnnn," Cythiria whined. "I want to show you something."

Judith shook her head and let out a resigned sigh. "Fiinnee. What do you want to show me?"

Cythiria hopped onto Blinky and straddled his back. She reached her hand towards Judith, who took it, a touch of hesitation in her posture. Cythiria pulled her up, quickly, easily, as if she were a twig. Judith straddled Blinky just behind Cythiria and wrapped her arms around her waist.

"Getting a bit touchy feely, are we?" smirked Cythiria.

"Oh, for fuck's sake."

Cythiria gasped. "Such language," she said with false admonishment. "Now where would you learn something like that, as one who has never left Griddish before?"

"I'm an Admin. I know all about the way things work on the Vars."

"Really!"

"Yep."

"Even Varling sex?"

"Of course."

"Then teach me."

"What?"

"Nothing." Blinky vibrated for a moment. His skin grew warm. He turned and hovered through the arch covered in writhing figures carved in bas-relief. A moment later, they were hovering over the grassy, green and brown plains of Ashen Fissure, the cool winds of Griddish *whooshing!* through their hair.

CHAPTER 42

Rising Concern

Var 7, Farth, Nissy

Chelss sat up on the bed, breathing heavily, sweat breaking on her forehead and neck. She could feel her heart beating heavily in her chest, a sense of fear and panic overtaking her as her eyes groped along the dark walls of Cythiria's former room. She touched her shirt with her hand. It was damp and cold. She shivered as she glanced out the window at the bright planetary ring, its light casting a cool, ghostly glow onto the surface of the bay.

She turned and jumped out of the bed. She looked around, finding a pile of washed and folded clothes. She picked up a pair of pants and pulled them on, followed by a t-shirt and a hoodie. She slipped on her own boots and pulled the hoodie up onto her head. She grabbed her backpack and slung it over her shoulder, tip toeing to the door of Cythiria's room.

She slowly pulled the door open, which creaked ever so slightly. She stepped quietly towards the front door, unlocked it, turned the handle, and pulled it. She cringed at the tiny squeal of rusty hinges. She stepped out onto the sidewalk and quietly pushed the door closed. When she was clear, she quickly walked to the street and turned towards the direction of the subway station.

"I have to get out of that house," she mumbled, recalling the nightmare, the visions of Cythiria holding her hand one moment, and then gone the next.

She hugged the pack to her chest as she walked down the damp, cobbled street, the pink and purple lights illuminating it with a neon glow. When she arrived at the subway station, she jogged towards the entry, jumping the turnstiles as she always did, just like Cythiria showed her. She ran to the platform and waited for the next car. She didn't care which train arrived, just any that would take her away from that house, the source of all her nightmares and anxiety.

The train *whooshed!* to a stop along the platform. Its doors slid open and Chelss jumped in.

The car rattled and swayed as it clattered along the tracks. The cabin's LED lights blinked off and on, and the pink and blue neon light flickered through the smudgy, rain-stained windows as it emerged onto the aboveground tracks. Chelss sighed as she gazed with large, hazel-colored eyes at the bright white planetary ring. Its milky lanes stretched across the cityscape, dwarfing it into insignificance.

The hard metal of the spike pressed against her chest as she pulled it tighter. *I just couldn't bear it any longer, waiting. Waiting for what? For some guy? This Jeremiah, like what can he do?*

Chelss started to nod off as the rhythm of the train rocked her to sleep. The chilly breeze from an opening door wafted against her. She shuddered and opened her bleary eyes, raising her hand to wipe away a crust of dried spittle from the corner of her mouth.

She squinted into the dark corridor of the cabin, near the sliding doors that closed between adjacent cars. Dark fabric rustled and formed an amorphous shape. She blinked hard and stared into the corner. And then, it moved.

"It's him," whispered Chelss, her hazel-colored eyes opened wide. Her body stiffened, and her heart thumped inside her chest. Her neck and cheeks grew warm. She shuddered as a chill ran along her back and neck. She stood up.

The man surged forward, glancing at Chelss through the flaps of his hood. The slender, silvery glasses flashed in the light of the planetary ring as he lunged through the open door of the train.

"Wait!" shouted Chelss. She darted towards the door, turning her body as she slipped through the *whooshing!* panels. They slammed shut and the train hummed and then clattered away.

Chelss pulled the pack onto her shoulders. She glanced up and down the platform, which was damp and dripping from the cool, moist air. She sniffed. A smell of piss and decaying garbage assaulted her nose. She coughed and a small puff of steam blew from her mouth.

Her body stiffened as she glanced at a billow of dark fabric which flowed down a dark corridor. She ran towards it, turning into the corridor, which was dimly lit by blinking and buzzing purple LED lights. She could hear the echoing patter of footsteps in the distance and the tip-tap of dripping water onto the concrete floor, where it puddled into small, turbid pools.

She shuddered again as she charged down the corridor. She hopped over a turnstile and stumbled onto a slippery, cobbled street. She glanced along the tall, dark buildings, which surrounded a wide courtyard. Upon the walls, weak fluorescent light flickered, revealing broken, graffitied walls and rusty, torn fences. The hum and clatter of cars echoed along the walls, and the click clack of solitary footsteps could be heard along the bitumen surface of the street.

Chelss took a deep breath. The cold air burned her throat, and as she exhaled, steam poured from her mouth. She stepped towards the sounds of the footsteps.

"Hey!" she shouted. "Stop running! I know who you are." She stepped forward, cautiously, one foot at a time. At the end of the courtyard, she paused, glancing into an unlit gateway.

"I see you have discovered me," came the warm, friendly voice.

Chelss jumped. She pressed her hand against her chest and took a few quick breaths. "What the fuck!"

"Indeed, this is a most opportune time," he said, pulling his hood away from his head.

"You said you would take me to Cyth," she started, her hazel-colored eyes glaring into those of the man named Jeremiah. "And then you disappeared."

"Some things are not simple. They require patience."

"But you said you could help." Chelss paused, her hazel-colored eyes pleading. "I…," her voice cracked. "I want to see Cyth." She sniffed, and her eyes grew damp.

Jeremiah paused. "I see you have the Perispike." Chelss nodded. "Then I suppose we can begin."

༽

Natty Mick pushed his hand through his thick, black hair, smirking as he gazed into the courtyard where Jeremiah and Chelss stood a moment ago. The fluorescent lights flickered and buzzed under the milky white glare of the planetary ring.

"So, you've started your ascent back to Griddish," he mumbled. *And to think you're bringing that little brat along with you. What use could she be to you, One to the Power of One. That is what you are called, is it not?* Natty scoffed. *And still, you lurk in the shadows of this forsaken city like some criminal. It is what you are, after all.* Natty sighed with exaggeration. *Not that I'd interfere with your plans. Far be it from me. However, Rive likes to see things play out. So, let's let this situation play out. Who knows? Perhaps some interesting effect can come about because of you and your endless nonsense.*

Natty turned and walked towards the turnstile of the train station. He hopped over it and walked up the long, dark corridor, his boots clicking on bitumen and sloshing through stagnant puddles. He stepped to the edge of the raised track. The warm breeze of an advancing train whipped along the platform, brushing through his thick, black hair, and billowing through his coat. The train rattled to a stop, and the doors whooshed open before him. "And so it begins," he mumbled. "We're moving towards a point of no return. That should make Rive pretty happy."

CHAPTER 43

Revealing Truth

Griddish, Ashen Fissure, the Ashen Plains

Judith wrapped her arm around Cythiria's waist. The Vérkatros swayed gently across the plains, the green-brown grass whooshing! below its chassis. She glanced at the broken cityscape of Ashen Fissure, the thin, spiked buildings that once reached ambitiously towards the apex of Griddish's dome. Now, it appeared as a skeletal corpse, left to decay into the grassy plains from which it rose.

Judith sniffed the cool breeze. Her nose twitched at the smell of decay. "The systems are falling apart," she muttered. *We are losing our ability to control the mechanics of Griddish. The Tenddrome does not cooperate, not as it once did. Not while the world was stable.*

"The world." *Nothing but a disk spinning through space, a purpose that has lost its point. And us. Why are we still here?* Judith sighed.

"What's the matter?" said Cythiria, as she gazed forward, a thin smile crossing her face.

"Nothing," mumbled Judith.

"That sigh was not nothing."

"It's just…."

"Just?"

"Never mind," said Judith. She tightened her arm's grip around Cythiria's waist, pressing her shoulders against the Mechanic Class Slave's back. "I'm just so tired sometimes."

"Lay your head on my shoulder."

Judith snorted. "I'm sure you already think I'm weak. I don't want to make your perception of me any worse."

"It's already pretty bad," said Cythiria, chuckling.

"I know. I'm pretty lame. I admit it."

Judith nodded to the sway of the Vérkatros. She shook her head and pinched her cheek between her thumb and forefinger. *Blinky. That's what she calls it. Or, him.* She touched Blinky's back with her hand, stroking the warm, almost flesh-like skin. Flesh, yet metal, like all Vérkatrae. *Where does machine begin and Vérkatros end? It's a silly question. One we don't know the answer to. Not anymore. Not since they were made eons ago. And yet, they must have changed over time. Just like us. Just like the Tenddrome.*

"You're awfully quiet," said Cythiria, her voice breaking the whispering silence of the Ashen Plains.

"Just thinking."

"Oh, no. Don't go doing that. It won't make things any better."

"Typical."

"Why typical?"

"Aren't you Mechanics all like that?"

Cythiria snorted. "I suppose we are. We live passionately and die young."

"Is that so?" said Judith, a touch of irony in her voice.

"Sure, it is."

"Well, then, I guess I should say it was nice knowing you."

"Ha! As if. Wherever I go, I'm taking you with me. Remember, I said I would take care of you. Or did you forget already?"

"How could I? But honestly, that doesn't really sound like *taking care of*."

"It's *my* way."

Judith felt her neck grow warm and her chest tighten. She fought a smile that was curling up on the corners of her mouth. "By the way, where exactly *are* we going?"

"To a special place."

"Why's it special?"

"It's a surprise."

Judith sighed. "Fine. I'll try to act all excited when we get there."

"Good. I like that."

Judith nodded as Blinky hovered along the grassy plains. Her heavy eyelids drooped, and she leaned her head on Cythiria's shoulder. She wrapped her other arm around Cythiria's waist.

"We're here!" came the shout. Judith jerked her head up. Her mouth felt dry. She lifted her finger and scratched away some crust that had formed at the corner of her mouth. The Vérkatros, Blinky, paused, his six legs set solidly on the grass below. Judith blinked her eyes hard and rubbed them with her balled-up knuckles. She yawned. Cythiria, who stood on the grass below her, reached her hand towards Judith. "Come on," she said, her eyes bright, a wide smile crossing her face. Judith took Cythiria's hand and slid off Blinky's back, landing her booted feet quietly on the grassy surface below.

"See?" said Cythiria, nodding forward.

Judith looked up at the tall, slim tower. Near its apex, which was barely visible from below, opened an eye-like portal. "A Slipshot?" said Judith, raising her brow as she glanced sidelong at Cythiria.

"Not just any Slipshot. Come on."

Cythiria pulled Judith towards the wide, metal-tiled platform. Judith felt her hand grow hot and sweaty inside Cythiria's, and she drew it away. She followed Cythiria, her light steps emitting a tinny echo along the platform. The two paused as they approached the array of black posts that formed a circle, at whose point of convergence, a smudge of black spread across the ground's surface, looking as if it were the location of a bonfire or an explosion.

Judith sniffed the air, which smelled of stale burning metal and oily smoke.

"Well, what do you think?" said Cythiria, as she gazed at the point of convergence.

"Um…, well, it's definitely a Slipshot." Judith paused. "I mean, it seems as if it's not used all that often."

"It's not just an ordinary Slipshot. It's the Slipshot to the Var I came from."

Judith turned her head and looked directly at Cythiria. "Where you came from?" She tilted her head and grimaced. "Weren't you initialized here, in Griddish?"

"Well, yeah, I guess."

"You guess?"

"I don't really remember much from that time."

Judith paused. "From that time? What time, exactly, are we talking about?" she said, firmly, as if she were lecturing a child.

Cythiria sighed. "I've been on Var 7 nearly all my life."

"All your life?"

"Just about. I went to Var 7 when I was a child. I don't remember what happened directly after that. My memories…." Cythiria's voice started to crack and her lips quiver. "My memories…were broken into so many pieces. And…" She paused, lifting her hand to her forehead. "…that's where I got these scars."

"The scars…."

Cythiria turned towards Judith. "I just wanted you to know. I never told you about myself. I thought maybe…."

"Maybe?"

"Maybe I should, you know, tell you why I'm not normal." She wrapped her arms tightly around her own waist. "Maybe it would explain why I'm such a failure and why I can't access the Tenddrome…."

"Oh, Cyth." Judith reached towards Cythiria and touched her arm. "You're not a failure."

"I just want to access the Tenddrome. I want to make Rive proud of me."

"Why, Cyth? Why do you want the approval of *that* woman so badly?"

"Rive saved me. She came to Var 7. She taught me how to be strong. She taught me how to survive."

Cythiria opened her arms and reached out towards Judith, enveloping her. Cythiria's raspy breath tickled her neck, and warm droplets dripped and splashed upon her shoulders. She could feel her own pounding heart as she pressed her body against that of the Admin Class Slave. "Please forgive me."

"Cythiria," whispered Judith, as she wrapped her arms around the Mechanic Class Slave's waist. "There's nothing to forgive."

꛰

Rive Amber slowly opened her eyes. The darkness fizzled and melted away, revealing the stark, stone walls of her chamber in Sanguine Heap. She took a deep breath and unfolded her legs from their lotus position entanglement. She stood and walked over to a window that overlooked the rolling and verdant Ashen Hills. Littered along the horizon, if Griddish could be said to have a horizon, stood clusters of Slipshot Silos. Like phantoms, they stood silent, waiting, overseeing the world that existed for them alone.

Rive sighed deeply. "So, she's taken a liking to that little Admin. Judith is her name?" *You shouldn't expose yourself, my dear Cythiria. You cannot access the Tenddrome, so you don't realize how each Slave is just a Node in a vast network. We are conduits to each other, wrapped in a comfortable, decaying cocoon. And yet, we see through each other's eyes, and share each other's knowledge and experience.* Rive paused. "And still, you are a puzzle, Cythiria," she muttered. *Perhaps you are the one who can relieve us of our ancient yoke. Var 7 changed you. It destroyed the old Mechanic Class Slave and forged a new Bestiar.*

Rive stepped away from the window, her jaw clenched, a quivering scowl forming on her upper lip. "I suppose I should make my way to Var 7's Slipshot Silo. If anything, that girl…no, that *woman*…could be a catalyst to change. She only requires a tiny push."

"If Rive Amber is right about Cythiria, then there's one place we need to be," said Matere, scratching his stubbly chin with his hand.

"And that is?" asked Betel, her cool, gray eyes pausing at Matere's gesture.

"The Slipshot to Var 7. That's the bottleneck, the place where it'll all happen. And besides, without a Capsa, we won't be able to open the portal anyway. And it's probably best that we shouldn't, even if we could. I have no doubt that Rive Amber will be waiting in the wings."

The pair trudged up to the top of a grassy hill. The Slipshot Silo stretched towards the sky and below, a pair of tiny figures crossed the wide platform. Matere and Betel crouched down and lay prone on the grass. Matere gestured and a holographic screen fizzled into view just in front of his face. "Well, would you look at that?" Betel followed.

"She's with someone."

"Indeed."

"Seems pretty innocent to me."

"You think so?"

"Yes. They're just two Slaves walking together on the platform. So what?"

"I would say there's a little more between them than that."

Betel sighed with impatience. "And so what if there is? How could that possibly affect the outcome of anything?"

"They're changing, Betel. The Slaves are no longer what they were originally designed for."

"That's what we call evolution, my dear scientist," said Betel, a tone of mockery in her voice.

"And we all know that evolution is a catalyst for change. Not just change on the surface, but deep, existential change."

Betel paused. "So, what are you really saying, Matere?"

"That we're at an important pivot point. One wrong move, and that Var 7 Slave could ruin things here in Griddish. And maybe all the Vars in the universe."

Betel snorted and shook her head. "Very scientific of you." She paused. "So, what do we do now?"

Matere paused, glancing along the Slipshot Silo's platform below. "There's not much we can do. Other than help things along a little."

Betel clicked her tongue. "As always, you play the role of the instigator, Matere."

"Adaptability is the key to survival, my dear council member."

"Except that you enjoy it too much."

CHAPTER 44

Missing

Var 7, Farth, Nissy

Jillian jumped up from the sofa in the living room of the small bungalow. Her head felt heavy, her eyes bleary. She blinked hard, as the room came into focus. She sighed quickly and walked towards Cythiria's room. She opened the door and looked around, her eyes scanning the room, the bed, the empty chairs, the corners into which clothes were once dropped carelessly and left to mold.

She turned and walked quickly towards the other room, kicking open the door and glaring at a disheveled pile that lay on the bed.

"Chelss is gone," she said.

The pile moved. "What?"

"Chelss is not here."

Fredrick sat up. He rubbed his eyes and scratched his stubbly cheek. "She's…gone?" He stood up and walked into the living room, pushing past Jillian. "But…why?"

Jillian sat on the sofa. "I don't know. She must've sneaked out when I was asleep."

"And the Perispike?"

Jillian glanced around the room. "Gone, it looks like." She paused. "It's my fault. I should have looked after her. I don't know how I could have let her get away."

Fredrick sat on the sofa next to her. "It's not your fault. I'm sure she was just tired of waiting around. Or maybe she got scared."

"What should we do?"

"We could go look for her."

Jillian clenched her jaw and punched her leg with her balled fist. "First Cythiria, now this. Why? Why do they always run away when I'm around?" Jillian's eyes grew damp, her nose a shade of pink.

Fredrick sighed. "It's not what you think, Jillian."

"Cythiria tried to *kill* herself, Fredrick," said Jillian, her voice cracking. "And when I showed up at the hospital, when I went there hoping I could bring her back home, she ran away and then disappeared." She looked at Fredrick, her eyes pleading. "What did I do wrong? How could I have saved Cythiria?"

Fredrick sighed. "You can't, Jillian. You just have to let her figure out her own way."

Jillian turned and rubbed away the tears with her fingers. "I only wanted the best for her. I wanted her to thrive in this world. We had it so hard here…."

"*You* had it so hard here, Jillian. For me, life wasn't any different than it was back on Earth. I was always a nobody. I never had much to lose. But you, you were always so privileged. You always had people invested in your decisions. You always had people making sure you would succeed in life."

Jillian snorted. *"People,"* she said, her voice filled with spite. "If you're referring to my family, *those* are not the people who really cared. All they ever worried about was themselves, about how they appeared to everyone else in the world. They never cared about me."

"And yet, you force your own regrets on Cyth. Did you ever think that maybe she just needed you to accept who she was? That maybe she couldn't live up to your dreams, or gain what *you* lost because now you're just a common refugee in a strange world?"

"*My* dreams?" shouted Jillian. "I lost my dreams when we came to this fucking nightmare of a place. I have *nothing* that I can give to Cythiria."

Fredrick shook his head. "I remember what you told me, way back when we were on Earth. In your apartment in San Francisco. You said your family never could own up to their mistakes. You said you felt betrayed by your mother, because she decided to defend your brother in spite of what she knew to be the truth about him. You said your family was only out to protect their own position in society."

"And I *hate* them for that," grumbled Jillian. "More than you can imagine."

"But you're no different. You're trying to protect Cyth from harm by imposing your own version of reality upon her. You can only accept what you already know to be the truth, the one real path in life." Fredrick paused. He sighed and placed his elbows on his knees. He gazed down at his worn socks and his smudged and stained sweatpants that he wore as pajamas. "That night, when I looked around your apartment, and I compared it to how I lived, I said I could never be equal to you. Not just because you were used to a certain lifestyle, but because you saw the world in a particular way. And that way is the *only* way. You said you were a coward because you wouldn't give up your lifestyle, but that wasn't it really. More than that, you were dishonest because you could never believe that there might be some *other* way to live, to see the world, other than what you already knew."

Jillian paused, a look of distant reminiscence crossing her face. "I…I'm sorry, Fredrick. I…don't know what to say…."

Fredrick turned and put his hand on her shoulder. "You don't need to say anything." He reached his other arm around her waist and pulled her close to him. He felt her body quiver as she pressed her face against his shoulder and sobbed. "Now, why don't we go look for Chelss? I'm sure there's a simple explanation."

Jillian pulled back and gazed into Fredrick's eyes. Her own deep, green eyes were bloodshot, her nose a shade of pink. She frowned and then looked down at the floor. "I *am* sorry," she said.

"I know," said Fredrick, gently rubbing her arms with his hands. "Let's get ready and go look for Chelss."

Jillian sniffed. "Ok." She stood and walked to the front door of the small bungalow, pushing it open while Fredrick quickly pulled on a pair of socks and some shoes. She stepped down the stairs and onto the walkway. She glanced behind her. Fredrick, his loose hoodie pulled up over his head, his golden locks flowing out of the sides, stumbled behind her. She paused.

"If we take my truck, we can get around more easily. At least we'll have a better chance of catching up with her."

She turned and stepped onto the pocked bitumen of the street. She stopped. Fredrick walked past her a few steps, paused, and poised his body defensively.

"Well, if it isn't the little Varling duo everyone is so fond of," came the voice of a man. He smirked and pushed his hand through his thick, black hair.

"It's you," grumbled Fredrick.

"Don't be so happy to see me. I'm sure you've missed me as much as I've missed you." He turned to face Jillian. "Such fire," he said, his eyes glancing over her red hair. "You haven't changed one bit since we last met."

He gazed distractedly towards the sky and lifted his forefinger to his chin. "Lemme see. It would have been when that *brat* was still a little shit." He sighed dramatically and rubbed his forehead with his thumb and forefinger. "Of course, your little husband, I know quite well. In fact, we've had a few rather engrossing discussions quite recently."

"He's not my husband," Jillian grumbled, her teeth clenched, her green eyes burning.

"Oh?" said Natty. "How hurtful of you, considering how much of his own life our little Varling has committed to you." Natty sighed dramatically again. He shrugged his shoulders. "Varlings. What can you expect of them? Such fickle creatures who know nothing of loyalty."

"So," started Fredrick. "I assume you are here for a reason?"

Natty smirked. "Quite. I only want to share with you a little bit of information that you might find useful."

"What *information*?" grumbled Jillian.

Natty snorted. "Such a terrible, ungrateful attitude. And to think that I am the gift bearer here, and yet I am so mistreated."

"Could you get to the point?" said Fredrick, his hands balling into fists.

"Well, I assume you are looking for that other brat, um…." Natty clicked his fingers in rapid succession.

"Chelss Brimwater."

"Right. Forgive me, I have a hard time telling the difference between Varlings."

"And?" pressed Jillian.

"Well, she's not alone. In fact, she is with someone who is particularly close to you."

"And that would be?"

"Hmm." Natty pursed his brow and raised his forefinger to his chin. "I believe you know him by the name Dr. Jeremiah Onu." Fredrick and Jillian exchanged glances. Natty smirked. He raised his hand and brushed it through his thick, black hair. "It seems they've devised a little mission that they would be doing together. Do you know what that is?"

"The Perispike Dome," mumbled Fredrick.

"Um…what is the appropriate word for this moment? Bingo! I believe it is." Natty stretched his arms and let out an exaggerated yawn. "Well, I think my job is done here. I'm sure we'll be meeting again very soon." Natty raised his hand and waved, turned, and walked along the pocked, bitumen surface of the road, turned, and was gone.

"The Perispike was discovered near the hospital where Cythiria…." Fredrick paused.

Jillian gazed into Fredrick's eyes. She placed her hand on his arm. "Then, let's go."

Jillian took Fredricks's hand and ran towards her truck. She gestured. A door whooshed open. Fredrick climbed in first, followed by Jillian. They sat and gazed out the front window, along the cityscape of Nissy, and the milky white planetary ring that streaked across the sky. Fredrick sighed. "If Jeremiah is preempting us, then he must have some plan to use Chelss to gain some specific goal."

"But what goal?"

Fredrick shook his head. "He said again and again that his ultimate goal is to completely end the influence of Griddish in the universe, including the Slipshot and all the Vars. If that's still the case, and I doubt much has changed, then he's decided that Chelss must somehow be a part of his overall scheme." Fredrick sighed.

"Then, let's go." Jillian gestured and the truck hummed to life. She pulled at the steering wheel, and the truck lurched forward, rattling across the pocked bitumen and into the urban canyons known as Nissy.

CHAPTER 45

Arrival & Departure

Var 7, Farth, Nissy

"Do you have the Perispike?"

Chelss looked up at Jeremiah with large, hazel-colored eyes. The parking garage smelled of dirty oil and must. A cool breeze wafted through the concrete corridors, carrying with it a scent of decaying seaweed. The milky white planetary ring grew bright with the settling evening and the tall, spiky buildings blinked a purple LED glow.

Chelss felt her chest tighten. The sound of her heavily beating heart pounded in her ears. She felt her neck and face flush. She glanced at the glowing cityscape, the pop of flashing lights, and her ears pricked up at the distant rumble of a city in motion. The city breathed its own rhythm, and Chelss breathed along with it.

She pulled the pack off her back and let it fall onto the bitumen of the garage floor. It clanged as the objects within clashed against each other. Not just the Perispike, but other items, like headphones and glasses that she used to connect to her school's network. *School.* It seemed so distant now. So irrelevant. *Cyth. She was such a loner. She seemed to hate everyone. I was the same. Alone. I never had a friend, not a close friend. Not someone I could trust. Not until I met her. And even then, I never was sure if I could trust her.*

Chelss bent over and reached towards the pack. She lifted the top flap. Her hands trembled as she reached inside and grasped the cool, metal object in her thin fingers. She stood up, holding the Perispike in two hands, as if she were about to present it as a gift. She sighed quickly. Her stomach turned and her legs trembled. She felt her neck and back grow damp with a cold sweat. She shuddered.

"Are you ready?" came the deep, calm, and steady voice. "Do you realize what you are about to do?"

Chelss nodded her head. "I don't care. I only want to see…her."

"Is she that important to you?"

"Yes. She is. The only friend I ever had. The only one who confided in me. The only one who wanted to know me for who I was, not just some face or some body."

"Then we should begin. Hold the sharp end of the spike to the ground's surface."

Chelss knelt on one knee and held the Perispike just above the concrete platform. A moment later, a sharp, metallic clap echoed through the garage's corridors, and the spike had embedded itself into the floor.

The whirring truck rattled along damp and cobbled streets, the tires clacking cacophonously through pink and blue fluorescent corridors. Jillian pulled at the wheel of the truck and turned sharply onto a road that led up a long, grassy hill. The dewy moisture reflected the white light of the planetary ring, imparting upon it an almost ghostly glow.

"Over there," said Fredrick, pointing to a large, square building that jutted upward from the hilltop. "The hospital."

The truck moaned as it climbed the hill. Once atop, Jillian pulled the wheel and the truck stopped its steady crawl.

"That's the garage," said Fredrick, pointing towards a multi-level, concrete parking structure. "That's the one Chelss was talking about."

"There's no way we can drive up that."

"Then let's run."

Jillian gestured and the doors of the truck *whooshed!* open. Fredrick jumped down, and Jillian followed. They jogged along a narrow, curving road and into the structure.

"Chelss!" he shouted, his voice echoing along the empty, concrete corridors. "Chelss!" he shouted again. Jillian glanced around and pointed towards a door. The two ran towards it. Fredrick kicked the door open and stepped into a stairwell. He sniffed. The dank, stale air smelled of urine. A weak buzz emitted from the shallow, blinking fluorescent lights above, casting a sickly, white-green hue onto the dilapidated stairwell. He dashed up the stairs, kicked open the door, and stepped onto the concrete platform. Jillian stepped next to him.

Jeremiah closed his eyes. A moment later, a plasmic arc shot from a port on the side of the Perispike, reaching and striking the next, then the next, until it connected each of the Perispikes to the other. A wash of blue light fizzled and grew into a wall that enveloped the two. Chelss gazed at Jeremiah, her eyes wide, trembling. She held her breath as the smell of burning metal assaulted her nose. The world grew silent.

Fredrick squinted into the corridors of the garage. "They're here," he said, nodding towards a shadowy image of billowing fabric in the depths of the corridor. He sniffed. The air smelled of burning metal. A white flash banished the shadows for a split second. Another followed, then another. And then, a thin, blue light, like some closing window, fizzled into view in front of them.

Fredrick lifted his hand and held it towards Jillian. A gentle, calming smile crossed his face. "It's time to go." Jillian gazed at Fredrick with sharp, blue eyes. She took his hand into hers. Fredrick ran forward, Jillian a step behind, as they dived into the blue light that flickered before them.

※

"Well," came the calm, deep voice. "It looks like we have some visitors." Jeremiah turned towards Fredrick and Jillian, who stood before him, their hands clasped together. "I must say, it is good seeing you again, Mr. Munchen, Ms. Crenshaw." Jeremiah bowed shallowly towards each.

"Never mind that," said Jillian, releasing her grasp of Fredrick's hand. "What is your purpose here?"

"My purpose?"

"Yes. Why are you putting up the Perispike dome? What do you intend to do?"

"Only what I've always *intended to do*, as you put it."

"And that is?"

"Since when has my goal been so opaque? I'm frankly surprised that you, one of my best students, Ms. Crenshaw, would ask such a question."

"Are you bringing Cythiria back here?" said Fredrick. "Is that why you abducted Chelss, so that you could get the Perispike?"

"Abducted?" Jeremiah smiled. "Certainly not. This young woman merely expressed to me a desire to see her lover again. How could I not oblige? As far as bringing that Mechanic Class Slave back here, I have no intention of upsetting the order of Farth enough to enable such a disastrous end."

"*You* have no intention of upsetting the order of Farth? Since when?" said Jillian.

"Let me put it this way. That Slave is staying where she is."

"And Chelss?"

Jeremiah turned towards Chelss, who gazed at him with large, hazel-colored eyes. "What is your decision?"

Chelss's eyes quivered and grew damp. Rivulets of tears started to stream down her cheeks. "I want to see Cyth."

Jeremiah smiled gently, raised his hand and placed it on her shoulder. "Then so it shall be."

He reached into his billowing cloak and pulled out a small capsule. He held it between his thumb and forefinger, pinched it, and tossed it onto the ground. It clattered and bounced, once, twice, three times, and then rolled to a stop. A moment later, it jumped and then popped. A plasmic arc shot from the inner apex of the Perispike dome and struck the ground. The smell of burning metal filled the air. A thin, black, vertical line fizzled into view and then spread apart, revealing a black portal. Chelss stared into it, her eyes groping for something to focus on, some object, some streak of light. The hole seemed to want to suck her into it, pulling at her hair and skin and clothes like tiny, grasping fingers. Her breath grew raspy, her heart beat rapidly in her chest.

Chelss looked back at Jeremiah. A gentle smile crossed his face, and he smiled warmly. "Now is your time. Take your opportunity."

Chelss turned towards the portal and stood in front of it. Her body trembled and tears streamed down her cheek. *I have nothing left in Farth now. I just want to see you again, Cythiria.* She stepped forward, falling into the darkness before her.

"How could you!" shouted Jillian. "How could you let this happen? She doesn't belong in Griddish. She belongs here."

"It was her decision," said Jeremiah. "It is one which I must respect."

Fredrick clenched his teeth. "Then we're going after her."

Jeremiah turned his steady, calm body towards the pair. His cloak billowed in the pull of the Slipshot portal. "That, I'm afraid, I cannot allow."

CHAPTER 46

A Final Meeting

Griddish, Ashen Fissure, the Var 7 Slipshot Silo

Cythiria felt her neck and face grow warm. She pulled Judith close, pressing her cheek against Judith's head. She closed her eyes and smiled gently as she felt the Admin Class Slave's arms wrap around her waist.

A blue plasmic arc burst from the eye-like portal atop the Slipshot Silo and struck the first post in the array, echoing a sharp, tinny ping along the metal tiles of the platform. Cythiria released her grasp of Judith and turned, stepping in front of the Admin Class Slave, her arm poised as a defensive barrier. Her body tensed as she watched the electric blue arc connect each of the posts in the circular array and then join at the point of convergence.

Cythiria's eyes grew wide, her body tense. The pulse of her racing heart pounded in her ears. She sniffed. The air smelled of burning metal. She coughed and then held her breath.

A thin, black line fizzled into view at the point of convergence and then spread apart, expanding to a dark portal. Cythiria gazed at it. She blinked hard as her eyes groped around the portal. Her stomach turned at its sheer blackness, at its eternal depth and nothingness.

A body tumbled out, falling onto the platform, and after a moment of stillness, rose to its hands and knees and then heaved.

"Chelss?" mumbled Cythiria. "Chelss, is that you?" She darted forward and ran towards the person before her. "Chelss!" she shouted as she fell to her knees. She took hold of her shoulders and lifted her towards herself. A face, eyes bleary, gazed back at her. The light brown hair was pulled back into a ponytail. The large, hazel-colored eyes stared distantly towards her, and her lips murmured some broken words. Cythiria's chest tightened and ached. Tears welled up in her eyes and streamed down her cheeks. She pulled Chelss close to her and sobbed.

"Cythiria," whispered Chelss. "I came for you. I…."

Cythiria pulled her closer, tears flowing down her cheeks in slender rivulets, dripping onto the hair and face of Chelss. "I never thought I'd see you again," she whispered hoarsely.

※

"Nothing like a tearful reunion," said Matere, as he looked upon the platform from the grassy hilltop through his field glasses. "It warms the cockles of my heart."

"The what?"

"Never mind."

"So, what's our next move?" said Betel.

Matere paused. "I'd normally say that we should leave well enough alone."

"Sure you would."

"Except…" He scanned the horizon through the holographic screen in front of him. "…There's a certain *someone* who is fast approaching."

"That being?"

"The one who sends shivers down my spine."

"Not an easy task, I'd say. Who is this person who has so much power over the *great* Matere Songgaard?" said Betel, a tone of mockery in her voice.

"Rive Amber."

"So, then?"

"Let's go."

∼

"Who is this person?" mumbled Judith Merlon as she watched Cythiria from afar, the way that she embraced this new arrival. She glanced at the Vérkatros, Blinky, who stood beside her, his skin a shade of gray, his large, round eyes gazing vacuously forward. He seemed to shudder a moment and then grow silent.

Cythiria never mentioned anything about a Varling that she was close to. What kind of relationship could these two have? Judith felt her stomach turn, a rising pang in her chest. *Is she a friend, or…something else?* She shook her head. "Don't be stupid," she muttered. It's not like Cythiria and I have anything going on. We're just friends. "But still, I wish she'd told me."

Judith sighed. She felt a breeze brush gently against the side of her face. She turned to face its direction. "Rive Amber?" she whispered. "Why is *she* here?"

∼

Cythiria wrapped her arms around Chelss's body. She buried her face in the Varling's hair. She could feel her body tremble. She could hear small whimpering. "I never thought…."

And then, a sharp whistling sound like electricity slicing through air, echoed its tinny ping along the surface of the metal-tiled platform. Chelss's body stiffened, she gasped as she gazed up at Cythiria through tear-drenched eyes, and her body grew limp.

"Chelss?" said Cythiria. She pushed the body an arm length away and shook it. "Chelss!" she shouted. The head bobbled on limp shoulders. Cythiria pulled Chelss close to her, pressing her hands against the Varling's back. She pulled her hands away and lifted them before her eyes. They were wet and crimson colored. "Chelss!" she screamed. Her face and neck grew hot, her heart pounded in her chest. She lay the body down and looked into the face, into the lifeless eyes. Tears streamed from her eyes and dripped on Chelss's face.

And then, she looked up. In front of her stood Rive Amber, grasping an ignited Plaxis Strand in her hand. Rive's jaw was clenched, her chin held high. A scowl crossed her face and quivered upon her upper lip. Her brow was pursed.

"You," hissed Cythiria. "You took Chelss away from me." She jumped up, a tooth-baring snarl growing on her lips. She spread her legs to a defensive stance and lifted her clenched fists to her face. "You take *everything* away from me."

Rive scoffed. The Plaxis Strand fizzled away, and she tossed its grip across the platform, where it tumbled and clattered to a stop. "You had nothing to begin with. What has really changed since then?"

Cythiria surged forward, raising her right fist, and aiming towards Rive's jaw. Rive ducked and turned, striking Cythiria's legs with her foot as she stumbled forward.

"I don't care," said Cythiria, her eyes ablaze with fury. She scowled, followed by the sound of grinding dentine. She surged forward again, raising her left elbow. Rive stepped aside and struck Cythiria in the torso with her knee. A cracking sound echoed along the metal-tiled surface of the platform. Cythiria fell on one knee and gasped for breath as she glared at Rive.

"You have no right," growled Cythiria through raspy, gasping breaths.

"I have *every* right," said Rive, slapping her own chest with her open hand. "*I'm* the one who brought you back to Griddish. *I'm* the one who saved you from yourself, when you were barely able to keep yourself alive. The Vars slowly kill us Slaves. I was not about to stand around and watch that happen again. Not again, Cythiria."

"All I wanted was to be happy," said Cythiria, her lip quivering, tears streaming down her cheeks, her voice cracking and trembling. "All I wanted was to belong, to be useful."

"You would *never* belong to the Vars, Cythiria. The Vars don't want you. But *I* want you. I want you here with me, by my side."

"But I don't belong here either. I'm useless. I can't access the Tenddrome. I can't connect with other Slaves. I can't even talk to Blinky."

Rive scoffed.

"And still, all you ever do is destroy everything I want and everything I love." Cythiria stood up, one arm wrapped around her own waist. Her breath was raspy and labored. "For that, I will always *hate* you." She charged forward, raising her right fist. Rive stepped to the side, lifted her foot and tripped Cythiria, who tumbled forward, falling to the surface of the platform, and lay on her back, her breath short.

"Isn't that enough, now?" a calming voice came. "You two have been at each other for too long. That girl," he said, nodding towards the supine Cythiria, "Is broken."

"Well, if it isn't the always meddling Matere Songgaard," said Rive, her lip quivering to a snarl, her eyes sharp with derision. "Don't tell me you've been watching us this whole time."

"At a distance. And I can say that your spat will gain you nothing, Rive."

Rive scoffed. "Oh, this is no ordinary *spat*, my dear Matere. This is much more than that, much more than you or *her*," she said nodding towards Betel, who stood just behind Matere, "Or any of you Engineer Class Citizens will ever understand."

Matere shook his head. "So be it. But if you don't stop this insanity, Rive, you'll bring us all to the brink of extinction."

Rive snorted. "I'd be doing the universe a favor then."

"And then what, Rive? What is your *real* goal here? Surely, it's not suicide, because people who want to kill themselves don't act the way you do."

"Is that a fact? Well, I'd beg to differ, Matere Songgaard, the most brilliant Engineer in all of Griddish." Rive's voice grew with spite and irony. "Only by uprooting the old can we make way for the new. It's really as simple as that."

"Including yourself, Rive?"

"Including myself, and all Slaves."

Matere sighed deeply. He turned his head and glanced at Betel, whose sharp, gray eyes remained focused on Rive.

Cythiria felt the cold, metal-tiled surface press against her back. She opened her eyes and gazed at the soft, white sky above her. Beyond, above the layer of mist and clouds that filled Griddish, was the inner apex of the dome. Shrouded, it was not visible from here. And yet, this slender veneer is what sustained Griddish for so long, from times that were barely just a broken memory in the Tenddrome, shared by all Slaves. Cythiria turned her head. On the surface lay the grip of Rive's disposed Plaxis Strand. She turned her body and reached for it. She grasped it, feeling the cool metal in her fingers. She closed her eyes for a moment, and then snapped them open. The Plaxis Strand ignited and whistled and pinged as it licked the surface of the platform.

"Very good, Cythiria," said Rive, her eyes following Cythiria's movements. "It seems your dreams are coming true. Only a true Slave can ignite a Plaxis through the Tenddrome."

Cythiria pushed her body up with one arm. She groaned as sharp, almost electric pain shot through her chest and back. She pushed herself up onto her feet and glared at Rive and Matere, who faced each other. She felt her chest grow hot. Her heart pounded in her chest. She felt the warmth of adrenaline rush through her veins. She glanced at Chelss's body, which lay in a humble, unobtrusive pile on the platform's surface, a crimson pool spreading under her back. *This is how you will be remembered, Chelss. Forgotten, like so many others. I won't allow it. Not now. Not ever.* She flicked the Plaxis Strand with her wrist. It whistled as it cut through the heavy, Griddish air. Her eyes burned with darkness, and her jaw clenched to a toothy scowl. "I will kill all of you!" she hissed and growled as she lifted the Plaxis Strand above her head. She stepped forward, and then….

She felt a grasp around her waist. A face appeared before hers. "Don't Cythiria. Please." She looked down at the face, at the pale skin, the light-colored, pleading eyes. "Don't do any more, Cythiria."

"Judith. I…."

"Please stop." Judith's eyes grew wide. They trembled, as tiny rivulets of tears rolled down her cheek. "Please don't do this."

"But I…."

"I don't know who she was to you, but you've got to stop. Otherwise, you'll get killed, and I don't want to lose you. Not now. Not like this."

Cythiria gazed into Judith's eyes. Her body quivered and the Plaxis Strand fell from her hand, its grip clattering on the surface of the Slipshot Silo's platform. She pushed Judith and tore herself away from the Admin Class Slave's grasp. She turned and ran towards Blinky. His skin flashed red and orange and purple and then green, the fear and anger and sadness that penetrated his very being. She took hold of his body and pulled herself onto his back, rolling to a prone position. Blinky stepped forward, vibrated and then hovered. His legs retracted under his body, and he *whooshed!* away.

"I need to find Chelss." Fredrick glared at Jeremiah. His body held a defensive stance, his hands balled into fists.

"There is nothing you can do for this Varling now," said Jeremiah.

"What do you mean?" said Jillian, her eyes sharp, her brow pursed.

"I am afraid a price has been paid for an outcome that will bring chaos to the world around us."

"Stop speaking in riddles!" shouted Jillian. "Tell us where Chelss is."

"Your little Varling is nothing more than a memory now."

Fredrick sighed deeply, his eyes and face drooping to a quiet sadness. "Buy why? How could you have let this happen? You, the all-powerful Vérkatros?"

"Power cannot change the inevitable."

Fredrick sighed deeply. He glanced at Jillian, who cast a dark glare upon Jeremiah. "And what about Cythiria?"

Jeremiah smiled gently. "If there is anything that is unknown in this universe, it is the future."

CHAPTER 47

The Great Re-frag

Griddish, Ashen Fissure

Cythiria grasped Blinky's back, feeling his warm, fleshy, yet metallic skin under her fingers. She sobbed, as tears streamed down her cheeks and dripped and puddled in the pocks and crevices of Blinky's skin. She felt the cool breeze of Griddish blow through her hair. Her body shivered and ached, her breath was labored and raspy.

"I don't care anymore, Blinky. I don't want to be a part of this. I just want to go. I want to leave, forever. Why won't Rive just let me go? Why? Why does she have to torment me like this? I did everything she wanted. I tried to be the person she wanted me to be. I fought for that. But all she does is take. She takes everything away from me. Everything that I love and value. Why, Blinky?"

Cythiria lay prone on Blinky's back. The sway of his body, the warmth of his skin, was comforting. Cythiria's eyes grew heavy, her body bruised and exhausted. The world around her grew dark, and then faded.

And then, she opened her eyes. The hiss of swaying grass enveloped her, its fragrance fresh and warm. She pushed herself onto her side, groaning. She stood, while her body seemed to creak and fold under her own weight. She glanced around the tall, waving grass.

"Blinky?" He stood in the distance, still, stone-like. Alone. "Blinky? What's going on?" The gentle Griddish light faded around her, and she was enveloped by an inky darkness. "Is this…?" Far away, dots of light fizzled into view. A few, at first, and then more, forming into clusters that were so far away, so large as to be unobtainable.

The clusters of light spread out before her and formed a sphere, which twisted and turned upon itself, with plasmic arcs licking the surface and then diving into the darkness of the center, like some colossal storm. And then, more clusters of light formed on the perimeter of the central sphere, blinking colors of light, those reds and oranges and purples, like Blinky, innumerable, calming, beautiful. And there, among them, was Blinky. He was small, a tiny dot in an eternal chain of tiny dots that flashed and pulsed in unison.

The darkness fizzled and faded away, replaced by the gentle, white light of Griddish. A calming, fragrant breeze blew through Cythiria's hair, and her bloodied clothes. She glanced around the grassy field. "Blinky?" she said. She stepped forward, her arms spread out as if she were swimming through long blades of grass. "Blinky!" she said, urgently. "Blinky!" she shouted. She ran, but her body did not feel pain. She stumbled forward, into a wide, circular clearing. She sniffed and coughed at the smell of burnt grass. "Blinky, what did you do?" She sat down on the edge of the blackened clearing. She pulled her knees to her chest and rested her forehead on them. "Blinky, what did you do?" She sniffed and sobbed. "And where did you go?"

It was like a deep, thumping pulse, an invisible wave that struck the Slipshot Silo as it shuddered and groaned. Matere and Betel were knocked from their feet. Rive tumbled backward, and Judith fell to her knees, grasping at the metal-tiled surface of the Slipshot Silo's platform. When the wave had passed, Judith stood. She looked towards the direction of its source. "Cythiria," she mumbled. "What happened?" She closed her eyes, falling into the inky blackness of the Tenddrome. Clusters of light blinked and sparkled in unison. The Tenddrome. It's different, somehow. It's…changed. But how? And why?

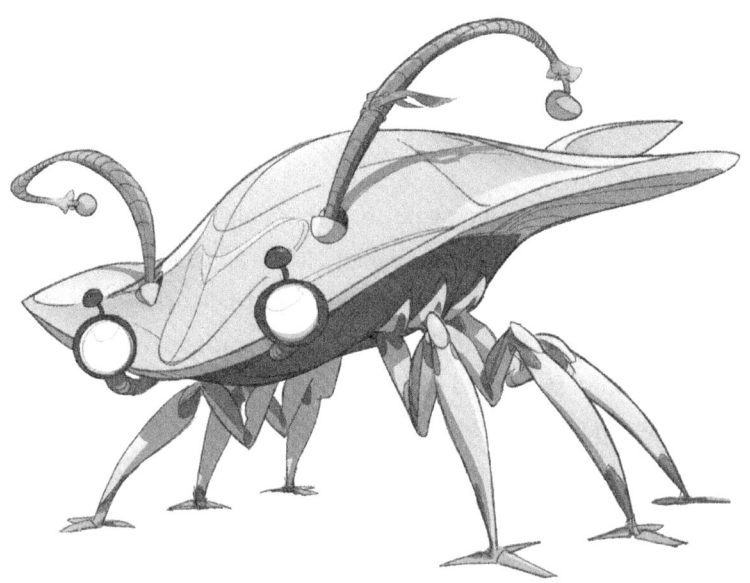

CHAPTER 48

A New Place

Griddish, the Ashen Hills, Stoic Planar

Cythiria Crenshaw gazed up at the white walls of Stoic Planar. They seemed to burst from the top of their verdant hilltop, overlooking the Ashen Plains and the sprawling horizon that was always littered with slender, needle-like Slipshot Silos.

Cythiria sighed as she gazed across the grassy plains, at the cityscape of Ashen Fissure that felt eternally still, as if it were frozen in time. She turned and walked towards the wide archway that led inside an ancient Griddishian temple called Stoic Planar, unused by the modern-day technocrats and warriors of Ashen Fissure. She crossed the threshold into a wide chamber upon whose floor was cast rainbows of colors filtered from a glassy skylight far overhead.

"So?" a voice came from behind her.

Cythiria snorted. She glanced up at the statue that was placed against a wall at the far end of the chamber. Upon its forehead were carved two tiny portals, and from those portals, two beams of light. "I'll never get used to that," she mumbled.

Judith smiled. "Well, you'd better get used to it. Since Rive's war ended so suddenly, you're some kind of hero, and now you've got nothing to do."

"I can hardly believe that."

"Believe it." Judith looked around the large, airy chamber. "To think they installed someone like *you* into a place like this."

"Gee, thanks."

"Don't mention it."

Cythiria paused. "Has the Tenddrome really changed that much since that day?"

"For now," said Judith. "But who knows? The Vérkatrae seem to be in a state of calm, at least temporarily."

The Vérkatrae.

"So, what exactly did happen?" said Cythiria.

Judith shrugged. "Who knows?" She looked at Cythiria. "Maybe it's up to you to find out."

"Up to me?"

"Why not?"

"I think that's probably above my level of schooling."

"Probably."

"You're feeling awfully mean today."

"Just paybacks, my dear Mechanic Class Slave." Judith paused. "And besides, that's why you have me."

Judith smiled and rubbed Cythiria's arm with her hand. She turned, stepping lightly along the glossy, stone floors. Cythiria sighed deeply and then walked through the echoing chamber until she arrived at a large window, from which she could see, almost as tiny, dark specks, The Bastion, Sanguine Heap, and beyond, the place where everything changed so suddenly.

"Where did you go, Blinky?" Cythiria mumbled. *I feel like you are out there somewhere. Maybe you are still in the Tenddrome. Even so, I'm not able to access it, not fully. So, I can only hope that you will return to me, someday.*

⁕

Griddish, The Ashen Plains, Sanguine Heap

"So?" said Natty Mick as he pushed his hand through his thick, black hair. "Now what?"

Rive Amber placed her hands behind her back. She held her chin high, and her lips curled to an almost permanent scowl. She gazed across the plains, her eyes stopping at a wide, dark circle on the otherwise yellow-green grass. "Whatever happened, it was monumental," she said.

"Monumental?"

"*Something* changed our world dramatically, yet we barely noticed." She sighed and turned away from the dark, stony portal, her sharp, dark eyes locking onto Natty's. Natty looked down and away. "That Vérk had something to do with this," she continued. "And yet, he is nowhere to be found."

Natty scoffed. "Maybe he just blew himself up."

Rive shook her head. "It's not that easy to destroy a Vérkatros. Especially like this. Especially when they are bound by the Tenddrome to stay within their boundaries." She paused. "But that Vérkatros, it somehow crossed over." A crooked smile crossed Rive's face. "Such magnificent power. It's hard to imagine, don't you think?"

Natty snorted. He pushed his hand through his thick, black hair. "Whatever. So now what?"

"I suppose we wait and let things play out a little."

Griddish, Sanguine Heap

Chelss opened her eyes. The dark walls were blurry at first. She breathed deeply, her chest heaving under a seemingly heavy weight, her body languid and numb. "Where am I?" she mumbled.

She heard footsteps echoing through the corridor. They were certain, confident, measured. And then, a face, one that she had seen before, but where?

"I see that you have awakened," came the voice. "You've been through quite a bit."

"I…what happened?"

"Some unfortunate circumstance, perhaps. But you are here with me now." Chelss pushed herself up, but then fell back onto the palette, her shaky arms giving out under the weight of her body. "You should rest now, and let your body recover."

The owner of the voice turned and walked away. Chelss lifted her arm and touched her face. She felt her chin, her cheek, her nose. Her hand stopped at her forehead. She ran her fingers along her brow, stopping at two, smoothly textured points. She fondled them with the tips of her fingers. They were cool to the touch, almost metallic.

Chelss sighed deeply. Her chest hurt, and then, she fell into a deep sleep.

Rive Amber looked into the mysterious, gray eyes of a slenderly built man, momentarily glancing over his white hair, and then returning her gaze to his. His expression was gentle, unassuming, soothing.

"It seems that you've actually pulled it off, Benj," she said. "I have to congratulate you for your accomplishment. Imagine being able to turn a simple Varling into a Bestiar by connecting her to the Tenddrome. Your skills are absolutely breathtaking."

"That Varling has not been turned into anything other than what she already was. The only difference is her ability to interact with the Tenddrome."

"Oh, Benj," said Rive, "Isn't it true that the only real difference between Slaves and Varlings is the Tenddrome itself?"

Benj sighed. "What's your goal, Rive? Why do this?"

"I simply wanted to make sure that our dear, little Varling continued to live her life after her very traumatic ordeal. That girl should not have to suffer for the decisions of others."

"How kind of you," said Benj, his voice lacking a tone of sarcasm that a statement like that would have had coming out of anyone else's mouth.

"Now let's let her rest. I have plans for her."

*

Griddish, the Former Council of Engineer Class Citizens

Betel sniffed the air. A fragrant breeze wafted across the grassy green hills and whistled through the rusty, corroding corpse once known as Development of the Council of Engineer Class Citizens.

"I suppose this is it," she mumbled as she stepped across a shattered, cobbled street and into the dank, skeletal shell that once contained arrays of laboratories and experiments. She raised her hand and gestured. A blue, holographic image fizzled momentarily into view and then faded. She sighed and pulled a small device out of the pocket of her trousers. With cool, gray eyes, she gazed at the screen. It projected a three-dimensional line graph that hummed and jumped nervously as she held it in the palm of her hand. She placed the device back in her trousers and glanced around. "There," she whispered, as she walked towards an open shaft. She looked down into it, and then up, both directions seeming to plunge into darkness. "Well," she said. "I guess there's only one way to go." She stepped to the edge. Her legs trembled and her chest tightened. Her stomach turned. She held her breath and then jumped.

The ground under her feet was soft and her feet *sloshed!* as she turned the heels of her boots. Her eyes groped around in the dark. A weak, blue flash of light caught her gaze. She walked towards it, her feet made heavy by thick mud.

"Well, what have we here?" she said, as she gazed at a square shaped object. She reached her hand towards it and grasped it. She lifted it, turned it, and gazed into it. Inside, between prongs that interlocked, was a sphere that emanated its own, weak glow. "So, this is it," she mumbled. *The source of all these new energy patterns in Griddish. I wonder if this is the only one, or are there more? And if so, why doesn't that old man Matere know about it? I suppose we'll find out soon enough.*

A NEW PLACE

Glossary

Ashen Fissure – A state within Griddish. Each state has its own government center, and is responsible for managing the large collection of Slipshots that are placed throughout its lands.

The Bastion – The technology logistics center of Ashen Fissure. All technical processes, such as the environment, the Slipshot, the Griddish dome, and numerous others are managed from here.

Beauty World Variations – A class of worlds that share a high level of life-flourishing qualities.

Bestiar – See Slave.

Capsa Ungere – Also known as Capsa. A small capsule used to initialize a Slipshot portal by igniting a connection between the Silo and its adjacent platform.

The Council of Engineer Class Citizens – Also known as The Council. The center of government of Ashen Fissure, divided into two sections, Governance and Development. The function of Governance is parliamentary and legislative. The function of Development is the invention of new technologies that will advance the overall purpose of Griddish, which is to propagate the human race throughout the universe.

Earth – One of the Beauty World Variations, also known as Var 8.

Engineer Class Citizens – The class of people in Griddish who fulfill mostly the technocratic function of state as well as oversee the development of new technologies.

Farth – One of the Beauty World Variations, also known as Var 7.

The Great Re-Frag – A heretofore mysterious event that changed the state of Griddish from one of war to one of relative peace. It has been suggested that a Transport Class Vérkatros, named Blinky by former Mechanic Class Slave Cythiria Crenshaw, was at the center of the event. His specific role, however, is yet undetermined.

Griddish – Also known as The Realm and The Griddish Realm. Griddish is the entirety of the world. It has been described as a wide disk covered by a protective dome. Griddish consists of a wide variety of land features, ranging from mountains to plains to seas, as well as a number of administrative states and districts.

Init Caster – Also known as IC. The device, approximately 4' in height and 4" in diameter, is used to wake Vérkatrae from their stasis, either self-imposed or imposed external to themselves.

Mechanic – See Slave.

Nissy – A large city in the Var 7 Beauty World.

Node – A point of interaction on the Tenddrome. Slaves are considered Nodes on the Tenddrome, as are other non-sentient objects, such as Slipshots, certain computer devices, and deeply functional machines.

Perispike – A device that, in conjunction with others of the same joined in an array, forms a perimeter around a Slipshot entry point which freezes all activity outside of itself, as well as temporally aligns Griddish with its target child world before a Slipshot entry.

Plaxis Strand – Also known as Plaxi. A weapon used in close, hand-to-hand combat scenarios.

Sanguine Heap – The military center of Ashen Fissure, currently controlled by Rive Amber.

Slave – A class of people who oversee the operations of Griddish on a daily basis. There are many sub classes of Slaves in Griddish, such as Mechanics who oversee the mechanical health of Vérkatrae and Slipshots, as well as all associative "real world" technologies. Bestiars are a new class of Slaves known for their warrior training and abilities. Admins manage the technical processes of Griddish. Psyches, a subclass of Admin, provide mental health and medical services to Slaves.

Stoic Planar – An ancient, quasi-religious center in which Cythiria Crenshaw was installed for her role in the Great Re-Frag.

Tenddrome – The manner and space in which all Slaves of Griddish connect to each other. The current state of the Tenddrome is unknown, and it may have evolved into low level sentience since it was established eons ago. Engineers and Vérkatrae are restricted from utilizing the Tenddrome.

Var – Also known as Variation. A world that is developed by the Engineer Class Citizens and placed and maintained in the universe by the Slipshot, which acts as an umbilical cord delivering its DNA to the child world. The two main Vars that Ashen Fissure manages are Var 7, known as Farth by its Varlings, and Var 8, known as Earth. However, there are many Slipshot Silos in Ashen Fissure, some experimental, others closed, still others leading to nothingness.

Vérkatros – Vérkatrae (plural). The machines originally developed by the early Engineer Class Citizens of Griddish to manage the creation and dismantling of Vars, as well as deep level creation tasks of Griddish itself, and low-level maintenance. There are many classes of Vérkatrae that serve multiple functions. Transport class Vérkatrae fulfill transportation tasks for Mechanics who engage in Griddish maintenance; Constructor class are charged with world building tasks; Sleeper class, evolving into proxies and translators, act as distraction intermediaries between Vérkatrae and Varlings during the execution of world dismantlement projects.

Waftring – A kind of crop obtained from the Waftring Heap region of Griddish. It is said to have psychedelic effects on Slaves. It can be addictive if not consumed in moderation. It has a strong, spicy aroma similar to cinnamon.

3

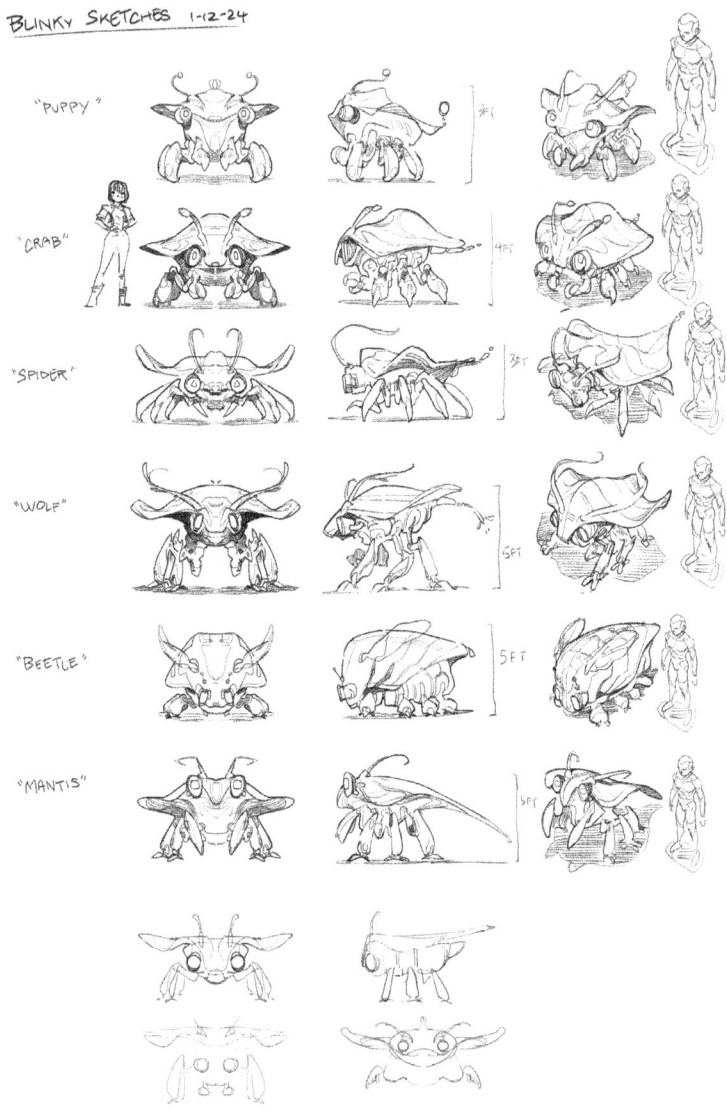

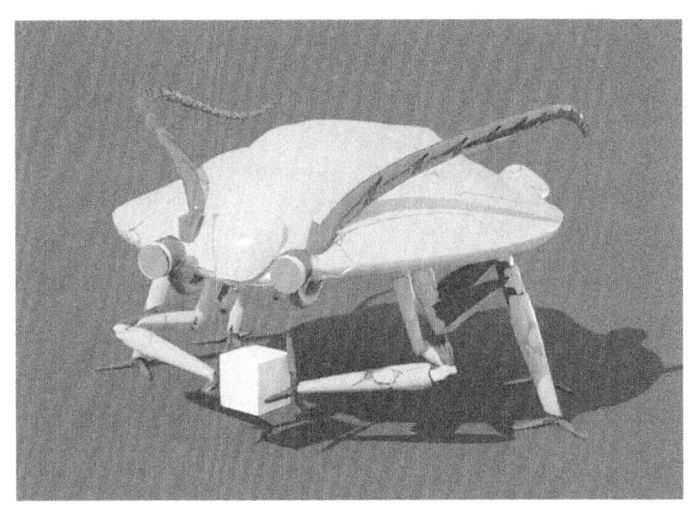

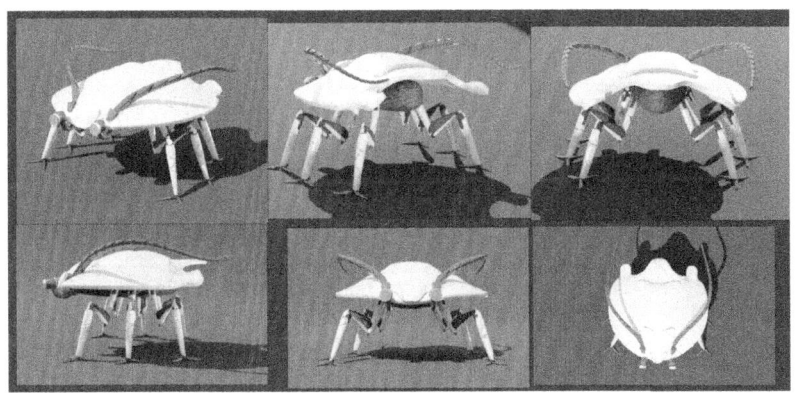

THE SLIPSHOT UNIVERSE AWAITS

An ancient technology. Countless worlds.
And the ones bold enough to defy it.
Across timelines and tangled portals, they're the ones chasing the truth.

Let's go through the Slipshot—together! www.slipshot.io

Made in the USA
Middletown, DE
21 September 2025

17164019R00209